The Hidden Truth

The Hidden Truth

The Mysteries of Bella Rose Estate

Book #3

PHYLLIS DEWEY

This book is fiction. Names, characters, places, and incidents either are the product of the author's imagination or are used factiously. Any resemblance to actual persons, living or dead, events, or locales is entirely coincidental.

Copyright © 2021 Phyllis Dewey
ISBN 978-1-7364347-6-5 paperback

DEDICATION

The Hidden Truth is dedicated to my sister and brother-in-law, Donna and Rich Kammer.

As I looked for ways to continuing the series of Bella Rose Estate I was reminded of a special place in a house were they once lived. That place was the inspiration for The Hidden Truth. Truths only discovered beyond a door hidden from the rest of the world.

We never know what lies beyond the doors that open in our everyday life.

Prologue

"There's More – Keep Looking."

Heather woke from her dream with those words still on her mind. The last thing she remembered was locking up after the wedding reception and coming home. She had been so tired she barely remembered going to bed.

She kept her eyes closed as she envisioned the scene of her dream. The note with the key under it was as vivid in her mind as if it were real. She had never had a dream make her feel as she did now. She lingered in bed a few minutes longer, deep in thought.

Her family had discovered the secrets her parents tried to keep hidden. They had unlocked everything they had found that took a key to open. Life had finally settled down, and they had each begun to move on.

Sara smiled as she drifted off to sleep. The last few years had been filled with the unexpected. Just when she thought life was settling in, something new would happen. Her family had gotten beyond all the twists in their lives. With her new husband by her side, she was confident that life would be amazing and perfect. She rolled over onto her side and watched Randall sleep for a moment as her eyes closed.

A new day was dawning. Bella Rose Estate was once again coming to life. The walls creaked as they settled just a little more. If walls could be heard, those at Bella Rose still had something to share.

Chapter One

A quietness fell over Bella Rose Manor. The wedding was over, Sara and Randall were on their way to their well-deserved honeymoon. All the guests had either gone home or to their rooms at the manor. Sara's siblings were relaxing in the living room. It had been a long day for all of them. A long, busy few months if the truth be told. Everyone was exhausted. One by one, the family moved off the comfortable sofa and chairs and said goodnight, heading to their own homes. Rachelle was the last to leave. She had bid Heather, Ben, Andy, and Karen a good night, locked the front door and turned off all the lights before going to her place. Tomorrow was a new day—the start to a new beginning for all of them.

Sara and Randall entered their cabin after enduring a delayed flight caused by a mechanical issue on the plane. Their short flight had turned into several hours, mostly spent waiting in the airport. The rental car was not what they had ordered, but they were so tired they took the one offered. Everything had gone so well for the wedding. Why did their honeymoon have such a rocky start? As they collapsed on the bed and heard the bed break under them, they had only one choice – laughter! What else could go wrong? No, wait, they didn't want to think that way. They just wanted to celebrate the start of their new life together like any newlyweds who had waited—Sleeping!

Sunday morning dawned on the mountains of Tennessee. Bella Rose Estate welcomed the beauty of her surroundings. Blessed with love for so long, and now the family had grown by one more, Bella Rose hoped life would find a new normal for everyone, and she could tell them her truths. She had to encourage them to keep looking. It wasn't up to her to just come right out and tell them. So far, her hints had not worked. Everyone was too busy to notice. A few more weeks, yes, a few more weeks, and she would get their curiosity stimulated again. Life was about to change – again. Bella Rose Manor, commonly and lovingly called 'Bella Rose,' had more to tell with its life of secrets held within her walls. No one yet knew–the truth.

Heather was up early. With her older sister Sara and Randall on their honeymoon, she and Rachelle were in charge of the Manor's operations, ensuring it all ran smoothly. She made a fresh pot of coffee when she got to the main house. The family decided to call it that since the manor often referred to the entire estate. The main house was where all their guests stayed and where the family often gathered in the large kitchen for family meetings.

As the coffee brewed, she reflected on the recent past. Heather loved that her family was all together and growing. Life certainly had changed over the last several years. If anyone had told her just five years earlier that she would be here, she would have laughed. But life, and her mother, had a vision, and now it all was coming true. Bella Rose Estate was a popular destination vacation spot and soon would be a destination event and wedding location. At least that was the rest of Heather's dream. She poured herself a cup of coffee and walked out the front door to take in the front view, then meandered around to the side facing the gazebo. She laughed when she saw a leftover balloon from the wedding reception stuck on the post and bobbing in the slight breeze. Life was good.

Sara and Randall woke up on the first morning of their honeymoon in a cabin hidden in the middle of the woods. Sara had a smile on her face that revealed her happiness. She turned and watched Randall as he opened his eyes and turned to face her. They reached out for each other, and without saying a word, they could feel the love they shared.

Sara had not slept well, but it did not matter. She was spending time with the man she loved. If someone had told her, at the time of her divorce from her abusive husband, that she would be married again, she would have told them they were crazy. It was amazing what had taken place in the last five years and how everything led to where she was now—in the arms of a man who had loved her all her life.

Ten years. She had divorced in that amount of time; both her parents had died and left Bella Rose Manor Estate to her; she had found her brother and convinced him to move to the manor. She had moved her sister, brother-in-law, and their one son to the manor. Her sister had given birth to another boy. They had expanded the Manor to include a chapel and a recreation hall. They had searched through the attic and found some secrets about the Manor and their family history. Her brother had gotten married. Then they found out that her brother was only her half-brother. Through all of that, she had met and obviously, made a lasting connection with Randall. And she had found a long-lost non-sister. She smiled, realizing that news was hard to explain. Rachelle was her father's second wife's daughter from a previous marriage. How do you explain that relationship? Through the attic's secret letters and journals, she had also found out that her parents had divorced and her father had remarried. And her mother had had a relationship that produced a child.

4

That information had explained a lot and raised so many other questions over the last few years.

Sara shook her head briefly as she was thinking of her recent past. Wow. All the things that had happened and it led to her present situation. Her honeymoon in the middle of nowhere with the man of her dreams! Life was good—finally.

Randall opened his eyes a bit more and saw that his bride's eyes were a million miles away.

"What is on your mind? I'm not sure I can read all of your looks yet, but that one is very perplexing."

"My mind is full of memories of the last ten, and especially the last five years of my life. How you and I met because of the one major event, that being my parents' deaths. And how life is good." She turned toward him and smiled.

"Okay, your thoughts are almost morbid for being on your honeymoon. Although it was indeed the death of your parents that brought us here." Randall laughed.

"Why are you laughing?"

"I was just thinking. When people ask us how we met, I can see their faces when we tell them we met while going over your parent's wills after they died.

Sara snickered and shook her head. "Sorry. You weren't quite awake yet, and my mind just wandered. I won't let that happen again. From now on, during our honeymoon, I will think only of you. And come up with a better way to tell people how we met." She reached around his bare chest in an attempt to show that he was the only thing on her mind.

"I know that is a nice thought to only think of me, but I also know you, and you will find time to think of other things. And I'm okay with that. It's not like we are teenagers or even in our twenties anymore, and love was all googly eyes and romance. We are more mature. We, well, you, have been through a lot in your life already. I don't expect you to be all romantical."

"Romantical? Is that a legal term?"

"No, not that I know of or that I have used in any legal document or court case I've handled. But it fits."

A brief moment of silence came between them, and then they wrapped their arms around each other and cuddled. "This is what I'd like to do all day."

"No, you wouldn't. You're a man. Men want more than to cuddle."

"Okay, you're right. What time is it?"

"I don't know, why?"

"Because I have plans for us today."

"You mean there is something to do in this middle of nowhere place?"

"Well, no, not here. We have to be somewhere else for that." He rolled over and looked at the clock resting on the nightstand. "In about 90 minutes!"

"An hour and a half? Are you kidding me?" Sara rolled away from him and jumped out of bed. "I have to take a shower! How far away is this place?"

"You look just fine to me. But, for the general public, yes, you need a shower and to do something with your hair." He snickered.

Sara grabbed a towel off the towel rack just inside the bathroom and tossed it at him hitting him in the head. "Thanks!" She laughed. As she walked into the bathroom, she saw herself in the mirror. Yes, she certainly needed to do something with her hair. It looked like she had tossed and turned and had a rough night. Oh, wait, she had. But it was a good rough, sleepless night. She was smiling as she climbed into the shower.

Andy and Karen were resting at their home. With permission from Heather to take the day off, they planned to enjoy the day by doing more work in the nursery. Now that they were expecting twins instead of only one, they had to add another crib and dresser. They could do with one changing table, but it seemed everything else now needed to be twice what they anticipated. How were they ever going to manage it?

"You need to stop worrying. I can see it on your face. I am fine. We will be fine. The babies will be fine."

"Wow, you can read my mind. Honestly, I was thinking about all the things we now will need in double amounts. Food, clothes, diapers, college tuition."

"Silly boy! We have a few years before we have to worry about college tuition for them. I told you to stop fretting over it all. We can only do so much at a time to prepare for them. Is Ben coming over and helping you today?"

"Yes, Ben will be here soon to help out. He is excited to help. I think he likes to give me advice about being a father. Since he already has two kids, he thinks he has all the answers. I will admit he has more answers than I do. But I know that twins are going to be different from having two single boys."

"Yes, from what I've read, this twin thing will take organization, planning, and learning as we go. But I'm sure we can do it. After all, we do have a large family around to help us."

"That we do, and I'm so grateful. I wish Larry and Grace could be here more often. We could never get them to sell the marina in Pennsylvania to move here. That place is their baby. Maybe now with twin grandchildren, they will change their minds and move."

"That would be nice. We do have a lot of your family here to help us. I wish my family could have been here. But that was not to be. God had other plans for my life. Being raised without my parents may have made me stronger. I do know I was grateful for Larry and Grace being around when I needed someone. They were always there for me. I wish they could and would move closer. Think we can ask them again?"

Just as Andy was about to respond, he heard a knock on their door. It was Ben coming to help with the nursery. Andy went to let him in. Karen went to the kitchen to make them coffee. Changes were about to take place in the nursery. Karen was looking forward to the final result. She had other plans while the men worked.

Karen headed to the manor after she had poured coffee for the men. She was going there to help Heather and Rachelle prepare for the new guests arriving. They had purposely been vacant for a few days following Sara and Randall's wedding. They needed to clean, prepare food, and get everything perfect for the guests and for when Sara came home. They wanted to impress Sara and let her know that she could be away from the manor without worrying. Karen knew Sara had not taken more than a couple of weeks away in the last five years, if not more. After her divorce, she had moved back with her parents to help them, throwing herself into her work. Once her parents died and left the manor to the three siblings, they all worked together by taking only a few breaks away. It was time for more changes.

Randall could not wait to see Sara's reaction to his next surprise for her. He had a rental car so he could take her on a tour of the area. He knew it was an area that Sara had never been to. He had only been there once, and that was just a month before they got married. He had flown up there to inquire about a few things about it and meet a few people. He had not told Sara where he was going when he told her about his quick trip and was surprised when she had not asked for any details. Maybe it was because she was so involved with the wedding plans and getting everything organized at Bella Rose so it would run smoothly while she was gone. Whatever the reason, he was glad he didn't have to come up with a lie. He was not sure he could ever lie to her. He loved her too much for that. He had waited his whole life to be with her; he wasn't about to do something stupid to ruin what he had with her. He planned for a lifetime together.

As soon as Sara was ready, they were on their way to a quick breakfast and their adventure. Sara had no idea what was in store for her. She was just excited to be away from Bella Rose and work. As much as Sara loved the Manor, it was a lot of work. She realized she was excited not only to be married and on her honeymoon but just to be away from her hectic life. It was a break that was long overdue.

Chapter Two

With its steeple rising high into the sky, the church was the oldest building in town and now served as the courthouse. The brick stairway led to the vast brick floor entrance. Memorialized on several of the bricks were the names of former residents. The foyer revealed a modernized area but held remains of the old, and the original lingered through the exposed bricks that lined the halls. This building was the first stop in the tour Randall had planned for his bride.

Randall parked the car in front of this old building and smiled as he noticed Sara's inquisitive look. "Why are we stopping here?"

"This is the first stop along our journey today. I have something to show you." He got out of the car and walked around to open her door. By the time he reached for the door handle, she had opened the door on her own. "How can I be a proper gentleman if you are going to open your own doors?"

"Sorry. I've been on my own for so long I'm not used to anyone doing things for me."

"Well, Mrs. Williams, you need to get used to it. I plan to spoil you and treat you like the lady you are for the rest of our lives together."

Sara heard his words and had a flashback to her first marriage, hearing her first husband again telling her the same thing, then, only a year later, turning on her and becoming abusive. She shook her head to erase those thoughts and images as she rose from the car. Randall was Not her first husband. Randall was different. He treated everyone with respect. That was one of the characteristics that drew her toward him.

Randall spoke with the clerk at the front desk inside the courthouse, who then motioned for them to have a seat. Sara looked around the room while they waited. For a courthouse, it was beautiful. Her image of a courthouse was not this. To her, they were for legal battles and never for good experiences.

Her curiosity was getting the best of her when an older gentleman walked into the foyer waiting room to meet them. They rose as he approached with an outstretched hand to shake Randall's hand. "Hello, Mr. Williams. Good to see you again. Would you and your wife please join me in my office?"

"Yes, thank you, Mr. Daniels; this is my wife, Sara."

Sara looked at Randall and then at Mr. Daniels as she reached out her hand to meet his to shake. Had she heard him correctly? She would let it go and ask about that later.

"Good to meet you, sir."

"You too, Mrs. Williams."

Sara smiled. It was only the second time she had been called Mrs. Williams. It felt good but unnatural. "Please, call me Sara."

"Okay, Sara, Randall, let's go to my office." He motioned toward his office just down the hall. They followed as he led the way. It almost felt like being called to the principal's office, but she followed the two of them down the hall. Once they were inside the office, Mr. Daniels closed the door and motioned them to a seat in front of his desk.

Mr. Daniels sat behind his large mahogany desk and went straight to the reason for the meeting. "Sara, I contacted your husband a couple of months ago about something that concerns you and your family." He reached for a folder that was lying on his desk. Sara looked at him and then at Randall. She was confused.

Mr. Daniels continued. "When I called him and explained the reason for my call, he told me that you have been wondering about your father and what he was doing with his life when you were a child, and he was an absent father. Your husband said you and your mother never knew for sure what Glen was doing. All he ever told your mother was that his work provided great bonuses and paid for the extra things for the family. Your husband also told me that when your parents divorced, he remarried, but later your parents reconnected and remarried. And at that time, he stayed home."

"Yes, all that is true." She looked at Randall again while more questions ran through her mind. "What is this all about? And why did you tell this man all of that?" directing the question to Randall. She was confused, lost, and felt exposed. Here was a stranger who knew an awful lot about her family's history. What else did he know? She looked at the file that he had not opened and wondered what he had for her?

Mr. Daniel noticed her expression. "Let me explain," he continued. "Glen, your father, worked in this town. He owned a piece of property here that his father had given him as a gift when he turned eighteen. It was his father's idea to give him land that would only increase in value over time. He had no idea what his son would do with it but knew that land was a much better investment than simply giving him a new car or money that would be spent or end up in the junkyard over time. He had been a land investor and hoped that what he had taught his son would pay off. Well, pay off, it certainly did. Glen knew how to turn land into money."

"What are you saying? Daddy never lived here. Are you sure it was my father? Glen Fairchild? I don't understand." Sara was full of questions.

Mr. Daniels opened the file lying on his desk and took the top paper out, handing it to Sara. "This is the deed for the original property your grandfather gave to your father." While Sara glanced at it, Mr. Daniels turned another paper toward her. "And this is what he developed from that original piece of property."

Sara glanced at the second paper. In disbelief, she looked up at Randall and then at Mr. Daniels. Sara still did not understand what she was looking at and what it meant to her. She assumed her father's money had gone to the Bella Rose Estate and her mother when he died. "What am I looking at? What are these numbers?"

"That is the value of the land that he developed here."

"So, who owns it now, and why are you showing me all of this? Daddy's been gone for over five years."

"Well, the land was set up in a trust with the town in charge of it. The town took care of it and continued its development after he moved away and even after he died. He had the trust set up separate from his will with the stipulation that the family did not know anything about it until five years after he died. I thought that was a bit odd. But it was legal. He entrusted me with managing the trust, and there was nothing I could do until now. I contacted Randall a month ago as he was the attorney Glen told me to contact when the time came." He looked at Randall. "He didn't even know anything about it until I called him. He flew up here two weeks ago to discuss it and arranged for our meeting."

Sara looked inquisitively at Randall. "You knew about this?"

"Not completely until two weeks ago. I changed all the plans for our honeymoon and made this our destination when Mr. Daniel's called me."

Sara was still looking at the paper and only half-heard Randall as he spoke. She wanted more information. What other secrets did this town hold for her and her family?

"Sara, Sara," Randall called her name.

"Yes, what?" Sara looked up and focused on him as she cleared her mind.

"There is more." Mr. Daniels spoke. "The residents had a meeting last week and have asked what they are to do with the property now? So there are papers to draw up after you make that decision."

"What do you mean what do they do with it? Isn't a town always a town?"

"Yes, and no. Your father developed this area. He ultimately left it to you and your family. Since the five years are up, it is up to you and your family to let us know if you want the town to stay as it has been, if you want to sell the property, or if you want to make changes."

"How can I decide what a town should do? A person can't close a town, can they? That would be ridiculous—too many lives and livelihoods involved. I can't hurt people. So, of course, the town has to stay."

"That is good to hear. Now the other issue at hand is will the area still be in charge of itself, or will you and your family be running it? It's a very small area, but it still needs to be managed. We are unincorporated, which means it is not considered a town like you would associate with a town. If you had time to look around, you noticed that there wasn't much to the town besides this building. I use it for my office; locals call it the courthouse, and it's the only church near here. And the church is not like most churches either. It is non-denominational and just a place for the locals to gather on Sundays to worship."

"I noticed the church reference on the door, but I thought that was in the past."

"No, it is what we have. The room down the hall and to the left is the church sanctuary."

"How interesting." There wasn't anything else she could think of to say to that. She felt it was a bit sad but also quaint.

She looked at Randall, searching for answers. Or other things to ask.

"I don't have any answers for you at the moment. This news is quite a surprise. Plus, I will have to discuss all of this with my sister since she is also Glen's child."

"Yes, of course. We understand that. We, I, would like to show you the area and have you meet some of the people. Then you can go home and talk with your sister and let us know what you decide. We would like to have an answer by the end of the year."

"Of course. I would love to see the area. After all, from the looks of it, I now own this?"

"Yes, you do. You and your sister own this now. Like I was explaining, this is not an official town. We are an area that is a large community within the county. We can remain as we are, or you can petition to make it an official town. You will need thirty-three and a third of the residents to agree to it. And that is the beginning. I can get you the written procedure if you would like. It gets a little complicated.

"Randall, do you mind?"

"Mind? I'm the one who brought you here, remember?"

"Yes, you are. Not the normal honeymoon—that is for sure."

"Who said anything about me or us being normal?" He laughed.

"You are right. We are not your normal family. And by the looks of all this, we just became more abnormal."

The three stood up. Sara handed Mr. Daniels the papers. He held up his hand in refusal. "You can hang on to them. I have copies for my office. This whole file is for you to look over. It shows the history, the work already completed, the town's area size, and a list of the people who live here. And there are a few pages of ideas the people have had for what to do with the land. We don't want to be incorporated, but we would like to be more of an official town; a few shops, a library. I think we can add those with the township's permission. A lot of red tape, rules, and regulations and such, I'm sure as well."

"We can discuss all of that later. I would like to see what I'm dealing with first. I need to see the land, the buildings, and meet the people."

Randall grinned as he realized Sara had changed into her business mindset. He glanced at Mr. Daniels and nodded his head. Her being in business mode was a good thing. She would be looking and thinking with her head and not just her heart. Once she saw the land, her heart would leave the land the way it was. Her head would see the potential. The combination would enable her to make a good decision to take home and present to her sister.

The three left Mr. Daniels' office and got into his car. They spent the rest of the morning touring the countryside. It certainly was not a town. There were just a few buildings on that street, followed by woods with houses partially hidden beyond trees. No rhyme or reason to where each one was. Some were visible from the road, while others were built off the road at the end of long dirt roads. Like Mr. Daniels had told them, the only buildings in the town were the courthouse and a small diner. The post office was a small building just off the main road. Mr. Daniels told them that an older couple lived in the back of the post office. The schools were in the next town. This little place had, well, it had nothing. Just land. Woods, flat land, meadows, and a small pond. Sara was just as perplexed when they finished the tour as she had been while looking at the papers. She would have to think about what she wanted to do with this inheritance. How was she going to explain this area to her sister?

When they finished the tour, they all talked for another half hour. Sara told Mr. Daniels that she would have to think about everything she had learned and seen that day. The people they had met were friendly enough and glad to meet her. They all asked what her plans were, and she honestly told them she had to discuss the matter with her sister before making any decisions.

Randall and Sara bade Mr. Daniels goodbye and told him they would be in touch in two weeks.

When they were back in the rental car, Sara spoke. "That was so surreal. I suddenly have more property to handle. What in the world am I going to do with it? It's so far away from where we live I can't manage it from home. I'd have to hire someone to look after it. There is nothing there. A few homes, a courthouse/church, and a diner! Oh, and a post office. What is that all about? There has to be more to make it profitable. The way it is, there is no real income." Sara was thinking out loud, and Randall was smiling as he was listening. He knew not to reply while she was thinking out loud. He was the same way. He didn't like to be interrupted while he was deep in thought. To see his new bride's mind work made him smile.

"Shall we go find a good restaurant for dinner?" Randall asked as he entered the next town over.

"Yes, that would be nice. If we stop nearby, we can find out more about this area from talking with the residents."

"That's an idea. But I think we need to get away from here and deal with what we have seen and what Mr. Daniels told us. And I think we need to spend time enjoying our time together. This trip wasn't supposed to be a work trip."

"You're right. It is our honeymoon." Sara leaned back against the headrest in the passenger seat. So far, her honeymoon was a whirlwind of things she had not expected. She could write notes later. It was time to enjoy her honeymoon.

Chapter Three

Life was returning to normal at Bella Rose Manor when Sara and Randall set out on their honeymoon. Heather, Karen, and Rachelle met in the kitchen to organize their cleaning and prepare for guests arriving in just a few days. The girls had excused Ben and Andy from helping that first day as they had a more pressing job to finish. They were busy building a second crib and making adjustments in the nursery for Andy and Karen's twins. When they were expecting one baby, it was an easy remodel to the room. With twins on the way, a few things had to be changed to have enough room.

While the girls were cleaning, their discussions turned to talk about the attic and what secrets might still be hiding.

"You know we never did finish going through everything in that room upstairs," Rachelle commented as she was dusting the living room coffee table and picked up the antique candy dish. The dish reminded her of old treasures—something she had little of when she was growing up. Something that she now found a connection to, thanks to her new family.

"You're right. We never did. We need to get back up there. I wonder if we should go explore again when we finish cleaning," Heather chimed in.

"Do you think Sara will mind if we go without her? I mean, it is a big part of her life as well."

"I'm sure she will be fine. She has other things on her mind right now."

"Speaking of Sara, has anyone heard from them?"

"They're on their honeymoon; I don't expect to hear from them." Heather tilted her head at the other ladies.

"True. I'm used to her keeping her finger on the manor even when she is away. It feels odd with her not being in touch with us. I hope they, oh never mind. I'm sure they are having a good time. Randall told me he had a few surprises up his sleeve for her."

"Oh really? I wonder what they are? I wonder if she will tell us when she gets back? They may be 'private' surprises, you know."

"If they were private, I don't think Randall would have told me anything."

"Very true. Now you have my curiosity up. And that is not good."

While they were still chatting and cleaning, the phone in the kitchen rang. Heather went to answer it.

"Do we have a new guest coming?" Rachelle asked when Heather came back into the living room.

"No. That was Sara." Heather said as she sat down on the sofa.

"We were just talking that she wouldn't call. Was she checking on us?"

"No," Heather said quietly while just staring into space.

Karen noticed her distant look. "What's wrong, Heather?"

Heather just sat there in silence. She was doing her best to digest what Sara had just told her. It was unreal that her family history and parents could become more complicated and mysterious, but it just had. "Oh, just that our family just got more interesting."

"Oh? How's that?" Karen asked as she and Rachelle both sat down on the sofa with Heather.

"It seems the surprise Randall told Rachelle about had to do with our father, Glen. He was the owner of an entire town."

"A whole town? How is that possible?"

"I don't know for sure. All Sara told me was that she and I have a major decision to make when she gets home about what to do with it. She said something about it not being incorporated, so it wasn't like most towns we know. But it was a large parcel of land, a few buildings, with several families living there. So she said she was bringing home the documents. And she was emailing me some of the information so I could look it up and do some research before they even got home."

"Wow! That is a lot to take in. I didn't know he owned anything more than Bella Rose." Rachelle commented.

"Bella Rose belonged to my mother's family. Daddy married into it, and when Mama inherited it, she had it put in both their names. That way, if she died first, it would go to him automatically and remain in operation. I thought that was the only land that we owned. Sara said this property is land that Daddy owned but never did anything with, I guess. I don't remember him ever talking about it."

"Where is this land?" Karen wanted more details.

"The far western part of the state," Heather said absently. Her mind was still trying to understand how her father could own a whole town. She shook her head. "Well, in the meantime, we have work to do. We can't dwell on this until we get more information." Heather stood up, and the other girls followed.

The men finished their work in the nursery and wandered into the kitchen of the manor. Andy was already cooking up a meal for everyone when the ladies joined them. It seemed odd that Sara wasn't there with Randall, but everyone knew they were having a good time. Everyone except Heather. She knew they were in the middle of a mystery.

"What's going on, Heather?" Ben asked. "You look lost in another world."

"She is—sort of. If you consider the other side of the state another world."

"Oh, the west side of the state IS a different world. Totally. Hot, humid, flat. Why do you mention the west side?" Ben asked.

"Sara called me today. It seems Daddy owned land over there. A whole town. Sara says she and I have a decision to make about it after she gets home."

"A decision? About what? And if Glen owned it, why are you just now finding out about it?"

"The decision is what to do about it. And the reason why it has taken so long is a mystery to me. Sara didn't say, and I was so confused that I didn't think to ask about the delay. We'll all find out when they get back."

"Dinner is served," Andy announced to everyone. They were already sitting around the island, but he enjoyed the announcement anyway.

"Thanks, little brother. You are the best. If you weren't here to cook for us, we'd all be skinny." Heather laughed as she filled her plate with the stir fry he had made. She loved when he made it because he always made extra rice to make the amazing rice pudding that their mother had made. His version was quicker and just as good.

The conversation turned to a discussion about the attic and the journals and letters as they all ate. The ladies talked about that earlier in the day, and now the men brought up the subject.

"You know we should see what else is up there before Karen can't get up there anymore."

"Hey, what are you saying? That I'm getting fat?"

"Babe, you're not getting fat, you are carrying twins, and everyone knows that with twins, you get bigger and have to be more careful."

"Okay, you talked your way out of that hole," Karen said as she snuggled up to Andy's side. "You're such a sweetheart. What would I do without you?"

"I'm not sure, and I hope you never have to find out."

"Me either. Now, do you think we can go to the attic before Sara and Randall come home? I mean, if she has a new piece of property to deal with, she may not have the time to help us look."

"You're right about that. Maybe, while business is slow, we can go up and continue to dig. What is on the calendar for tomorrow?"

"Just making sure the guests are taken care of in the morning. They are on their own after breakfast, and so are we. Shall we set a time to meet and go back to investigating the room?"

"Sounds like a good plan. What do you think, Heather? Do you think Sara would mind all that much?"

"Considering what she has to deal with now out West, she may appreciate us looking without her."

"Okay." Heather conceded. "I guess we can go on the search again."

"Can anyone join in this search?" Rachelle asked. She had not been a part of the other searches. She had been the result of one of the discoveries in the attic. She wondered what else they could find. She did not know of any other secrets in her family. She wondered if Susan had any other secrets. There were times she felt like a third wheel around her new family, knowing in truth that she was not related to any of them, but they made her feel like she was one of the sisters. Yet, when it came time to explain the family relationship, it was impossible. It was best to call her a friend of the family. Yet, now they included her in the attic's secrets and the searching for more. To be included felt wonderful. To help would be amazing.

"Of course, you can join us. You are part of the family now."

After dinner and dessert, they went their separate ways to get some rest before morning dawned and another adventure began in their lives.

The next morning, after the guests were on their way to their destinations for the day, it was time to explore.

Rachelle joined them as they walked to the third floor to the attic. The door to the right was the secret room they all called the attic, even though it was not on a separate floor like most attics. It was just a spare room that Susan had transformed into her writing room and after her death had become the secret room, locked until the whole family had moved to the manor and it became operational again. Now they wondered what new secrets they would find. And Rachelle's main interest was seeing the room that had led them to her.

Heather did the honors that had been left to Sara before and unlocked the door. Rachelle followed them all inside and closed the door behind her.

Inside, Rachelle was amazed by the room. She did not know what she had expected, but this was almost magical. She could sense the time when Susan would have been in the room sitting at the desk that stood to the left. She sensed that no one had ever used the bed in the corner. The dressers and the armoire had an elegant flare, with the woodwork details of raised swirls, a touch of gold plating. The bookcase that stood in the other corner still had some books and journals on the shelves. She imagined the shelves filled with books as well as more journals. She noticed an indentation in the wall just to the right of the writing desk as she continued to look around. She slowly moved so as not to disturb what remained and what had once been.

"Where does this lead?" She asked in general. She assumed they had been inside it before and removed whatever was inside. Maybe that is where they found the papers that led them to her.

"Where does what lead?" Heather asked as she turned to see what Rachelle was referring to.

"This little door?" Rachelle reached down to open the door and noticed there was no door knob.

"I've never noticed it before. Andy, did you see this?"

Andy joined them as they studied the indents in the wall. "I never noticed it before. Maybe we had the dresser in front of it when we were up here."

"Who moved the dresser?" Heather asked.

"Sara must have moved it. I wonder why she never mentioned this to us."

"Maybe she didn't notice it. Can you open it?"

"I don't see a door knob. Maybe you just push it open." Andy pushed gently. The small door opened. He had to duck down to get through, but once through the door, there was a whole other room on the other side. He gasped when his eyes adjusted to the darkness while he searched for the light switch.

"What is in there?" Heather called out as she bent down to enter. As she walked into the full-size room and stood up, Andy found the switch, and the single lamp sent light into the room. It was Heather's turn to gasp.

Karen bent down to look in. "I don't think I can fit through the opening. What is in there?"

"You won't believe it. You need to come in. The room is full size once you get through the door."

Karen bent down and turned and barely managed to enter the newly found room. Rachelle followed behind.

The single lamp shed enough light to reveal several cots lining two walls, two dressers along the right wall, and a desk near the door. In the middle of the right side wall was a window hidden by a sheet of plywood nailed to the window frame. There was dust covering everything inside. A four-drawer lateral file cabinet stood in the back corner.

"What is all of this?" Rachelle asked, doing a fast sweep with her eyes.

"I have no idea," Heather answered. "Andy, can you get that plywood off the window to let more light inside?"

"I will need a hammer or nail remover, but it should not be a problem. Let me go downstairs."

"I have a hammer in the craft room next door; I'll go get it." Heather offered.

While Heather went next door, Andy was busy looking at the opening of the small door. He could not figure out how anyone brought the furniture in through such a small space. Even in the dim light, Andy saw the evidence of a larger doorway. What was the reason for the added secrecy? Heather returned with the hammer while he was trying to imagine the purpose of the room. He removed the nails and then removed the board to reveal a window with a view of the mountains. With the board down, it added a lot more light to the room, and they could make out more details of what was inside.

"What do you suppose was the purpose of this room?" Rachelle asked.

"Storage? Maybe the cots were used when couples had young kids that stayed with them in the guest rooms."

"That makes sense. But why were they hidden behind a secret door? And why was the window blocked off?" Karen asked.

Karen walked to the file cabinet while the others looked around the room for any clues. The drawer was stuck but easily opened on the second tug, catching Karen off balance. She held on to the drawer-pull to steady herself as she peered inside at a space full of hanging files. She pushed them back to read their labels and noticed journals lying below the files. She carefully pulled out a few of the thinner files, leaving the journals.

"Hey everyone, look what I found."

"What is it?" Andy asked as he walked over to his wife. She handed him one of the files. Heather and Rachelle joined them and looked at the files they had. Heather then reached in, pulled out a journal, handed it to Heather, closed the top drawer, and opened the second one. More files and a couple of small boxes. She pulled out one of the boxes and opened it. Inside were letters—a lot of letters.

Chapter Four

Sara had not slept well since learning about the property her father had left to her and her sister. Her thoughts about what to do with it were mixed. A part of her wanted to be able to keep it and develop it. Another part told her to let it go to the townspeople and let them do what they wanted with it. It was a beautiful area, even if it did not have the mountains of East Tennessee that she loved. She knew the people they had met loved the area.

Randall woke to find his bride looking into the woods from her seat on the side chair at the window. He got the sense that she missed home already, but he was unsure what she was thinking. The surprise he had thrown at her was life-changing. He hoped the next one was more pleasant.

"Good morning, beautiful. I take it you didn't sleep well?" Randall spoke just above a whisper from where he lay, leaning on his elbow watching her. He did not want to shock her away from her thoughts.

Sara turned away from the window and looked at him. "No, I can't get that land off my mind. I'm torn about what to do with it."

"I'm sure whatever you and Heather decide will be the right move. I have faith in you."

"Thanks. Glad someone does. I don't. At least not concerning this. What am I supposed to do?" Sara stood from her chair and walked over to join her husband on the bed. She sat next to him as he sat up and put his arm around her.

"You are going to take all the information home with you, plus the photos you took while we were touring the property, talk to Heather and maybe the others, and come up with a solution that works best for you and for those that live here on the land."

"Such faith. I wish I had some of it."

Randall hugged her shoulders. "You do have that faith. Tap into it." He then turned away from her as he got out of their bed, announcing, "Now you need to get ready so we can go on our next exploration."

"Where are we going now? I can't take another surprise like the one yesterday."

"No, nothing like that. Just a good time out and about."

"Okay. I'll get ready. I love you."

When they were ready to start their day, Randall took her out to brunch at the Country Store. He had heard they had the best country buffet with some unique dishes. An older lady welcomed them as they walked through the entrance. She asked if they were there for brunch or to shop. Then directed them to the dining area when Randall told her they were there to eat first but would shop when they finished.

Sara eyed the buffet as they walked beyond it to their table. She had never seen so much food for a brunch. Her first thought was of Andy and how he would love it here. So much to choose from. Once they were seated and ordered coffee and orange juice to drink, they filled their plates at the buffet. Scrambled eggs, shredded potatoes with cheese, blueberry muffins, chocolate chip muffins, apple strudel, cheesecake donuts, fresh fruit, bacon, ham, sausage, omelets that the chef made to order, and even chocolate cake! She took a little taste of almost everything to decide what was best.

Randall looked at her plate when they got back to their table and laughed.

"What are you laughing at?"

"You do know you can go back up for more food. You didn't have to put it all on one plate."

"I didn't. I avoided the chocolate cake." Sara laughed as she took her first bite. "Oh, my, these potatoes are amazing! What did they put in them? It's a lot more than just potatoes and cheese. Do I taste sour cream? Onion? A hint of garlic?"

"And you say you can't cook." Randall teased her.

"I can't. But Andy has taught us all well over the last few years, and we are getting to know how he cooks and what he cooks with."

"You've learned well."

They finished their meal, including a slice of chocolate cake they shared, then went to the shopping area. There the bride and groom saw a lot of locally crafted items for sale. It was more of a specialty store than your run-of-the-mill general store. The items for sale were not something you could find just anywhere. Sara picked out a few things she wanted to take back home, including a few things for her nephews and the babies. She had to be gender-neutral as she didn't know what they were yet. She was hoping for at least one girl, but she would love them no matter what.

Randall stayed off the main highway when they left the store, choosing to take the back roads. He wanted his bride to see the beauty of the extended area. To emphasize that while it was beautiful, there was not a lot of activity in the area. Not like she had at home. He was hoping it would help her make her decision. He knew what he wanted her to do with the land, but he would leave it up to Sara and Heather. Even though they were married, the land was hers and Heather's inheritance, and it was ultimately up to them to decide what became of it.

Sara was quiet as Randall drove. She was enjoying the scenery but was thinking of Bella Rose Estate. More than that, she was thinking of the secret her father had kept from her. He had kept it even from her mother! How could he do that? And why would he do that? Was he getting money from the land all those years? And if he was, what was he doing with it? Why had he not told his family about it? Was it a treasure he didn't want to share or an eyesore he wanted to keep hidden in his life? If he didn't like it, why had he not sold it while he was still alive? So many questions. And no answers. She took a deep breath as they rounded the bend. She gasped at what she saw.

In front of them was the most beautiful lake. The water held the reflection of the blue sky with the white clouds in its stillness. The trees stood tall along the shore. A few docks jetted out into the water. A white-sailed sailboat coasted along the middle of it by the gentle breeze, evidenced by the easy swaying of the tree branches.

"This place is beautiful! Can we stop and get a closer look?" Sara asked as she reached over and touched his arm. I'm so glad you told me to bring my camera. This place is perfect for a photo shoot. Do you mind?"

"Of course, I don't mind. It's why I brought you here. I knew you would love it."

"You know me well."

Randall stopped the car in the pull-off that had been made just for this reason. It was the site of a few well-known photos taken and placed for sale that he had noticed in the gift shop. Now his bride could capture her own.

Sara had always been interested in photography and was reluctant to switch from film to digital when it became popular. Now she was glad for the digital age. She didn't have to waste film on photos that were not perfect, and she could take as many shots from different angles to her heart's content. While she was clicking away, she turned the camera to focus on Randall. When he finally noticed, he ducked to hide. She told him it was too late; she had already taken several photos of her love.

Chapter Five

After finding the treasures in the attic, they each carried an armload down to the main kitchen. Rachelle told them she would make room in the office to store them while they began to read through each one and figure out what the pages hid.

Andy had spoken with Ben and convinced him to cut the door out to the size it should be and put a regular door on it, giving them easy access to the secret room.

"Did you notice the dates on these letters?" Karen asked.

"Yes, the ones I found dated back to when the Bella Rose was just a single dwelling that my grandparents built. I wonder why she kept them all for so long?"

"I wondered that as well. Maybe the letters will give us the answers."

"I hope so. I know I'm curious. So you think Sara would mind if we started to read them without her here."

"I hope not. I don't think I can wait that long."

"Good, me either. I thought I'd clean out a file drawer in the office so we can store them in there. We can organize the bundles according to the dates and maybe read them accordingly if there is an order. And the journals, I would assume, are by each year. Maybe by each person?"

"Why would there be so many different ones if they are by person? You think these are from family or the guests?"

"I have a feeling they are from the guests. You know we have the tradition that we thought Mama had started with each guest writing something in the journals we leave in each room. Maybe it was her Mama that started it, and these are from that time. They could tell us a lot about the history of this place and maybe even the area. That would be amazing." Heather was getting excited.

"Okay, let's at least clean off as much dust as we can before we take them to the office.

"Let me make some room inside there." Rachelle headed to the office. She wasn't sure where to find room in a file cabinet, but she would do her best. Maybe, she thought, for now, they could sit on a shelf in the bookcase.

They took some of the found items down to the kitchen island while Rachelle cleared space in the office. Later, with the island free of all the treasures and the air free from dust— it was dinner time. Marc and Maddex were busy playing in the living room when a couple of the guests came in from their day trip. Ben was keeping an eye on the boys and welcomed the guests back.

"How was your visit in town today?" He asked them.

"It was wonderful. We found some treasures in the antique stores. Things we remember our grandparents having when we were little. We've not seen them since they died several years ago until today. I know they are not the same pieces, but we bought them for the memories."

"We hear that a lot from folks. There are a lot of treasures downtown in those shops."

"Our grandmother told us about this place. She told us she and a friend had come here once a long, long time ago. Said it saved her life to be here."

"Saved her life? How's that?"

"She said she was having trouble at home, and her parents sent her here to stay awhile. She never did say why but said it changed her life. She told us to visit if we ever had the chance and if this place was still here. She said she would love to come back someday, but she lives too far away, and it's hard for her to travel anymore."

"What is her name, if you don't mind me asking."

31

"Her name is Rhea Brown. I'm not sure what her maiden name was. We can ask her next time I see her. I'm not even sure what year she was here. I never thought to ask.

"Do you remember her friend's name?"

"No, sorry. She never gave me her friend's name. I do know it was a female friend and not a boyfriend or her husband. So she must have been young. Teenagers, maybe?"

"I know we have some of the records from several years ago, and all the guests had to sign in. Maybe we can find her name someday. Maybe we can make arrangements for her to come to visit again."

"That would be awesome. You have our contact information with our reservation. Could you call us or email us if you ever find it? I'd love to know when she was here and for how long. Wouldn't it be something if we were staying in the same room?"

"Well, when your grandmother was most likely here, this building wasn't built yet, or at least not complete the way it is now. This portion was added after Heather and Sara's parents were the owners. They would have stayed in the old part. Or the other building, which is now where Sara lives. The old part is what is now the office, this living room, and the kitchen. They had a couple of rooms upstairs. And on the third floor are two rooms we use for storage now." Ben explained. He didn't tell them that the others had just found letters and journals in one of those rooms. And he wasn't about to tell them that it was all in hiding. He was going to remember her grandmother's name.

Later that evening, Heather got a call from Sara. She was surprised to hear from her again. Some honeymoon she was having, she had called home twice now.

"Hey, Sis. What's wrong? Why another phone call? Are things not going well?"

"No, they're going fine. We are enjoying our time away." She sounded distant.

"But....?"

"Well, ever since I found out about the land, I can't get it off my mind. I want to come home and talk to you about it."

"Okay, and this can't wait?"

"Not when it's eating at me, no. And, well, I was talking with Randall and told him I have a funny feeling about the manor. I'm not sure what it is, but I feel I need to be there. Is something going on?"

Heather pulled the phone away from her face. She hadn't wanted to make Sara cut her honeymoon short because of what they had found; when she hadn't even mentioned to Sara that they were going to look, but she was coming home anyway.

"Heather. What's going on? Everyone alright? Karen and the babies okay?"

"Everyone is fine. Babies and Karen are fine." Heather left it at that.

"So, what are you not telling me? Spill it."

"Okay. I hope you're not going to hate us. But, we went into the attic again today."

"The attic? Why?"

"We got talking and decided it was a good time to go back up there and see what else we may find. Karen will be too pregnant if we wait too long and then way too busy with the twins. The rest of us will be busier as well, helping her and chipping in while she is out with the babies."

"Okay, I see your point. But you couldn't wait until I got home?"

"Simply put, no." Heather chuckled. "I know, just like at Christmas and not being able to wait to open the gifts."

"My thoughts exactly. So what did you find? It must have been something interesting the way you hesitated to tell me."

"We found a secret room."

"Another secret room? Where?" Sara had been reclining on the bed until she heard 'secret room.' She sat straight up on the bed. Randall came to her side and just looked at her waiting to hear more as well.

"It was in the attic room, just beyond where Mama had her desk. It was a small opening with no doorknob, but Rachelle noticed an indentation in the wall. So Andy pushed it open. We had to almost crawl to get inside, but there is a full-size room beyond that opening."

"Was there anything in there?"

"A lot. Cots, two dressers, a desk, and a filing cabinet."

"Wait, cots? Like we use when parents come to stay and want their kids to stay in the room with them?"

"Sort of. But these are old, and some are falling apart."

"Okay, so they must be the old ones that Grandmama used to use. No big deal."

"But we found some things in the file cabinet."

"What is in there?"

"Letters and journals. The letters are in bundles, and the journals are just small journals. We took several of them out and put them in the office downstairs so we can read them."

"Good plan."

"You aren't mad that we went searching without you?"

"Heather, with what I just found out about the secrets daddy was keeping, I have enough to deal with and more questions about his life. Of course, I'm not mad. I am curious about that small opening."

"We are too. We talked to Ben, and he is going to make it the full-size opening again so we can go in without ducking and so we can get the furniture out if or when we decide to do so."

"Good plan there as well. Don't let Ben do that until I see the little opening. I want to see that. Well, that settles it; we will get a flight home tomorrow." She looked at Randall with pleading eyes mixed with her flirting look that he could not resist.

"Are you sure you don't want to stay on your honeymoon?"

"Not now. We can go on trips later. We have a lot to deal with, and as you said, we need to do as much as we can while Karen can help us the most. See you sometime tomorrow. I will call you and let you know what time."

"Sounds good. I'm so glad you are coming home. And glad you are not mad at me."

"Even if I was mad at you, I cannot stay mad at you. You are my sister. I don't think staying mad is allowed." She laughed

"I love you, Sis; see you tomorrow."

"Love you too. Sweet dreams."

Sara hung up the phone. Randall was right there like a little kid wanting to hear what was going on.

"What was that all about? And I take it we are going home tomorrow?"

"Yes, I'm sorry. I know you wanted this honeymoon to be special. And it was. You are full of surprises. But, I can't get this land out of my head, and now Heather says they found a secret room in the manor."

"A secret room? Where?"

"Attached to the attic. It seems there was a small door that didn't even have a door handle that led to a full-size room. They found more letters and journals in a file cabinet. They also found old cots, dressers, and I don't know what else."

"Yes, we need to get home. We can do another honeymoon later. I know how you are about the mysteries and secrets in your family and the manor."

"I love you. I'm so glad you understand me."

"I do my best. Love you too. Now let me make a call and change our flight home."

Heather was smiling when she hung up the phone.

"Well, your look of concern has changed now that the call is over. What is going on with Sara?"

"She and Randall are coming home tomorrow. She is not mad at us for going to the attic, by the way. I was worried about that. Anyway, she is consumed with the land that Daddy owned, and now we own, I guess. I don't know if she and I own it or what that deal is all about. She wants to talk with me about that and help us go through the treasures we found today. Oh, and she wants you to wait to open that door larger. She wants to see the small opening herself first."

"Not a problem. I wasn't going to get to it tomorrow anyway."

"Now, I think it is time to get some rest. The boys are asleep. They fell right to sleep when I put them down. I must have worn them out today. Or they wore me out. I'm exhausted." He laid his head on his pillow and watched Heather finish getting ready for bed. He smiled as he watched her. He felt so lucky to have her in his life. He was so blessed that he had not lost her in that car accident a few years earlier. That had been a true test of their marriage. He was still smiling as he watched her walk to the bed with the slight limp that no one noticed anymore. To him, it was still a memory of the time he almost lost her and reminded him of how blessed he was.

All was quiet at the manor. The guests had all called it a night. Rachelle was in her apartment, which was adjacent to the kitchen in the back of the manor. Andy and Karen were home getting ready for bed.

"Oh, my!" Karen broke the silence in their room.

"What? What is it?" Andy asked as he sat up with concern.

"I just felt the baby, babies kick. Come feel this."

Andy reached over and let her guide his hand to her growing belly. They both felt the next kick.

"I wonder if they are fighting?"

"I don't think so. At least not yet. I've only felt gentle kicks from time to time so far. This is the first time anyone else has been around to share it with."

"You are an amazing woman, Karen."

"What makes you say that?"

"Oh, I don't know. You gave up your life and moved to a new state with a family you had not known very long. You pitched right in to help us with running Bella Rose. You help me in the kitchen to cook for the guests. You've learned to decorate cakes for the special events Heather is organizing. You don't complain much about anything. And now you are pregnant with twins."

"I love you, Mr. Andy Fairchild."

"I love you, too, Mrs. Karen Fairchild. Now tell those kids to settle down for the night. We need to get some rest."

"Very funny. I hate to tell you that at this stage of the game, the kids don't listen to me."

"Oh, just like when they become teenagers! Great!"

"Yes, just like that. Remember how you were as a teenager?"

"Oh, please, don't remind me. That was the age I began running away from home and learned to live on my own off the land. It was not the best decision I ever made. You, my darling wife, are the best decision I ever made."

"And you are mine. Good night Andy. Sweet dreams."

"Good night Karen. I hope those little teenagers don't keep you awake for long." He reached over and turned the light off.

"I hope not too. I've heard it gets a lot worse." She laid down and rubbed her belly as they both fell asleep.

Chapter Six

Sara and Randall were able to catch an afternoon flight home. When their flight to their honeymoon destination only took them to the west side of the state, she wondered why they had not driven. Now, she was glad they had flown as it saved a lot of time. She felt good to be home, especially when Randall surprised her again by lifting her and carrying her over the front door threshold. She knew then that even though they had cut the honeymoon short, the romance was still there. He was a keeper in her book.

She called Heather to let her know they were home and asked if everyone was getting together for dinner. Heather told her that they were, and Andy had made a special treat for them. While waiting for dinner time, she and Randall unpacked and set out a few of his things around the house he had brought over before the wedding. Sara had insisted on being old school before they got married and had not allowed him to move in. She wanted her life with him to be special and different from her first marriage, which had ended in disaster. She smiled at her husband, knowing they were off to a good start.

Dinner time always brought the family together. While they did not do it every night anymore, it was great to have the occasional large family meal. It gave them time to talk about life and the business, make plans, and enjoy time together at the end of the day. Any stresses anyone had were usually gone by the end of clean-up.

"Welcome home, Sis and Brother," Heather said when she entered with her family in tow.

Sara met her with a hug. "Thanks, Sis. It's good to be home—I think."

"Of course it is. Well, maybe not since you cut your honeymoon time short, but I love you for it. I can't wait to hear more about what you discovered in West Tennessee. But, first—let's eat!"

"Sounds good to me. Gather around everyone. Dinner is served," Andy said as he set the main course on the table. Karen had set the island up for everyone, complete with the stool for Marc and the high chair for Maddex. It wouldn't be long before Maddex would be big enough to sit on a stool like his big brother. He was probably ready now, size-wise, but he could not sit still for very long, so they kept him confined when he sat there to avoid an accident.

"Lasagna! Love it!" Randall said when he looked at the food and sat down. It's one of my favorites. How does it stand up to the Green Olive's Restaurant?"

"Better!" Andy defended himself. "Well, almost better. I was able to get the recipe from the owner, so I get it as close as I can."

"I think it's a bit better, Karen said as she leaned against her husband. "His is made with love." She smiled.

"And for dessert, dear Sister, I have made Tiramisu," Andy added, spoiling the surprise he had planned.

"Perfect! You're the best!"

After dinner, the conversation centered around the treasures they had found in the secret room. Rachelle went into the office and brought out a few bundles of letters and a couple of the journals, placing them on the island for everyone to see.

"Have you read any of the letters yet?"

"No, we were waiting for you."

"No time like the present to start. Hand me a bundle." Sara reached out for one. She untied the string and leafed through the letters. They were old, yellowed, and slightly torn. Most were in envelopes. Some of the stamps had fallen off from the glue drying out. Some letters didn't have envelopes. It was hard to read some of the envelopes as the ink had faded over time. Everyone was watching her as she looked at the first group she had unwrapped.

"These are dated when our Grandparents owned the manor. They are addressed to her and, nope, just her. I wonder why they are not addressed to GrandMama and Granddaddy?" She took the letter that was on top. Then handed the bundle to Heather, who was sitting next to her. "Here, I think everyone should take one to read. There are no secrets here." She looked at Andy. "Of course, these letters may tell us otherwise."

Heather took a letter and passed the rest along. Everyone took one and started to read to themselves.

Dear Rose,

Thank you so much for being here for me. I don't know what I would have done without you. My life was a shambles before I came here. My parents wanted nothing to do with me. My friends deserted me. My boyfriend left me. I was lost. I was homeless. Then I heard about this place and found my refuge with you.

After I left, I was able to start a new life. I know that what I did was the best thing for me and my little one. You were right. I needed to turn my life around. I could even reconnect with my parents before they passed away, and they forgave me and apologized for their part. It felt good to know that in the end, they still loved me.

I met a wonderful man after I left and now have two children. They do not know anything about Bella Rose and my time there. I hope you understand that I had to keep it all a secret. My life is good now, and I just wanted to let you know that I don't know if I could have survived without you.

I will always love you,

Rhea B.

Sara turned the letter over to see if there was more. The back was blank. She looked up and watched the faces of the others as they were reading their letters. They all had the same look she was sure she had. And all seemed to be as speechless as she was. What was this letter referring to? She waited for the others to finish before saying anything.

"Is anyone as confused as I am? Or was it just my letter that was mysterious?"

"No, I'm confused too. What did yours say?" Heather asked. Everyone else was still looking at their letters with confusion. They all looked at Sara.

"Well, my letter made it sound like Grandmama had rescued a young girl from her parents who had kicked her out."

"Mine too. Who wrote yours?"

"A Susan signed mine."

"Mine was from a girl named Debra."

"Mine was from Jo Anna"

"Okay, Sara cut them off. So each letter in this bundle seems to be from a different person. What is common about the bundles? Time frame? Address? Contents?"

"Let's set them aside and open the next bundle."

"Yes, let's," Sara said to Rachelle. Rachelle handed her the next bundle, and Sara did the same thing as with the first bundle. Everyone got a letter to read.

Dear Rose,

First, let me say, "Thank You." Thank you and Robert for your hospitality while I was there with my family. We had such a wonderful time. We were at a loss of what to do when our daughter told us she was 'with child.' We could not let her stay at home with us. We had a reputation to uphold in our community. You were the first person to understand that and let us bring our little girl to you to live until the baby was born. We are so grateful to you for that. You encouraged her to continue her schooling and make plans for her life when she could come home and start over. It was easier to explain to family and friends that she was away at a special school than it would have been to confess that we were bad parents and allowed our child to have a child out of wedlock. That is just something that is not tolerable in our circle.

Again, thank you.

Sincerely,
Mrs. G.
(Shirley's Mother)

Sara lowered the letter and noticed everyone was looking at her. They could have heard a pin drop in the room. What were they all reading?

"Sara?" Heather raised her letter as she asked. "What is all this about?"

"I'm as lost as you are. What did your letter say?"

"Mine was from a mother thanking Grandmama for helping them when her daughter needed help. There weren't a lot of details, but that's the gist of it."

"Mine was basically the same thing. It was from a mother. This first letter was from the girl that was here. How about the rest of you? Same grouping?"

"Yes, that must be the common ground of each bundle."

"But what do you make of them so far, Sis?"

"So far, it sounds like Grandmama and Granddaddy had a place for homeless, pregnant girls."

"I agree. But the first ones made it sound like the girls gave their babies up for adoption? Is that legal? Or was it legal back then?" Sara looked at Randall. "Do you know about the legalities of adoption in this area back then?"

"I don't, but I'm sure I can find out. I agree that so far, that is what the letters make it sound like."

"But why the secret room? Why not just house them in the standard rooms? I know Bella Rose was not very large during that time, but I'm sure there would have been rooms for them."

"Maybe more of the letters will tell us."

"Or the journals."

"Yes, the journals," Sara said. While she was looking around, she noticed the time. "The journals will have to wait. It is late. Heather and Ben, you need to get those boys to bed. Karen, you need your rest. And, last I knew, we still have guests to feed in the morning."

"Spoilsport. Just when I was getting into this investigation."

"I know, I am a spoilsport. But as much as I'd like to solve this tonight, I have a feeling this will take a while. It will also take all of us working together."

"Yes, it will. I'm glad to have another project to work on."

"Funny. I know we are all busy, but we can work on this in our spare time. I don't think it is a priority. But, I do want to know more."

"Sounds like a plan. We will see you in the morning. Come on, boys, time to get going. Say goodnight to everyone." The boys did as their mother said and gave hugs to everyone. Heather was hugging her sister and asked her about the land she had found.

"I will talk to you about that in the morning. Like the journals, it will also wait."

"Okay. Love you, Sis. Good night."

"Good night all."

Chapter Seven

Morning dawned with another sleepless night for Sara. She now not only had the land to think about, now the secret room! She simply could not figure it out.

"Good morning, Beautiful," Randall said as he handed her a cup of hot coffee.

"Good morning. Did I keep you awake last night?"

"No, I slept well. Why? Did you not sleep again?"

"Well, I have a lot on my mind. I think I spent the night trying to figure it out. Then when I finally fell asleep, I dreamed that the land was being used for the young girls to hide from family. All the buildings were in the middle of the secluded land. There were watchmen stationed around the property lines to keep all strangers out. It was confusing. Almost as confusing as the letters themselves."

"Well, maybe today you can read a few more and find out more. For now, how about bacon and eggs for breakfast?"

"I don't feel like cooking." She said absent-mindedly.

"I wasn't asking you to cook. I can cook. And you, my lovely wife, need to eat. I can't control your sleeping habits, but I can make you something to eat. Now, while I cook, you go get your shower."

Sara gave him a quick kiss. "Thank you. I'm not sure how I survived without you taking care of me."

"At this stage, neither do I." He laughed as he walked into the kitchen to start cooking. Sara just shook her head and pretended she didn't hear what he said.

The guests enjoyed another wonderful breakfast and were on their way to enjoy the rest of their visit going to their destinations. Downtown was the most common destination, but some traveled further west to enjoy the day in the Smoky Mountains, hiking, sightseeing, or shopping. Summers were a very busy time for everyone.

Sara and Randall arrived hand in hand at the Bella Rose kitchen. Randall was still on his honeymoon time off from work so that he could join his new family. He had no idea what he was in for, but it didn't matter. He was happy.

Rachelle saw Sara come in and motioned for her to join her in the office. Rachelle wanted to show her the letters and journals she had hidden in the file cabinet.

"That is quite a lot of letters. Did you leave any upstairs in that room?"

"We left a few only because our hands were full. We got all the journals, though. When are you going up to see the room?"

"I think I'll wait for Heather to get here. Any idea when she will be here?"

As she was speaking, Heather walked in. "I'm here. Are you ready to go investigate that room?"

"Yes, most definitely. I didn't sleep well last night thinking about it and dreaming about it when I finally did fall asleep."

"You need to get your rest, dear sister." As they talked, they walked up the stairs to the secret room. Before they got there, Heather asked her about the land in West Tennessee.

"What is it about that land you were telling me about?"

"Well, it seems that Daddy owns, owned, land in West Tennessee. The town is unincorporated, so it isn't an official town. There is no school, no post office, no stores, except a small convenience store. And while they do have a courthouse, it doubles as a church."

"The courthouse doubles as a church?"

"Yes, as I said, it is not incorporated. So there are no major businesses. No factories or jobs to speak of. Very few residents live on the land, and everyone works outside of the area in the next two towns."

"So, what did Daddy want to do with the land? Why did he have it to start with?"

"I'm not sure. The attorney we spoke with only knew that he had owned it and set it up for people to live there with few rules, regulations, and taxes. You know, no restrictions. But the families that live there are taking good care of their homes and the land. There is a lot of vacant land."

"So what are we supposed to do with it? And why were we not told about all of this when Daddy died? Did Mama know about the land?"

"No, there is nothing that indicates that Mama knew anything about it. And we were never told about it because the people who live there and the attorney were told that after he died, they would have five years to continue to live there. At that time, we were to be told about the land and to decide what to do with it."

At that moment, they were at the attic door, and Sara stopped talking.

"So this is where the secret room is?"

"Yes, inside. Are you ready?"

"I'm ready. We've been through a lot. This discovery should not be too difficult to handle."

Together they walked into the attic. They had spent a lot of time inside there already. Sara could not believe they had missed the secret door until she walked in.

"So, where is the secret door?" She asked Heather as they walked in. It wasn't visible at first glance.

"It is to the right of Mama's desk over here. I'm surprised you didn't notice it when you moved the bookcase."

"Moved the bookcase? I never moved the bookcase."

"You didn't?"

"No. I would not have a reason to move the bookcase."

"Well, none of us moved it either. Of course, Ben was not here when we asked everyone, but he never said he had moved it when he found out about it. We just assumed you had."

"Not me. So if none of us moved it, who did? Who has access to this room?"

"No one. The attic is kept locked; the key is in the office, which is also locked when no one is in there."

"Okay, this is getting spooky. Show me the room."

Heather reached over and pushed the little door. It did not budge. She pushed a little harder, and finally, it opened. She walked in, and Sara followed close behind.

Sara gasped. She saw the cots lined up along the two walls and a few more folded up behind several of them. Sara saw the desk and the dressers. She also noticed a few suitcases under some of the cots in the back near the file cabinet. She just stood in silence, taking it all in. What did it all mean? Why was this here? What was her Grandmama hiding? And why had it not been opened before now? Or if it had, why was everything still here? Did her parents know about this room? So many questions ran together in her head.

"So, what do you think?" Sara jumped when she heard Heather ask her a question.

"I'm not sure. This is all so out of place. What was going on here? And for how long? It certainly had ended before we were born. At least I don't remember ever hearing anything about it. Do you?"

"No, I don't. I'm as shocked as you are."

Sara started to walk through the room, touching the cots, running her fingers across the desktop. She sat at the desk and opened the top drawer. Inside were papers, office supplies, and a key. Sara shook her head. The last thing she wanted to see was another key. What was this key for? She opened the top side drawer. There was nothing in there. She opened the bottom drawer. It was heavy. Inside was a safe that filled the whole drawer. She called Heather over to the desk as she lifted the safe and placed it on top of the desk.

"Do you have the key?" Heather asked when she saw the safe.

"Sure do. It was in the top drawer. Are you ready to see what's inside?"

"Sure, how bad could it be?" The sisters looked at each other, realizing that nothing was beyond imagination.

Sara used the key and opened the safe. Inside were papers and envelopes. She removed everything from inside while Heather made room on top of the desk. Sara slowly went through each paper while Heather looked on then took them from her, making new piles on the desk.

"What does all of this mean? I can't deal with more family secrets! Life was so simple just five years ago. What were our parents and now our grandparents thinking? What were they doing? Do you think all of this has something to do with why Bella Rose is so well known in town? Do the townspeople, especially the older ones, know more than they have shared with us? What do they know that we don't?"

"What are you trying to say? What makes you think the residents in town know more than we do about this place?"

"I've sensed a few of the older people talking behind my back when I'm shopping there or just walking around. Some seem distant. They have for years, but I've noticed it more since Daddy and Mama died.

"Well, we had lost our parents within months of each other. Then we searched and found Andy. We all came back home and are making a go of running Bella Rose. I just thought they felt bad for us or thought we would fail at running it. You have a vivid imagination."

"I'm serious. What if someone or someones in town knows more about this place than they have shared? Maybe they don't think we can handle the truth, whatever it may be. Or maybe they think we know the truth and are amazed at how we are still here and becoming a success."

"Where did you come up with all these thoughts? You worry me. We don't even know what all these papers mean. We don't know what the letters are referring to. We don't know much of anything yet. Let's wait until we figure more things out. I think I need to get Randall to look at these papers and see what they mean."

"Good idea. We can take that and the rest of the letters downstairs to the office. That way we won't have to come back up here for a while."

"Are you scared to be in here?"

"I'm not sure why, but yes. Being here bothers me. In fact, I have to get out of here. Are you ready?"

Sara scooted the chair back, and it screeched against the floor, making them both jump. "Sure. You get the letters; I'll take the safe. Heather, we will be, no, we are fine. Stop with your vivid imagination."

"I will do my best. But I'd like answers so I can let it all rest."

"And we will get the answers. I'm counting on these papers and the letters and journals to tell us the full story. Then we can get on with our lives."

"Don't forget we have that land to deal with now too."

"Yes, we do. We'll talk about that later today." Sara closed the safe while Heather held the letters and closed the drawer on the cabinet. Together they walked out of the room, closing the door behind them. They left the attic and walked to the first floor and into the office.

"So, what do you think about what's up there?" Karen asked when she saw them.

"Well, we found a safe in the desk that had more papers inside. I am going to have Randall look through them for us and hopefully answer some questions."

Hearing his name, Randall came into the office from the living room, where he had been playing with the boys.

"What do you have for me?"

"I have a safe with a lot of papers. I think I know what some of them are, but not all. I was hoping you could look at them and tell us what we may be dealing with."

"Sure, I'd be glad to. Is this the safe?" He asked as he spotted the safe on the desk.

"Yes, it is. And here is the key to it. We can leave the safe open if you want, and I can put the key in the desk drawer. That way, the key won't get lost."

"That will be fine. Let me take a look." Randall took the safe with him and sat in the guest chair by the door. He lifted the lid and glanced inside. Randall noticed old vehicle insurance cards, vehicle titles, envelopes with more papers inside, and another key inside an envelope from the bank. He lifted the key and looked at Sara. "I found another key."

"No! No more keys! What is that one to?"

"It was inside an envelope from the bank in town. I think it goes to a safe deposit box."

"Why didn't the bank president that we dealt with after Mama died mention a safe deposit box?"

"Maybe he didn't know about it. There are a lot of people in the area that use that bank. I don't think he knows everyone. Maybe he didn't think about it at the time."

"Okay, I'll give you that one. But it still doesn't help answer what might be in there.

"No, it doesn't. Are you ready for a short road trip?"

"I am. Let's go. Heather, can you lock up everything while we are gone? I need to find some answers. Or if you have someone to watch the boys, we will lock up so you can come with us."

"Are you sure?"

"Yes, you are a part of all this. You need to be with me. I think we need Andy to be there too."

"But Andy might not be a blood relative to this."

"Yes, I think this is related to Mama and Grandmama, not our Daddy. The land is related to Daddy, not this. Andy needs to be with us."

"Okay, I'll go find him when I find Ben to watch the boys." Heather was shaking her head.

"What is it, Sis?" You don't have to come if you don't want to."

"Oh, I'm coming. I'm just overwhelmed, I guess. Why can't life be simple anymore?"

"That would be nice. Maybe someday it will be again."

After everyone heard what they had found and the need to go to the bank, they piled into Randall's car and headed to the bank. They were silent for most of the short trip. When Randall parked the car, he turned in his seat to talk with them. "You know that you do not need to be inside if you don't want to be when we open this. You don't know what is in there."

They all listened to him talk about the legal specifics, but all agreed they wanted to be together to witness the findings.

The group walked into the bank. Randall went to the teller and asked for the bank president, explaining they were all there to open a safe deposit box. The teller told him that he didn't have to have the bank president there to open it. He said he knew that, but the president was his friend, and he wanted him there.

A few minutes later, the president joined the family. "They told me you had asked for me and that you needed to get into a bank deposit box. You do know any teller can let you in to open that."

"Yes, I know, but since this is related to Bella Rose manor and you had been the keeper of the will when their Mama died, I thought you'd like to be here for this as well. Plus, if I have questions, I'd like you to be here to answer them."

"Okay. Hello everyone." He said as he took the key from Randall and led them into the vault.

A moment later, they were all staring at the deposit box. It was a shallow, long, narrow metal box like the ones they had opened after Susan died. There could not be much in there. Sara thought. They all gathered closer as the President opened the lid. Inside was just one thing. One envelope; Randall reached in and pulled it out, and handed it to Sara. The president closed the lid while Sara carefully opened the envelope.

"You can take that home to open if you want," he said as he put the box back into the opening in the wall.

"No, I want to see what it has inside."

Sara took the neatly folded paper out of the envelope. The envelope and paper were old and yellowed, almost like what they had found in the secret room. She carefully opened it and began to read it to herself. Before she finished it, her knees started to buckle under her. Randall reached over and steadied her.

"We need to go home. I can't read this here."

"Okay. Let's go home." Randall started to lead everyone out.

"What does it say?" Andy asked.

"I want to be at home to read it. Please."

"Okay. We can go."

They all left the bank and got into the car. Randall drove them all home. No one said a word while they drove. When they arrived, everyone followed Sara to the living room, where she sat down. She was glad no one was there but family. The information was a shock to her system, and she knew it would be for the rest of her family as well. Although the few letters they had read had been a clue, she didn't think anyone had understood completely what it all meant. When she had skimmed over the letter at the bank, it all came together. It wasn't good. Somehow she knew this would change their lives unless they could continue to keep the secret. And why couldn't they? A million thoughts were going through her head as she just sat there in silence.

Everyone gathered around her, waiting and watching her. What in the world was in that letter? And how could she have had such a reaction so fast? Was it that bad? As Sara continued her silence, her family began to look at each other with silent questions.

"Sara, what's going on? What does that letter say?" Randall was sitting next to his wife and spoke quietly to her. He had never seen her like this. She was never silent for this long. Something was not right.

Sara looked down at the envelope where she had replaced the letter. She lifted it just a few inches and tried to speak. At first, nothing would come out of her mouth. She slowly opened the envelope and gently took the letter out. It was old, like the letters from the secret room. Since it had been inside the vault, it was not as fragile as the others, yet, Sara treated it with care. This letter could change the way her family thought about their family history. She opened the folds of the letter and smoothed it against her leg. Then lifted it so she could read it to the others.

Sara began to read the letter.

> *I don't know who will find this letter, or even if it will mean anything to the one who does. But, I have come to that point in my life that the truth needs telling. If this letter is found at Bella Rose Manor, you will understand what I am about to write. If you are part of my descendants, you may understand even more. Or it will bring you more questions and maybe some pain. I hope you don't feel the pain. I hope you see the positive.*

> *In a quick explanation, I will just say that I was part of something that some may find illegal or, at the least—wrong. I saw it as the only way to help people at first. Later I found it as the only way to save people. Young girls, specifically.*

You see, I was involved in hiding them from people who were out to find them and hurt them. Some I was even hiding from their own families who had pushed them away as if they were something they could throw away instead of showing them the love they deserved. All the girls I took in were either running away or being cast out by family because they were pregnant. They had no place to go. They all were told to get rid of their baby. And that is what I did.

Sara turned to the second page. One she had not looked at before. The first page is the one that had left her speechless. She hoped it would not be as shocking when she turned the page but knew it could worsen depending on the details. She continued reading.

When Robert and I moved here to Bella Rose, it was just a small house. It didn't have a name; it was just our home. It was our beginning. We planned on having a simple life in the country, raising our family like everyone else we knew.

Then one day, we heard a knock on our door. It was a young girl. She was alone. At first, I thought she was lost. But knowing where our house was, I couldn't figure out how she found our house. It was cold outside, and she was shivering. So I invited her in.

That was how it began. That little lost girl changed our lives. You see, she was with child. She was alone. Her parents had sent her away. She had little more than the clothes on her back. Her entire life was inside the bag she carried and inside her.

We listened to her story and had no idea what to do. Robert wanted to take her to the police station. I stopped him. This little girl needed our help. So we took her in. We had a spare bedroom that I was saving to make into a nursery when the time came for us to have a family. Instead, it was the first guest room we had.

A couple of months later, this little girl named Rhea gave birth to a perfect baby boy. She named him Benjamin Thomas. We had discussed her future before she gave birth, and she said she would not keep him. She told us that her parents would take her back after the baby was born, only if she had given the baby away.

Robert had done a lot of searching and found a couple who would take the baby, no questions asked. So after Benjamin was born, Rhea said goodbye to him, and we arranged to give him away. It was the hardest thing I had ever done. To let that baby go to an unknown family was both joyous and heartbreaking. We watched this girl, a little child herself, relieved that she could now go back home and get on with her life with her family. I also saw the heartache in her eyes. I could tell she loved her baby the moment he was born.

While she had been there, we had a gentleman come to the door asking for her. We told him we had no guests and to leave. When he insisted, Robert threatened to call the police if he didn't go away. I had hidden with Rhea until the man left.

After she left, Robert and I talked. Maybe helping girls like her was our calling. Maybe it was meant to be. But we just let those thoughts go, and as time went on, we forgot about that idea.

Until it happened again. This time a mother was standing at the door with her daughter. She was going to just drop her 'with child' daughter with a stranger and walk away. Of course, we thought the lady was heartless, but we took the child in and let the older lady walk away.

While we had not run with the idea of taking in wayward girls, we had thought to build on to our home and offer guest rooms to travelers who wanted a place to stay but did not want to stay in a hotel. In reality, Robert had already started to build it. So taking in another child was an easy decision.

Like the first, this baby was to be given away. Before giving birth, her mother arrived again, this time to take her home. She seemed genuine. She seemed to have had a change of heart. I let her talk with her daughter for a while before they both left together. The mother had given me her address and phone number to call later to check on her daughter and baby. And about a month later, I did just that; Only to find out that the mother had taken her daughter to a doctor to get rid of the baby. The procedure had not gone well, and they both had died. I was devastated! I vowed then never to let another girl be forced to go through that if she first came here. I would not let the families take back their children they had either dropped off or sent away because they were with child. I just wouldn't.

So while Robert was building the addition, he built a secret room attached to one of the rooms he had on the third floor.

If you are reading this, I know you have found the room. And you have found the other evidence of my actions.

I hope you will take the time to read the letters and the journals that the girls and I wrote. They were all beautiful little girls caught up in bad circumstances. They had no place else to go. Robert and I showed them love. We showed them that not all people were bad. We showed them opportunities they may not have had. And yes, most of them gave their babies up for adoption.

At first, the adoptions were also secret. The only information the new families had about their adoptive baby was the birth date and a name. They were free to rename the child, create a birth certificate and live their lives as if the child was their blood.

After a few years, we connected with an adoption agency to do it legally yet still secretly.

I wish I knew what happened to all those girls and the babies, but I don't. All I knew about them after they left was what they said in their letters. I prayed for them every day.

I want you, whoever you are, to know that even though it may have started as an illegal act to give the babies away, and I'm not sure what you would call our hiding of them, but it was for their protection, and I would do it all over again. Robert and I loved every one of the girls and their babies.

We stopped taking the girls in when our own children got to the age of not understanding that what we were doing had to be kept a secret. By then, we had started taking in regular borders and started what is now, or was, known as Bella Rose Manor.

So, now you know more of the hidden truth behind Bella Rose Manor and our family.

Rose

Chapter Eight

Everyone was silent as they tried to digest what Sara had read to them. How could their Grandmama be involved with that? On the other hand, she was saving lives and helping young girls live better lives. She was there for them when no one else was. She was a hero to so many. So if she was a hero, why were they in such shock?

"So, this changes everything," Sara said after she had looked at her family sitting in silence for a moment.

"Maybe. Maybe not. We can look at it negatively or positively. I prefer to think positively. Rose was a hero. A life saver." Heather responded while she was still busy mixing her thoughts.

"Yes, she was a hero. But, she also was involved in a possible illegal act." Sara said. She had looked at it only from the negative aspect when she first glanced at it. Now, maybe it was not such a bad letter. Maybe her thoughts of the illegal aspect were from her being with Randall. He was an attorney, and Sara had begun thinking more analytical instead of creatively. She tilted her head as she realized that life was not always black and white. Life had many gray areas where the view of things changed with different lighting.

"I want to look at her as a hero. Who cares if it was illegal at the time. She saved lives—a lot of lives. Yes, maybe Rose went about it wrong. Maybe she did not know of a better way to do it. Remember, this was a long time ago. There may not have been places for these girls to go." Heather added.

"That is true," Sara said.

"I think we need to take the high road here and consider our grandparents as heroes," Andy said. "But, it does make me wonder why she hid it? I mean, after a while, it should have been acceptable to be open about it. Do you think our Mama remembered it?"

"She must have, although she was an infant at the time. It depends on how many years it continued. She may not have remembered it. The letter says that they stopped once their biological kids were older and couldn't keep a secret." Heather said.

Starting their own family changed things." Karen added as she rubbed her growing belly.

"So, what do we do with this new twist to our lives? Do we keep it hidden?" Heather asked.

"No. I think we read all the letters and journals. Then I think we try to find the girls." Rachelle joined in after listening to everyone else voice their thoughts.

"Find them? Why? They may not want to be found. And they would be older than your parents. They could be anywhere in the world. Their names may have changed if they got married. And some may even have died already." Ben added. He didn't like to be morbid about it, but it was true.

"Maybe we can find the children that were born here and invite them here to visit," Rachelle said.

"That would be a miracle. Do you have any idea how hard it is to find people who have been adopted? Most adoptions were secret as far as who their birth parents were. And then there are the parents who adopt children but never tell them they are adopted." Heather said as she was trying to figure out how they would even start to search.

"I realize this, but I bet we could find a few of them." Sara had become excited.

"Always the optimist. That's why we love you." Andy smiled.

"So, what is our first step?" Ben was getting interested

63

"We read the letters and journals," Sara said as she sat up, putting herself into action mode. What had begun as a feeling of doom for her family had turned into something positive. "I also think, Randall, that we need to find out about the legalities of what she did back then. And if there is anything we should be aware of that we can and can't do with this new knowledge."

"I will get to work on it. I am still on a break from work for our honeymoon," Randall gave Sara a sideways look, "so I can take that free time to 'secretly' do some investigation." Randall winked at Sara. "Love you, dear." He was learning more and more that this family he grew up around had more secrets than even he knew.

So, what is our next step? Do we just read the letters out of curiosity, or do we actively search for these girls, now women, and the babies?" Ben asked and continued. "We don't have much to go on yet. Just a few names. We don't even have dates."

"No, but the letters and journals may tell us more. I say we divide and conquer." Karen said.

Rachelle had been quiet. She was listening and watching everyone as Sara had been reading. Rachelle had become a part of this family, but this was not part of her family history, not even an in-law or step-family part. She wasn't sure if she should offer to run the manor while they all investigated or offer to help read.

"Rachelle, you have been quiet. What do you think about all of this?" Sara asked.

"I am not sure what to think. You certainly have a lot to investigate and answers to find. I think your grandparents were amazing to do what they did. I mean, if it was illegal, they were risking everything if they got caught. I also think they were some special people who cared that much about strangers. It will be interesting to see what you find out."

"You are a part of us; you are more than welcome to help us read and search for answers."

"Are you sure? I'm not related at all."

"Neither is Ben, Randall, nor I, but we will help," Karen said.

"But you at least are related by marriage. I'm not even that. I'm just—I'm not sure what I am." Rachelle admitted.

"You, young lady, are our sister! You are a big part of our family. Family isn't just about blood. Family is about love, and caring, and well, family! You are family." Sara said as she walked over to her and put her arm around her shoulder. You belong here. We love you."

"Ditto, what she said," Andy added, more than laughed to lighten the mood of the room.

Rachelle turned and went to the office. She carried the file basket she had put the letters and journals in earlier to where her family sat. "Well, I say, let's get started. Everyone, take a bundle, but keep the bundles together."

"Good plan. Let's see what our grandparents achieved." Sara said as she reached in for one of the journals.

"Reminds me of when we first discovered the letters and journals in the attic. We still have not gone through all of those." Heather mentioned as she pulled out a bundle of letters.

"You're right. I think these will reveal the true beginning of Bella Rose. Later we can go through the other ones." Sara said.

"Our family seems to have quite a history. Who knew?" Andy added as he took a bundle for him and Karen.

"Happy hunting, everyone. Let's go read as you have time, and we can meet back here tomorrow night. Do you think that is enough time?"

"Are you kidding? I don't think I'll be able to put them down when I start. But I'll just get another bundle when I finish these." Heather said.

Everyone went their separate ways to read or take care of the regular tasks of the manor.

Randall went to his computer to do some research. Sara sat down in her favorite chair to read the journal.

I've never written a journal before, but here I go. For whatever reason, I think what Robert and I are doing with our lives at the moment needs to be documented.

First, a little background—

Robert and I had just gotten married when we bought this land we live on now. We built a small house with two bedrooms in hopes of one day having a child. We had enough land that we could add on to the house if and when we needed to. We had the house built on a hill with a beautiful view of the mountains in the distance. I loved sitting on our little back porch and just looking out and feeling God's love for us.

One day I heard a knock at our front door. A visitor would sound like a normal event to most people. Not for us. We lived at the end of a dead-end lane that winds up a small hill. You can only find us if you are looking for us and have a reason to be here. We didn't have many friends who dropped in uninvited, so when I heard the knock, I was surprised. I thought maybe something had happened to Robert.

I opened the door and saw this little girl standing there with a small bag in her hand. At first, I thought maybe she was selling something that she had made, or her family had made, and then they sent her out to sell it door to door because they were poor and needed money.

It was chilly out, so I invited her in. She was a little dirty, but she was a little girl, so I didn't hold that against her.

Then I heard her story.

She had been sent away from her home because she was with child. They wanted nothing to do with her and threw her out with just a few of her belongings, including a small teddy bear. She had no place to go. She saw our tiny lane and planned to follow it and sleep that night in the woods. When she saw our little house, she was brave to even knock on the door, not knowing who lived there.

I asked her what her plans were. She told me she had no plans but that she had to find someone who wanted a baby.

I was shocked and confused. The little girl then told me that her parents told her to leave and not return until after getting rid of the baby. They told her that she would ruin their family reputation and status in their town if she stayed and had the baby. They would tell folks that she had gone away to school or something.

I reached out and hugged her. By then, I had made her something to drink, and we were sitting by the window looking out over the mountains.

Well, when Robert came home, I told him about this little girl who by then was asleep on our sofa bundled under one of my quilts.

He listened and asked me what I planned to do. I told him I wanted her to at least spend the night to stay safe. He agreed. When the girl woke up, the three of us talked together and decided she would stay with us until after the baby was born. We told her we would help her and take care of her. Robert told her he would see what he could do about finding someone who wanted to take in a newborn baby.

She sat and cried when she accepted our invitation. It wasn't until then that she told me her name was Rhea.

Over the next few months, before she had the baby, we learned more about her. She was reluctant to tell us much, but that was okay. We were strangers to her.

Robert found a young couple a few towns away who had wanted a baby and were willing to adopt her baby. We explained to them that they would need to raise it as their own and never tell anyone the truth about it. They agreed.

When the baby was born, I helped deliver him. He was such a beautiful newborn. Not all newborns are cute. This one was. Rhea had told me that she wanted to hold him and name him before giving him away. I knew that might not be the best thing for her and knew that she might not want to give him away at the last moment, especially if she held him. Rhea held him for almost an hour. She talked to him, sang to him. And then she named him Benjamin Thomas. After calling him by his name, she handed him to me and closed her eyes to sleep. When she later awoke, she asked if Benjamin had found his home. I told her that he had and that his new parents would love him as their own.

Rhea left us a week after she gave birth and returned to her parents. I got a letter from her a few years later, and by then, our new way of life was in full swing.

See, that was how Bella Rose started— what had started as our simple house turned into a place for runaway girls who were with child.

Here is more.

The second girl was brought to us by her mother. When I opened the door to them and heard her mother tell me to take care of her daughter to save her the embarrassment, I was appalled. How could any mother think of her own daughter as an embarrassment? Of course, we took her in. The mother left without even telling her daughter that she loved her. I could see the pain and loneliness in that child's eyes. That night I heard her cry herself to sleep.

I talked with Robert about it and asked him to add on to the house. I wanted to be able to take in more troubled girls. We had been using the spare bedroom, and luckily the girls were only arriving one at a time. I had a strange feeling there would be more.

And there were more.

Robert built on to the house with a whole new building. We planned to provide a place for these girls by giving them a place to feel at home—complete with a few bedrooms, a living room, a kitchen, and a place for me to do the office work and be there for them if they needed me. I wanted them to feel the love of family. I ended up spending many nights there when it was getting close to their delivery times. They all were so young and scared.

Soon after Robert started to build this new addition, a new girl arrived—again, brought by her mother. The girl was there maybe for a month when the mother returned to take her home. At first, I was a bit leery about it. But when I spoke with the girl, she said she wanted to go home. So I let her go. I later learned that the mother had come to take her to have an abortion. A doctor did not do it, and in the end, it caused the death of the baby and that precious little girl.

When I found that out, I told Robert I wanted a safe room built into the addition. I asked him to put it off to the side of the one bedroom with a hidden door. That way, I could better protect the girls.

He thought I was silly until a young man knocked on our door demanding to see one of the girls one day. He said he was the baby's father and demanded to take her home. The more I told him we didn't have anyone there by that name, the angrier he became. Robert heard our argument and came to the door. He was able to tell this man to leave us alone and never return. Robert told him if he ever came back, he was calling the police.

Luckily, the addition was already being built, and he didn't even attempt to go there. We knew then that we had to secure the other building against that. So Robert built a locking gate around the front. He also built a breezeway between our house and the addition.

We would get letters from the girls from time to time after they had returned home and gotten on with their lives. We did our best to stay in touch with the adoptive parents while also keeping their secrets.

Usually, at Christmas time, we would host a large party and invite all the adoptive parents. We never said a word to them of the connection they all had to each other, and unless they talked about it among themselves, they never knew.

Several years later, our own family grew, and I gave birth to my biological child, Susan. She was the love of my life. As much as I loved each of the girls who had entered our home and felt love for all the babies, having one of my own was nothing compared to that. I was in heaven.

A year later, I was pregnant with another child. I had the stress of the girls who still showed up, the stress of finding couples who wanted children, and the thought that what we were doing was, in fact, illegal. I told Robert that we should get connected to a legal adoption agency and work with them.

While he looked into that, I was busy with taking care of Susan and being pregnant. All was going well until late one night.

I had such pain in my side that Robert had to drive me to the hospital. We took Susan with us, but the other girls stayed on their own. They were all old enough to fend for themselves.

Early the next morning, I received the news that I had lost the baby. I was devastated. My heart had never felt such loss. It wasn't something anyone discussed. I was alone. Yes, I had Robert, the girls, and Susan, but I still felt the pain of grief.

I put on my best face and went on with life. We continued being the home for wayward girls. At least for a while.

When Susan got old enough to talk and make friends outside the home, we knew we had to do something different. Having this special place for them had run its course. It was time for a change. And so we stopped taking them in. We closed the doors after the last girl left, following her baby's adoption.

Susan never knew about what went on in her home before she could talk. At least, I don't think she did. We never talked about it after we closed it down.

Robert and I converted the home into a Manor for regular guests. It was a slow start, but we had a full house almost every weekend and some during the week within a year. Susan was growing into a great kid, and life was wonderful.

I often think back to those days and the girls. I wondered how they would be doing over the years if they ever found true love, married, or had other children. I wondered if they ever talked about their time at our place. Or even if they remember. However, I can't imagine being able to forget such a traumatic time in their lives.

For several years I still got letters from a few of them. I even got a couple of letters from the adoptive parents letting me know how their babies had done. How they had grown and how blessed they felt to raise these children that at one time had been unwanted.

I used to worry that what we did was the wrong thing to do. But as time went on and with the letters, I realized that we did what was needed. We were blessed.

I hope, now that you have read this and know the details of how Bella Rose Manor got started, that you will feel blessed as we have felt. Bella Rose began with love. Love for family. Love for the stranger that knocked on our door. Love for each other.

If Bella Rose is still in operation, I hope it is run with the same love and brings joy to all who enter.

Rose

Chapter Nine

Sara had not put the journal down since she started to read it. Before she knew it, it was dark outside, and Randall brought her a plate of food.

"What's this?" She asked as she took the plate from him.

"You, my darling wife, have been so deeply into that journal that the place could have burnt to the ground, and you would not have noticed. That must be some story."

"Oh my, yes. You would not believe the history of Bella Rose!"

"It was a single-family house that your grandfather expanded into the Manor it is today. Well, almost. I know you and your siblings added a few things to the property after your parents died, but that's about it."

"Um. Good try. But, no."

"No?"

"Yes, No. You know those couple of letters we read earlier? From a girl that my grandparents helped and another one from a mother? And then the letter we found in the safe deposit box?"

"Yes, what about them? I know we were all confused."

"Now they all make sense. A long time ago, soon after my grandparents married and built this place, a little girl knocked at their door...."

Sara left her meal to sit while she told Randall what she had learned from the journal. When she finished, she leaned back with a large smile on her face.

"You mean to tell me that this used to be a home for wayward girls, and the secret room was to protect them?"

"That's how it sounds. We had assumed from the letters that they kept the girls and adopted their babies out, but now we know why the secret room. They were protecting them. Sometimes from their own families. Sometimes from the father of their own baby. It is so sad."

"Sad that the girls had to go through that, but great that your grandparents saw the need and did that for them."

"I agree. It does put a whole new light on what Bella Rose was meant to be."

"I almost wish they had kept it as a place for those in need. There are still girls in that situation. They still get tossed out of their homes; the baby's fathers leave them with nothing."

"Yes, but at least there are places for them to go now, right?"

"Yes, of course. You're right." He hesitated. "So what do you do now? Do you still want me to investigate if it was legal or not?"

"I'm not sure. It wouldn't make any difference. The fact that it may have been illegal makes me proud of my grandparents for risking their lives for those girls and the babies. Let me talk to the others, and we will go from there." Sara started to eat her now cold dinner.

As much as she wanted to call the others, it was late, and she didn't think they would have had time to read a lot of the letters. So she would let them be. They would all talk tomorrow. In the meantime, she also had the land on her mind.

"Randall, what do you think we should do about that land in West Tennessee?" Do you think we should just sell it to the residents?"

"That was a quick change of subject." Randall sat up straight. "I think you need to talk with Heather about it. However, if you want my honest opinion, I think you should go ahead and sell it. Let the residents deal with it, leave it as it is, develop it, whatever they want. We live so far away and are busy. And now, with these letters and a new mystery to resolve, you will have your hands full here."

"Thanks. I was thinking the same thing. Mainly because it is so far away from us. I would still like to know why Daddy owned it in the first place. What is over there that had his interest? If I sell it, I may never know."

"You can always talk to the attorney again. He was older and seemed to know your Dad personally. He may know the story behind that."

"True. Hey, is there any chocolate cake left?"

"Chocolate cake?" Randall just shook his head and got up to get her a piece of the cake they had brought home earlier. "Why are you so hungry?"

"I have no idea. Excitement, I guess." She did her best to slow down and enjoy the piece of chocolate cake. It was always better when eaten slowly. Her brother made the best cake!

Heather finally had the two boys in bed and started reading the letters she had taken home.

Dear Rose,

You will never know how much it meant to me to find you. You were my Godsend when I had no place else to go. I hope you know that you changed my life.

I was at an all-time low spot in my life when I found out I was going to have a child. When I told my parents about it, they tossed me out like week-old garbage.

They didn't even think about the fact the child was part of them. They just saw how embarrassed they would be with me not being married. And the fact that the boy who got me pregnant broke up with me and didn't believe me when I told him it was his child. He called me a...well, you know. I have never seen or heard from him after that day.

I am so thankful that you found a loving home for my little girl. She was so beautiful. I almost wanted to keep her when she was born, but I knew I had no way to care for her and that my parents would not have allowed her in their home.

I do hope someday, somehow, to be able to see her, at least again. I won't tell her who I am if she or her parents don't want that to happen. I just would love to see her and know she is alright.

Thank you again, Rose, for being there for me when I needed someone to care for me and show me that there is still love in this world. I will stay in touch if that is okay with you.

Love,
Shelly

Heather had tears in her eyes. Ben went to her to comfort her. He asked her why she was crying, and all she could do was hand him the letter. So he read it too. While he was reading that one, she dried her eyes and picked up the next one. It basically said the same thing. She picked up the next one. It was the same. All these girls were so thankful for Rose being there for them. Then she picked up the last letter that was in the bundle.

Dear Rose,

I don't know how to thank you. I was so scared that night when my boyfriend, EX-boyfriend tried to find me. I heard you at the door when he asked about me. He did his best to convince you that he loved me and wanted the baby and me back. You told him that he had the wrong address. When he tried to argue with you, Robert stepped in and told him to leave or else.

I know I was the reason you built that secret room that saved many girls from angry boyfriends and parents.

I learned a lot talking with the few other girls that were there when I was. It felt good to know I was not the only girl in my predicament, but it also saddened me to know that fact.

We formed a bond while we were there, not only with you and Robert but with each other. After I had my baby boy and left, I always wondered what happened to the other girls, if they were able to return to their hometowns, if they made a good life for themselves.

I also wondered what happened to all the babies that were born and adopted out. Especially my precious little boy. For you to allow me to hold him for just a little while and to tell you what I would have named him meant a lot. I know whoever adopted him may have chosen a different name, and that is okay.

I know now that what you did was unheard of back in the day. You could have gotten into so much trouble. I love you for what you did.

I hope the years have been good to you. You deserve it. Maybe someday I will make it back to see you and thank you in person. But, I live so far away now.

I will tell you that I have been able to go on with my life. I met this wonderful man, and we had two children—a boy and a girl. They are the loves of my life. But I will always have a spot in my heart for my first-born son, Benjamin Thomas. If someday I have the good fortune to find and be reconnected with my son, I would be thrilled. If I never do, I at least hope he knows his birth mother loves him.

I will always remember you, your love, and the mountains of TN. Take care of each other.

Love,
Rhea B.

She finished reading the letter and handed it to Ben. He took the letter and set it down as he hadn't finished reading the last one she had given him. She interrupted his reading.

"These letters are intriguing. I wonder what Sara has found out in the journal. I'm sure she has read it by now." Heather looked at the clock. It was too late to go over to Sara's. She would have gone over to her sister's without hesitation before Sara was married. Now she would not disturb her sister and new husband.

Just then, they heard Maddex crying. "I'll go check on him. You keep reading." Heather got up to check on their young son. It wasn't like him to cry at night.

Ben was busy reading and heard only a part of what she said. "Okay."

He put down the second letter and picked up the last one she had handed him. He noticed that it was longer than the others and that the paper was not as old and yellowed.

He began to read. He felt touched by the words on this one. It was slightly different from the other letters, as it included more details but said the same basic thing. The writer had come here while she was pregnant to find safety.

It was the ending that caught his breath. The child's name. And it was signed by 'Rhea B.' He stood straight up and rushed into where Heather was.

"I think I made a connection!"

"Shh, I just got him back to sleep! What are you talking about?"

"This letter! I think I made a connection!" He yelled in a whisper.

"Okay. Tell me out there." She whispered and pointed to the door.

Once they were back out in their living room, he started talking.

"This letter. It is signed by Rhea B."

"Yes, so?"

"The other day, I was talking with one of our guests. She told me that her grandmother had told her about this place just before she died and told her if she ever got the chance to look this place up and come visit."

"And....?"

"Let me finish. Anyway, this guest told me that her grandmother told her she had come here once for a safe place to stay. That she had been in trouble, and this place and the owners here saved her life." He looked at Heather, expecting her to know the rest of the story. When she just kept looking at him, he knew he had forgotten the main connection. He picked up the paper and pointed to the signature. "Her grandmother's name was Rhea Brown!"

Heather grabbed the letter out of his hand. Suddenly she was excited but speechless! After a moment of her looking at the letter and her husband, she spoke. "You mean to tell me that we may have the granddaughter of this lady here at the manor?"

"That's what I'm saying. But, we don't know all the details of any of this, and I don't think it would be a good idea to bring this on our guest and then it not be the right connection."

"You're right. I think we just need to let all of this sink in. We can talk to Sara about it tomorrow."

"Do I have to wait that long?"

"Yes. Yes, we do. Let's get some rest tonight. I have a feeling the next few days will be a whirlwind for all of us." He took the letter from her hand and just looked at it. There was something about this letter. To find that connection would be amazing.

Chapter Ten

Morning dawned early. Heather nor Ben had slept much. Sara and Randall had been awake for a while as well. Life was changing for everyone. Finding out this new information about their family and their home was a shock. None of them had even considered that for a reason the manor had begun. Why would they? To them, their grandparents had just expanded their home for guests to stay and enjoy the area. It was simply a place to stay and feel welcomed and at home, unlike a hotel that didn't have that welcoming feeling of home or homemade breakfasts and the chance to meet the owners and interact with them. Now there was new light shining through.

Everyone was early for breakfast. As soon as the coffee was made and poured, it seemed everyone wanted to talk at once. Randall raised his hands. "Hush everyone, I know we found out some new information last night, and from the sounds of it, so did you, but I think we need to talk one at a time. Sara – you first."

"Thank you, my Dear. Last night I read the small journal written by our grandmama, Rose. She revealed some information that is quite shocking but full of love. Like the couple of letters we all read yesterday, her journal confirmed what we, or at least what I, was thinking. She wrote of how the Manor started, how it grew, and why there is a secret room." She could tell she had all of their attention and could tell they all had something to say. "So, you each had the letters to read. Each bundle just had a few letters in them, so from your reactions, I have a feeling you had time to read them all?"

"Yes, we did," Andy spoke before Heather had a chance. "The few letters we read seemed to be written by mothers who had left their daughters here. They talked about not taking care of them or not wanting their family reputation to be scorned, so they brought their daughters here until their babies were born. All but one mentioned their daughters being able to come home afterward. One mentioned that she was thankful for bringing her daughter here and added that her daughter never returned home because her husband would not let her. She still misses her daughter but knows that it is better than if she had gone back home. That was so sad to read. None of them mentioned the secret room or any other details of this place other than just dropping them off and that they were glad it was a place of seclusion."

Rachelle spoke up when Andy took a long pause. "The few letters I read were from parents that talked of adopting babies from here. They talked of how grateful they were to avoid the waiting list and all the legal documentation involved in a regular adoption. They just were able to go away for a while and come home pretending they had adopted a child while they were away. No one ever asked them for the specifics. They created their own birth certificates with the baby's name, date of birth, and whatever else they needed to document and were able to get a real birth certificate. They raised their child as if it were their own, and no one ever questioned them. Most said they changed the names of the children when they got them. One said they kept the name because it fit. But they called him by the middle name. All said that as time went on, they did tell their child that it was adopted, but that passed records were sealed during that time, and they had no way of finding the birth parents."

"How sad that the kids would not be able to find their birth parents. I'm glad my mother told me I was adopted. She told me I could search for my birth mother if I wanted to, but that the last she knew, she had died. So I just never followed through. I would have loved to meet her. I think." Ben said, then looked around. Randall and Rachelle just looked at him.

"Yes, I'm adopted." He answered their looks.

"I didn't know that. Of course, there is no reason why I would know that." Rachelle said and just took it as a fact of life. There was a lot she didn't know about her family yet.

"Okay, Sis, what did you find out last night?"

"I thought you would never ask." She started. Our letters were from the girls who stayed here. They were all so grateful for a place to stay. One found the place on her own and seemed to be the first one to stay here. The next one was dropped off by her mother, who promised to come to take her home—once she got rid of the baby. The third one was the interesting one."

"And we think we have a connection," Ben interrupted.

"Connection? What do you mean?" Sara asked.

Well, that third letter talked about when her ex-boyfriend tried to find her, and that Rose kept him at bay for a while, and then Robert stepped up and told him to leave, or he would call the cops. The boy left, and they never let him know that his girlfriend was indeed inside. I am guessing that the secret room was built after that incident.

"Okay, is there another connection?"

"Yes, a big one. The letter was signed by Rhea B."

"And?"

"Let me back up a couple of days here. The other day I was watching the boys in the living room. I think it was the day some of you were up in the attic and actually found the secret room. Anyway, a couple of the guests came back from town with a few antiques from the one store. We started talking about the pieces they had, and the one lady told me that her grandmother told them about this place and said to visit someday if they ever got the chance. I asked her grandmother's name and told her I could look through the records and tell her when her grandmother stayed here. I asked what her grandmother's name was. Get this! Her name was Rhea Brown!"

Sara rubbed her arms that suddenly had goosebumps.

"You're kidding. Do you think it is the same person? Could our guest be Rhea B's granddaughter? But wait. Let me try to figure this out." Would the timing be right? And if Rhea is the grandmother, who are the parents? If Rhea's child was adopted out...." Sara was trying to figure it out.

"Rhea B. added in the letter that she had met a wonderful man and had two other children but always wondered and loved her firstborn son," Ben added.

"Okay, that helps. I think." Sara was still running all this information through her mind. For some reason, it wasn't very clear.

"Do you think we should tell the guest that we may have found out the story of why her grandmother was here?" Ben asked.

"NO!" Sara responded even without thinking. "We are not positive there is a connection. We don't know if she knows that her grandmother had a child she gave up for adoption. Not all babies who are adopted are told they are. Parents just raise them as their own."

"I was told I was adopted. I was also told that the records were sealed back then, so I can't even search for my birth parents. I'd jump at the chance to know who mine were/are."

"Not everyone is like you, Ben." Heather reached over and kissed him on the cheek.

"Gee, thanks, I think. So, we wait? We let this guest go home without saying a word?"

"Yes, we let the subject matter go for now. We keep the guest's contact information, but we let her go home. We have a lot more to figure out. Not only another couple of journals but a few more bundles of letters. Not to mention we still have all the stuff that is still in the main attic room upstairs."

Sara sat back in her chair. "I need more coffee." This discovery was almost too much to handle.

"Here you go, Sis." Andy handed her a fresh cup of coffee. "Yes, it is. I think we need to take the day and chill."

"Ha! Good luck with getting these girls to chill." Randall said.

"I know. It was worth a try." Andy laughed as he looked at his sisters and Rachelle.

Sara was sipping her hot coffee and trying to figure out what to do next. Randall might be right. It was too much all at once. She needed to chill. After a few moments, she had her composure. She turned to face everyone and set her coffee down on the island.

"Okay, here is the plan. Today we go about our work as normal. We weren't even going to meet until this evening so, since we met this morning we need to take the day and breathe. Ben, don't say a word to our guest. If she asks you if you had time to check when her grandmother was here, tell her you have not had time. Make sure you do have her contact information. And if she wants to tell you about her family, fine, but don't, DO NOT, tell her what we found. Heather, you and I have to talk about other matters. The rest of you – try to have a normal day. We'll talk more tonight."

Everyone stood up to go their separate ways. They all seemed perplexed but understood. It was a lot to take in.

Heather followed Sara back to her house so they could talk without interruption.

"So what do you make of what we found in the secret room, Sis?" She asked Sara.

"I don't know. I was excited about it when I realized how our grandparents had helped so many girls. Then, the fact that we may have one of the decedents from that time frame as our guest just got to me. I suddenly couldn't deal with it. Between just getting married, being on my honeymoon, learning that our father kept secrets from us, and even from Mama, and now the secret room? All too much and too fast."

"I see your point. So what is this about the land?"

They had reached Sara's house by then and were sitting at her kitchen table.

"It seems Daddy owned land that was unincorporated. It has a courthouse/church, several families that live there, and a small store. Everything else that would help make it a real town is in the next two towns over from it. The attorney told us that we have a choice. We can sell the land to those who live there or take over managing it and either leave it as it is and be the owners, and maybe sometime later sell it, or we can develop it to become incorporated. The last option would take a LOT of work. Work I'm not willing to take on. We have enough going on here. So my thought is to sell it. I know if we hold on to it, years from now, it will be worth more, but considering everything we have going on here and the location so far away, I'd say let's sell it. Unless you have another idea."

"Sounds like you have it all figured out for us," Heather said.

"No, just my opinion. If you have other thoughts, I'm willing to listen. We are in this together."

"Do you have a map of the place?"

"Sure, here are all the papers for it." She reached behind her to the countertop for the file and handed it to Heather.

Heather opened the file and looked at all the photos. "This place is beautiful. No mountains like here, but still beautiful. Are you sure you want to sell this?"

"That is my thought, but I'm open to discussion."

The two of them looked over all the papers and the photos. Sara told her all about the place and the people. As she listened to herself talk, she was almost talking herself into keeping it. But, she stood fast. She had enough to handle at the manor.

"So, I agree we need to sell this land back to them. It is beautiful but too far away for us to deal with all the time. Did you find out why Daddy owned it?"

"No, not yet. I talked with Randall, and he said we should talk with the attorney over there. He said there is an older attorney there who may have known Daddy personally. He might know why Daddy was there."

"Okay. Sounds like a good plan. Now, I'm going to change the subject. What do you think about what was in the secret room?"

"Whew! That was a lot to take in. I was fine just reading the journal, but it was overwhelming when everyone started talking about the letters. For some reason, it was too much. I like things organized and in order. Suddenly it felt like chaos to me."

"I got that from you. I am concerned about you. I do apologize for anything Ben may have done to cause it. He got so excited that we may have found a connection."

"I noticed. Why do you think that is? He's usually the more laid back of all of us."

"I don't know. Maybe because he felt a true family connection."

"He's been in this family for a long time now. He doesn't feel a part of us?"

"Oh, no, he does. He loves being a part of us. It's just that since he is adopted and unable to find his parents, he was hoping to be able to make a connection for our guest."

"I see. Now I understand."

"So, Sis, what are your plans now that your honeymoon was cut short?"

"Well, I think I'll call about the land in West Tennessee and start the ball rolling to sell it. Then I want to spend time in the secret room and reading the letters. I also want to get back to the letters in the attic that we haven't read yet."

"That is what we were planning to do when we found the secret room. I think it is so wonderful that Granddaddy built that for Grandmama and the girls. Maybe we should keep it as a safe place to hide."

"Why would you need to hide?"

"When we get overwhelmed and need a place to go to get away from everyone? Me, when the kids get too much." Heather laughed.

"Your kids are great! I don't see you needing to hide from them."

"Oh, wait until they get older; I'm sure I'll want to hide at some point."

By then, the sisters were both relaxed and laughing. It's what Heather had hoped to do for her sister. She had been so tense since coming home early.

Chapter Eleven

The days had turned into a few weeks. Bella Rose Manor had been busy with guests. Karen had been to her doctor about the twins and was told to take it easy or she would end up on bed rest with the twins. Reluctantly, she stopped helping in the kitchen with food prep and stopped making cakes. Instead, she spent her time reading—about child care and taking care of twins and books full of baby names. They had found out they were having a boy and a girl, and now they were stuck deciding whether to have their names close to each other, starting with the same letter or two unrelated names. And then, of course, they were careful that the babies' initials didn't form any bad words or words that would cause teasing or bullying. Why was choosing a name for a baby or two so difficult? She was laughing when Andy came home from the manor.

"What is so funny?"

"Oh, just sitting here trying to figure out what to name our children. It's not as easy as one would imagine. I mean, how difficult is it to come up with Andy or Karen? Did our parents stress over our names this much?"

"I'm sure they did. But, to their defense, they only had to come up with one at a time."

"Two makes it twice as hard. I hope raising twins isn't twice as hard."

"Funny. You're the one reading all the baby books. Are twins harder to raise?"

"Oh, believe me, some of those books are scary. It almost makes one question about having a child at all. But, by the time most people read them, it is too late to change their minds."

"I'm glad you waited to read them. I can't imagine not having kids, and we haven't had these two yet." He said as he rubbed her belly. Just then, the babies kicked.

"There they are. I hope they are not fighting inside there."

"Not yet. I'm sure I could tell if they were fighting. They are just moving around, trying to find enough room to keep growing."

Andy bent down to her belly and whispered to stop fighting and be nice to each other. He kept his hand and hers on her belly. Surprisingly the babies stopped moving. Andy and Karen looked at each other and laughed.

They laid back on the bed where Karen had been sitting when Andy came home. Andy reached for the book of baby names and opened it.

"Let's see about those baby names." He said.

They spent the next hour reading, talking, changing their minds, laughing, and trying out names. At the end of the hour, they had come up with the perfect ones—names that meant the most to them. They would let the family know in the morning. When they had finally come up with names, Karen felt the babies kick again. She laughed as she reached for Andy's hand to feel their children. He laughed with her.

As they lay there filled with the love of two new people they had never met, Karen started to have pains instead of just the feeling that came from the babies kicking. She moved suddenly and grabbed her belly.

"What is it? What's wrong?" Andy asked as he sat up.

"I'm not sure, but that was more than a kick. That one hurt."

"Is that something you were told to expect?"

"I was told there would be some pain, yes. It's gone for the moment. I hope they can hold out for the next eight weeks."

"We were told twins might come early. You know that."

"I know. But I don't think eight weeks early is what they were thinking. I just need some rest. Maybe we were laughing too much. Let me get some sleep and see how things are in the morning."

"You wake me if you need me. Don't do this all on your own. If those pains continue I will get you to the hospital or at least the doctor."

"I will wake you. Now get some rest as well."

Andy turned out the lights as he joined his wife in bed. Her eyes were closed, but he leaned over and kissed her, knowing she was just resting. She smiled.

In the middle of the night, Karen let out a sound Andy had never heard before, and he sat straight up in bed.

"Karen, what's wrong?" He reached for the light.

"It hurts, Andy, hurts bad. I don't know if it should hurt this bad."

"Okay, we are going to the hospital. Can you get dressed?"

"Sure." She rolled over so she could sit up. The pains had subsided for the moment, giving her a chance to get up and get dressed. The pains had not continued, and she was thinking how silly she had been and was about to tell Andy she was fine when another pain hit her. "Time to go—this hurts."

"Okay. Give your doctor a call and let her know we are going to the hospital."

"It's the middle of the night! I'm not going to call her."

"Call her. It's almost 6 AM; she may be up anyway. She's your doctor. She told you to call her if and anytime you needed her. I think this is one of those times."

"Oh, alright." She winced in pain but grabbed her phone and dialed her doctor.

"Dr. George, this is Karen Fairchild. I'm having some severe pains and Andy is taking me to the hospital. Can you meet us there?" She waited for her doctor to reply. "Thank you so much. See you in a few." She hung up her phone as she and Andy were getting into the car.

Dr. George was at the hospital when they arrived at the ER. She walked them into the exam room and pulled the curtain after asking several questions, doing an ultrasound and checking the babies' heartbeats, taking blood for blood work, checking her temp, pulse, blood pressure, and just observing her in general. Dr. George told Karen that she was fine. The pains were just what was known as Braxton Hicks' contractions. She told them it was false labor and not to worry about it. When those pains became worse or closer together, then it would be something to worry about. She told Karen to rest in the exam room while she monitored her and returned the test results. Dr. George also wanted to witness the pain, if one came soon, to assess Karen's condition fully. She didn't see any reason to think they were more.

Two hours later, Dr. George sent Karen and Andy home to get some rest. After they arrived at the hospital, Andy had called Sara, letting her know what was happening and requesting her to make breakfast for the manor's guests. Sara agreed but was concerned about Karen and the babies and asked Andy if he was sure Karen was okay. He said she was, and not to worry. He just needed someone to make the breakfast. He told her he would call her later.

When they got home, Andy called Sara to reassure his sister that all was well and tell her they would get some rest, but he'd be over later.

He got Karen situated in their bed and then laid down by her side. He watched her rest and thought about how beautiful she was, especially while carrying their babies. Andy knew their life was about to change and that it would be for the better. No more quiet time between them. He knew life would never be the way it had been for the last couple of years. Then he chuckled to himself. Being a part of this family was never the same. And normal? Ha, what was normal? Nothing in his family.

Later that day, Andy was at the manor when Karen called. Her voice told him something was wrong even before he heard any of her words. He dashed out of the door. Sara had been with him and followed him.

"Is she okay?" Sara called after him.

"I hope so. The Doctor said it was something called Braxton Hicks contractions before. I hope that's all it is this time."

They reached Andy's house, and Sara automatically followed him into the bedroom where Karen lay on the bed. She was rubbing her belly and moaning.

"Karen, what's wrong?"

"I don't know. All I know is it hurts—worse than last time," pain in her voice.

"Karen, are the pains close together?"

"No, I don't think so. They just hurt like no pain I've ever had before."

"Do you want me to have Heather come over? She's had two kids; she may be more helpful than I am." Sara felt lost but asked the only thing that came to mind.

"Do you mind? I think that would ease her mind." Andy answered.

Sara grabbed her phone from her back pocket and called Heather. It didn't take long for Heather to join them and sit next to Karen.

"Oh, the joys of pregnancy. I remember it well. Those fake contractions can be so believable. Take my word for it—it gets worse."

"WORSE?" Karen asked. It can't get worse." Agony showing on her face.

"Oh, honey. It does. Have you and Andy been to the birthing classes?"

"No, we were supposed to go but missed the first two and just never went."

"Oh, okay. Well, you now have your personal teacher and coach. Andy, get over here. It's time for birthing school for the two of you."

Andy went over to sit next to Karen. Sara stood and watched as her little sister helped her little brother and his wife with the steps of childbirth. She wished she could record these special moments. It was what family was all about. Love, caring, looking out for, helping each other, and dropping everything when others need you.

Heather took Karen and Andy all through the steps of how to breathe during her contractions. She had them practice several times. Karen had one of her contractions about halfway through it, and Heather helped her breathe through the pain. The next time a pain came, Karen automatically did the breathing she had learned and was amazed at how it helped.

"The biggest thing to remember when you have the contractions and when you go into real labor is to breathe. Don't wait for the pain to be intolerable. Breathe when the pain starts."

"You are amazing. Thank you, Heather. I was about ready for Andy to take me back to the hospital. Now I think I can handle the pains."

"Good. However, it is time to get to the hospital when those pains come in a regular rhythm, especially if they get close together. In fact, for twins, your doctor may want you in the hospital beforehand. I think they do that when you are having twins." Heather didn't say more. She didn't want to scare Karen or Andy. Heather knew that delivering twins sometimes came with complications and often required a c-section. She assumed their doctor had talked with them about it, but she didn't want to bring it up at this moment. She had just gotten them calmed down and able to handle Karen's current pains.

Heather and Sara left after and headed home as soon as Karen and Andy felt confident, and Karen was resting again.

"So, is Karen really doing alright? Nothing to worry about?" Sara had heard the conversation but was still concerned that Heather had kept something from Karen and Andy.

"Yes, she is fine. I left out that a lot of times, twins get delivered by c-section. But, I'm sure her doctor has told them all about the possibilities of what to expect. She was just surprised by the Braxton Hicks contractions. Those get us all. They got me even with Maddex, and I had them with Marc, but we get so aware of any little thing the closer it gets to the due date. So, I will warn you; she may overreact again. We do need to pay attention to her, though. She is far enough along in her pregnancy that she could deliver early. Although this soon may be too early. You never know what God and mother nature has in mind. We need to make sure she takes care of herself."

"Oh, we will. That's one thing I like about all of us living so close together. We all look out for each other."

"Me too. I never thought I would like to live so close to family, but now I can't imagine not living close."

"Mama knew what she was doing when she requested to have us all live here close to the manor. Smart lady."

"Yes, she was. I miss her so much."

"I miss her too. Miss Daddy, too."

"Speaking of Daddy, have you called that attorney about the property?"

"Yes, I did. The attorney said he was going to have the papers drawn up and send them to us to look over and sign if they meet our wishes."

"Good. Did you also ask him why Daddy owned it?"

"Yes, but he said he didn't know for sure. Just that Daddy spent a lot of time over there for his investment business and had land for a personal investment, he thinks Daddy had plans to develop it but never had the chance."

"That makes sense. I hope when we sell it, the people there will develop it."

"Oh, I don't know. It's so beautiful as it is. I hope the townspeople leave it alone."

"You may be right. Hey, I have an idea. How about if we keep a section of it for us and build a vacation cabin? We could rent it out or just use it for our family getaway."

"Like Randall has his cabin up in the mountains?"

"Yes. This land would be further away, but something to think about before we sign the papers. You may want to call the attorney and add that to the contract before drawing up the first draft. That would save going back and forth on changes."

"Interesting idea. But we'd have to fly over there and pick out which plot of land we want for us."

"Road trip!" Heather laughed and then hung her shoulder. "Like we have time right now for a road trip. Heck, you even cut your honeymoon short. Maybe we'll just let the land go. We do have all the land here. Plus, Randall has the cabin. We all get to use the cabin, right?"

"Of course, we all get to use it. Let me talk to Randall about the idea of keeping a piece of the land over there. I'll let you know."

The conversation ended, and they went their separate ways. Sara could not get the idea of keeping some of the property out of her mind. Maybe by keeping it, she could keep investigating why her Daddy was there.

Chapter Twelve

The letters. The journals. The questions. The intrigue. Sara was sitting in the attic, just taking in everything that surrounded her. They had dusted and cleaned both the attic and the secret room. Ben had remodeled the doorway, so it was easy to walk from one room to the other. They had folded the cots and lined them up against the walls. They left everything else where it was. They had taken photos of the rooms the way they found them before making any nostalgic changes.

As she sat there, she tried to imagine having to hide in that room. The fear the girls must have felt knowing that those that they loved were trying to hurt them and their babies. How could anyone do that to young girls? Here were girls who either ran away, got sent away because they made a mistake or were victims of abuse, and ended up pregnant. Sara had not thought about the abuse aspect before. She just assumed all the girls had been with their boyfriend and made a mistake. Girls that were young and didn't know better or thought that life would be great having a baby. Now, for some reason, the idea of being abused made her shudder. She hoped none of the letters or journals told of those circumstances.

She had taken the first batch of letters and journals to her house instead of leaving them in the attic or office. She now reached for another bundle to read. She had taken the day off to do this. Something was driving her to find out more details. It was all so revealing of what Bella Rose had been and maybe needed to be again.

Yes, maybe Bella Rose needed to be a place for unwanted kids. She shook her head. No, Bella Rose was doing great as it was. Heather was expanding what they offered with the event planning. Karen, once the babies were a bit older, planned to continue the cake decorating. No, Bella Rose was fine just the way it was. 'Don't take on more than you can handle,' she told herself as she opened the first letter to read. She hoped to find out more, get to know the girls who had been here. And learn more about her Grandmama and Granddaddy in the process.

Dear Rose,

My life. I owe it all to you. If it had not been for you, I would have no idea where I would be today. Sometimes I think I would not be here at all, that my life would have ended somehow.

I was at the lowest point in my young life when I found you and your home. When you took me in without asking questions or judging me, I felt love for the first time in my life. I thought I had people who loved me before but found no love from any of them. Not like the love you and Robert showed me.

I was broken. I was young. I was depressed. And like the other girls there and those you told me about, I was with child. The 'love' of my life used me and tossed me aside. He knew my home life wasn't good, and I thought he was my way out. I soon found out that was not true either. I then lost faith in people. I had no place to go. I was on the streets.

Then someone told me about you, and I did everything I could to get there. How I survived the trip, I don't know, but I did. And it was the best trip I ever made.

The only thing for me to do was to give up my child when it was born. I knew that. But, I never stopped loving that little one and never stopped looking for her. I knew the adoptions were secret and the records sealed, but I never lost hope.

Rose, I wanted to let you know that through prayer and never giving up, I was able to find her several years later. I had found my way in the world. Went back to school. Found out how to live and love for the first time. I searched. I looked at every child that was her age. I looked for someone who looked like me when I was little. I had no idea where to look. Heck, I even knew she could be anywhere in the world. But I kept looking.

I found her. She was 16 at the time. I was teaching high school and also a student counselor. She was a new student. The minute she walked into my office, I felt something. My heart jumped. I knew there was nothing I could do at that moment, so I held on to my thoughts. But, I learned about her. I met her parents. I was happy for her and the good home she had, but I longed for her to know who I was. I had no right. Yet, my heart longed for that connection—for her.

One day her mother came into my office. She said she had something to tell me about her daughter. My heart sank. I thought something was wrong. She sat and proceeded to tell me that her daughter was adopted and wanted to meet her birth mother. I held it in and just listened. This wonderful woman then said the most amazing thing. She said she knew I was her daughter's birth mother. I asked her how she knew. She said she knew it the day they came to register her, and she met me. She told me we looked too much alike. She said she watched me work with the kids and noticed the similarities between her daughter and me.

I asked her what she wanted to do. She told me she had kept all the papers regarding the adoption and had a few questions for me. When my answers agreed with her story of the adoption, the location, the birth date— everything, we just sat in my office and cried. We held each other. And we bonded.

She told her daughter, and we connected as mother and daughter two weeks later.

It has been such a blessing. Our daughter still lives with her adoptive parents, but we see each other all the time. Her family has included my family and me in special events and holidays. We have formed a big happy family filled with love.

Thank you so much for all the love you showed me that was possible. I hope you are doing well. I would love for my daughter and me to come to visit sometime. She talks about wanting to see where she was born, and I have told her the full story. Maybe someday we can do that.

Love to you and your family from Daisy and me,

Amelia D.

Sara was in tears by the time she finished reading the letter. She was so proud of what her grandparents did for the few years they did it. She wished they had done it longer but understood why they didn't. It would have been difficult to have their biological children keep it quiet if their work with the girls had been done secretly. Part of her heart went out to all the girls. Life had been so hard for them. She couldn't imagine being sent away or feeling the need to run away.

Then she thought of Andy. He had run away as a teenager. Life for him must have been difficult too. Of course, he wasn't 'with child' as the girls had been, but he was so young, doing his best to live on his own—on the streets. The strength those kids had just to keep going. To fight to live.

Sara spent the next hour reading letters very similar to that first one. Each one made her shed tears. That was what that particular bundle was about—girls who had been able to reconnect with their babies. There were only about five of them that had written to Rose about it. She wondered if more had been able to make that connection later in their lives.

She picked up the only other journal left. The first had been one her Grandmama had written. She opened this one to find her Granddaddy had written it! She almost was crying before she started to read it. She flipped through it and noticed that he had not written much, but he had drawn on several of the pages. She slowly looked at each drawing.

The first one looked like a sketch of her house. The house they had lived in when they first got married. Next were some floor plans drawn of the manor and followed by the plans for the secret room. She looked closely at that one. He had drawn a couple of beds, two dressers, and a desk. Just like they had found it, except the beds were gone, and cots were in their place. The next drawing was of a garden setting with benches, trellises, flowers, rose bushes. There was no color to the drawing, but she could picture the beauty. He was designing a rose garden for his bride. The last few pages were of people. She smiled when she recognized them. It was her grandparents and her mother.

She then turned to the front and read the few pages he had written.

Dear Me,

Who else am I writing this to? Who else will care? Whoever does get to read this, I hope you understand.

I met and married the love of my life many years ago. Rose was/is the most beautiful woman in the world. Her physical beauty hides how beautiful her soul is. The love she has for me and everyone she meets could outshine the sun. Because of this, I devoted my life to being there for her and helping bring her dreams to life.

Little did I know, and I don't think she even knew, what her dreams were until there was a knock on our door one day. There stood a little girl. She could not have been more than fourteen years old, but she looked so frail. She told us her story, and that little girl changed our lives. She was pregnant and had no place to go. How she found us, we never found out for sure.

It doesn't matter what her life had been like before she arrived at our home. What mattered for Rose and me was that we did everything we could to help her from that day forward as much as we could, and she would let us.

And so we took care of her. We found a home for her baby that she didn't want or could not keep. We taught her as much as we could, and soon after her baby was born, she left us.

But then another one came to us and then another. We took each one into our home. Rose and I knew then that God was sending them to us. We needed to build a place for them other than our spare bedroom.

And that is how Bella Rose began. From a little innocent fourteen-year-old girl with no place to go, no place to call home, and no one who loved her.

So no matter what you have heard about how Bella Rose got its start, you now have the truth. The hidden truth.

We had to keep it hidden. When we started, adoptions, as we did them, were not legal. At least I didn't think so. I was very selective about who adopted the babies. I had to trust them never to tell the truth. I feared for us. But, I knew if I believed that God was the one sending those girls to us, He would watch out for us and keep us protected. And He did.

Over the few years we were able to help these girls, we learned a lot. A lot more about love. A lot more about how cruel some people can be. And how hate often sneaks in where love should be.

When Rose and I had our first and only child, we knew our time of living this secret life was coming to an end. We could not expect our little girl to keep such secrets at her young age. And so we closed our doors to those girls. I found another place for them to go that was legal and safe, and as others still showed up from time to time, I would take them to the new location.

From that humble beginning, we then opened our doors to the general public to come and stay with us. I closed off the secret room and hid all the evidence of our secret life inside there. I know someday someone will discover it. And if you are reading this, I know you have found it. I hope you will gain something from learning the truth—the true meaning of loving and caring for others. I hope you can welcome in the stranger and show them that they are loved. I hope you let God into your life if He isn't already a part of it. He will bless you more than you can imagine.

Yes, we did have to close our doors, but we never closed our hearts. And we never stopped loving those girls and their babies.

I never once stopped loving Rose, appreciating her, and being amazed by her and her love for me and others.

Robert James--
The original owner of Bella Rose Manor

When she finished reading the short entry, she closed the journal and set it on the desk. She stood up and walked around the room, trying to get the feeling of their presence. As she reached the window, she felt a feeling of warmth. She looked out the window and saw the outline of rocks and a division inside the area. She saw the garden her Granddaddy had drawn. It had died away years ago, and since it was in the far back of the house, they had never done anything with it since they had taken it over after their Mama had died.

With all the remodeling they had done, this was never touched.

With a sudden idea in her head, she grabbed the journal and the letters and hurried downstairs. She had a job to do. And she needed Ben's help.

Chapter Thirteen

Karen awoke with a start and grabbed Andy. The sudden touch and hearing his name called had him wide awake and sitting up.

"What is it?"

"It's time."

"Time? Oh! Time! Are you sure? It's too soon." He jumped out of bed and went to her side of the bed. "Can you get dressed?"

"Yes, it's time, at least I think so. The contraction stopped for now." She slid off the bed and reached for her maternity pants and top. She smiled through her persistent pain as she thought it soon would be the last time she would have to wear such clothes. Oh, to be thin again, she thought.

Andy got dressed, grabbed her suitcase, and walked out of the room.

"Hey! Don't forget me!" Karen said as she waddled to the doorway.

"I won't. I was just going to put this in the car."

Just then, another contraction hit, and she had to sit down. "Or not," Andy said as he went to her side. "I'm calling Heather." He reached for his phone.

"I've called the doctor; she'll meet us there," Karen said, catching her breath when the pain subsided.

Andy called Heather to let her know what was happening. By that time, they were in the car. Andy hung up and drove as fast but as safe as he could. He was glad the hospital was not too far away. He did not want anything to happen to the babies or his wife.

Dr. George met them at the emergency room just like she had a month before. "Okay, young lady. Whether you have them now or we can stop the contractions for a while, you are staying here until those babies are born."

Karen looked at Andy, who looked terrified, and smiled. As scared as she was, the look on her husband's face was priceless. She hoped he would survive the delivery when it came time. Even though she was in pain, she smiled at him.

Dr. George wheeled Karen to the hospital admitting area and helped Andy get his wife checked into a room. They then went straight up the elevator to the maternity ward. This place was going to be her home for at least a few days.

After a few more contractions and a full exam, Dr. George said it soon would be time. Just to relax and breathe. She told them she would be back shortly but that the nurses would be with them soon. A few minutes later, she was summoned back to Karen's room. Her pain was worse. Dr. George notified the NCIU that twins were coming sometime in the next few hours as preemies. She needed all hands on deck to care for them, especially if there were any complications.

"Complications?" Andy asked when she hung up her phone. He had heard only part of the doctor's conversation.

"Just a normal routine. When it comes to twins, we always prepare for possible complications. Twins are usually early, but we take precautions with all deliveries. Yours are a little earlier than some, but I'm not overly worried. We've done this before." She tried to lighten his anxiety.

"Okay. I was worried." Andy returned to Karen's side and held her hand.

Karen and Andy laughed, talked, and when the pains came, they breathed through the contractions. They counted the minutes between them and watched the monitors. The family had arrived, visited, and were waiting in the waiting room. Rachelle had volunteered to stay and watch Marc and Maddex so everyone else could be at the hospital.

Karen grabbed Andy's arm and dug her nails into him. He held her as Karen winched in pain and then laughed a little as she loosened her grip. Andy looked at her as she pointed down. Her water had broken. The nurse who was there called for the doctor. Then proceeded to deal with the water on the floor and her bed. Somehow she managed to get the area under Karen dry while no one noticed.

Dr. George came in quickly. She summoned the two nurses with a lot of instructions that neither Karen nor Andy understood. All they knew was what Dr. George said. "It's time. Let's get those babies out, now."

What seemed like slow motion done in silence was anything but that. Dr. George was barking out orders; another doctor came in; incubators were wheeled in; more nurses arrived. It was utter chaos.

Karen was gripping Andy's arm. The sounds she was making were ones Andy had never heard before. He did his best to help her breathe through the contractions and pain. He didn't like to see his wife in so much pain. His heart ached for her. He heard Dr. George order Karen to push!

And then the sound of a baby crying—followed by silence.

Dr. George was right there waiting, telling Karen to push one more time. She knew Karen was exhausted. Dr. George knew Karen was in pain. She also knew the other baby might be in trouble.

"Push, Karen, Push. That's it. Push. Harder. That's it! There he is! She said and then was quiet. She reached immediately to the baby's neck and, with her two fingers, was able to unwrap the umbilical cord wrapped around his neck. "Thank God." She whispered.

Dr. George guided the baby the rest of the way out and turned him over, patting him on the back.

Silence.

Karen felt herself not breathing.

Finally – a loud cry!

110

Everyone in the room breathed. Karen was in tears, as was Andy. Their babies were finally here! The nurses were cleaning them, checking their vital signs, and wrapping them in their blankets. One by one, the nurses laid first their baby girl and then their baby boy on Karen's chest.

"Are they..... okay?" Andy asked

"Yes, They are a bit small, but not bad for twins. And everything seems normal. We will take them to NCIU in a few minutes to make sure, but from their crying, weight, and color, I think they are perfect! Congratulations!"

Dr. George turned and thanked the other doctor. "Thanks for being here. I wasn't sure how things would go when I saw the color of that amniotic fluid when it broke. That usually means the baby is in some trouble. But we were lucky. It could have been much worse. I've seen worse and try not to think of it. Today—today, this family was blessed.

A few minutes later, the babies were taken from Karen and wheeled away to the NICU for their first thorough check-ups. The nurses told Andy he could talk to his family while they cleaned up the room and made Karen a bit more presentable for visitors. He was happy to oblige. That experience was a lot to take in; he needed a break. He suddenly realized he was a Daddy! He left the room, walking on the clouds.

As he got close to the waiting room, he was spotted, and everyone stood up to meet him.

"Babies and Karen are fine!" was all he could get out before they surrounded him with hugs and congratulations.

"When can we go see them and Karen?" Sara asked.

"The babies were taken to NICU for tests to be sure everything was normal. Karen is getting more presentable, and you can see Karen in a few minutes. The nurse will let us know when we can see the babies."

"So everything is okay? Babies are fine? Karen is fine?"

"Yes, Sis, babies are fine. Karen can tell you all about it. All I know is it was amazing to watch. To see the birth of my children! Andy sat down and cried. Happy tears. Tears of relief. Tears of love and joy.

"And now, 'Daddy,' the fun begins," Ben said as he put his arm around him. "I'm here for you anytime. Tip number one – change their diapers. You'll score big points in Karen's eyes." He laughed. And so did Andy. His new life was just beginning.

A week later, the sign on the outside of their front door said, "Welcome home, River & Ryan.

The house was filled with gifts for the babies and a few for Karen. The nursery was complete with cribs and stuffed animals, and baby afghans. All were waiting for Karen and Andy to bring their babies home. The family was waiting as well. Food had been prepared and stored in the refrigerator and freezer so they would not have to cook for a while. A list of family members was posted on the bulletin board in the babies' room with times that each would be available to help.

Chapter Fourteen

Life had changed when the twins came home. Everyone stepped up to help out and give Karen and Andy time to enjoy their new family by helping with the child care and helping more with the manor. Rachelle stepped in to help cook the breakfasts for the guests and helping Sara with the reservations and all the paperwork involved. Heather helped with the cleaning at the manor more and organized and planned a few upcoming events. Ben continued to maintain the property and assure the rooms were ready for the new guests each time. He still made sure there were new flowers in the rooms for each new guest. He took pride in working on the landscape of the property.

When Sara approached him with her secret project, he was excited. She shared the drawing of the original garden with him, and together they added their ideas for improvements and additions. These included putting in a private playground for Marc, Maddex, River, and Ryan. Sara was so excited she could hardly keep it quiet. Luckily no one noticed the looks between Sara and Ben from time to time. Everyone was so busy no one noticed the new project.

Two months later, Sara called a family meeting, including the children this time. It had been a while since the family had an official meeting, that no one was quite sure what to expect.

"Welcome, everyone. I know it's been a while since we've all talked business regarding the manor or the attic or secret room. We have been blessed with River and Ryan coming into our lives, and they took center stage. And we love it, by the way." She added, smiling at Andy and Karen. "You are doing a great job with them."

"While everyone has been so busy helping each other, Ben and I have been busy, okay, Ben has been busy in the background. Literally, in the background. First, let me tell you what I found just before the birth of the babies."

She proceeded to tell them about the letters and the other journal she had found in the secret room, how their Grandfather had worshiped and spoiled their Grandmama, and the history of how Bella Rose began. She told them that all the stories they had heard from town and even what they had heard from their parents were not the whole truth. Bella Rose had a hidden truth. She told them some of what they already had discovered but added how much love was involved. Sara then read to them the letter from their Grandfather and then began showing the sketches. When she finished, she turned to Ben.

"Right after the twins were born, I got with Ben and told him about all of this and the secret garden shown here. I took him up to the secret room and showed him that when you look out of that window, the one that has been boarded up, you could see the outline of a rose garden. Just like this sketch. Well, I asked Ben to recreate that space." Sara concluded her part of the story and stepped back.

Ben took over telling the story. "When she showed it to me, I was happy to rebuild it, rose bushes and all. After I started it, I went to her and suggested making it bigger and telling her why and how. She agreed. The finished landscape is now ready to reveal. It was not easy to do with everyone around, but you all were so involved with work and babies that it worked in my favor. Believe me, keeping it all quiet was not easy. Heather often asked me what I was up to, and I would just tell her 'work.' Sorry for the lies." He looked at his wife and shrugged his shoulders.

"Those weren't lies, Ben." Sara cut in. "You *were* working. For me."

"Thank you, that makes me feel better about the cover stories I came up with."

"Before we go out to see what I have made, let me explain some of it. Granddaddy made the rose garden for Grandmama when they were first married. She tended to her roses and would sit in her flower garden. She could see them from her window in her office. And until the window got boarded up, you could see it from the window in the secret room as well. Over time the roses died, and that beautiful garden got forgotten. No one used the back of the house for anything. That is until now." He smiled. "Ladies and gentlemen, we now not only have the rose garden back, but I have made it much bigger, private to only our family, and have added a playground for our children!"

"A playground? That's amazing. Now the kids can play on their own and not have the guests always around. They can have their private space. You are so sweet."

"It will be a while until the twins can use it, but thank you."

"With the babies in mind, I included a couple of baby-friendly items there for them to enjoy. A special baby swing, baby size climbing areas, and even a space for a portable baby pool for them to have fun and get accustomed to the water."

"Let's go see it." Andy stood up with his son in his arms. "Let's go see your new playground," he said to his son, who was too young to understand what he was saying. The baby smiled and cooed, and everyone laughed. Maybe Ryan did understand.

They walked outside to see this private family space. It was perfect. Ben had installed swings, a slide, a place to play kid-sized basketball, a space for the kiddie pool, and even a couple of benches for the adults to sit on while watching the kids play. The garden area was fenced off from the play area so the kids would not walk all over the plants. There were a few rose bushes, Daisies, a Mountain Laurel Bush, and a

Rhododendron bush at the far end. A rock way laid out the path to walk through the plants. And four stones had been engraved with their parents' and grandparents' names on them. The stones were even a surprise to Sara.

"You made these stones?" Sara asked when she noticed them.

"No, I had them made by a local stonemason. He is a stone engraver and was happy to help."

"You did a great job, Ben."

"Thanks. It was fun to do. The hardest part was not getting caught doing it. Do you realize how close some of you were to seeing it while I was working on it? It may be private from the public, but it is very visible in the back of the house."

Marc asked if he could play and, of course, was given permission. It took no time at all for him to get on the swings. "That is their favorite thing to do lately. Take them to the park, and that is the first thing he finds. And the small one for babies is perfect. This whole garden play area is perfect." Heather hugged her husband. "I think I'll keep you around for a while." She smiled.

When Marc finished on the swings, everyone returned to the kitchen to talk.

"I've been thinking," Sara began. "Now that we know how the manor originated and about the girls, do you think it is time to search for the girls who wrote the letters?"

"Do you think they want to be found?"

"In the letters I read when I read Daddy's journal, it seemed that they wanted to come back. They made it sound like being here was a point in their life that changed everything, and they are grateful for it. I know not all the letters had that message, but many did."

"True, some did. First, I wonder what the other letters say that we found in the main attic room. We have not finished reading those. Maybe some of those girls have made it back, and we just don't know it."

"You'd think they would have said something."

"Maybe not. Remember, their life when they were here was a secret. They may have kept that secret and just returned to see how life here had changed. Or to relive part of what changed their lives for the better."

"True. I wonder if any of our recent guests have been some of those girls. Has anyone been keeping up with what our guests have written in the journals we leave in the rooms?"

Everyone shook their heads. "Sorry to say, I clean the rooms but never read what people write," Heather said. "I feel bad about that. Several of our guests have come back for the second and third time. I wonder if they can tell we haven't read what they wrote? Do you think anyone had left a message we should know about?"

"What do you mean by that? Like they are in trouble?"

"No, not really. Just a message that links them to the past here."

"Now that would be interesting. Also sad that we missed it. But even if we had read the current ones, we may not have caught the meaning. We just recently found out the truth."

"Point taken. I have an idea," Rachelle chimed in. "Why don't we divide up and read some more or investigate more. Some can read the attic letters, some the current journals, and I will volunteer to wander around town, talk to the town folk, and see what they may know. Or suspect."

"Do you think the town folk would talk?"

"Are you kidding? People always love to spread gossip and rumors. I can find out if anyone knows the truth."

"Let the mystery hunt begin," Sara said.

Karen raised her hand. "I volunteer to read some. I have the babies to take care of, but I can fit in some reading from time to time."

"Are you sure? You have your hands full."

"I know, but it will do me good to take some time to do something else productive. Plus, I have Andy helping with our kids. He has been so great with them. He's spoiling them and me. It's time we get back to helping all of you. It will give our minds something to think about besides feeding, burping, diapers, and sleeping." She laughed.

"You're on. I will give you some of the letters from the attic. Who wants to take on the journals from the rooms. The current ones?"

"I'll do those. I can read them as I'm cleaning; that way, the journals stay in the rooms and don't get forgotten or mixed up and returned to the wrong room." Heather volunteered.

"And I'll take the attic. Randall, you can help Heather and Ben. When you are home from work, you can also help me."

"How about if I help by also doing some searching at the courthouse and around town. I was going to look into the legalities of adoptions back then but never did. I can start there. Maybe some names will show up."

"Sounds good. It feels so good to have the family together again. I know we all work together here, but lately, we've not all been together. We need to change that. Now that the twins are a little bit older and easier to tag along." She looked at Andy and Karen. "I'm so glad they are healthy and growing. You two are blessed."

"That we are, big Sis. That we are."

Sara found herself in the attic again. She was going up there more and more in the last few weeks. Not only to read the letters but just to sit. She found comfort there. Almost like she was sitting with Mama, and sometimes she felt her Grandmama there. She wondered what it must have been like taking care of those girls, risking her own life for them, hiding them, and loving them. She wished she had known her grandmother longer. Or that she had known then what questions to ask her.

When you are young, you never know the questions to ask. You think they will live forever, and you have all the time in the world to find out their stories. Then they are gone, and you have only wishes and memories and the stories you were smart enough to listen to and remember.

Heather picked up the journal in the first guest room she was cleaning. It was the room they rented out the most. Not that people requested it, but because it was the closest one to the main area of the manor, and simply just the one they rented first if it was available. She figured it would have the most entries. And from the looks of how full it was, she could be right.

She began to turn the pages and skim the writings. Some entries were written in cursive. Some were printed. She began to look for the ones written in cursive, thinking an older person would have written those. That would tell her if it could be one of the girls. Chances were that none of them had come back to visit. But the intrigue kept them going.

She flipped through page after page of printed words. Most pages said the same thing, 'Love it here. Great food, great people, great town. Will be back.' That sort of review. Nice to read, but not what she was looking for. A few pages were written in cursive but said the same basic thing as the others. She completed the journal and was a bit disappointed. Nothing led her to believe the guests were related to any of the girls or the adoptions.

Ben was busy helping Heather clean the room and picked up another of the journals. He also skimmed through it and found nothing. He laid it back down and went on to the next room. Same there. Nothing.

Heather had gone through two rooms and found nothing. She was losing hope. The last room on that floor was open. Ben was already inside cleaning and had just taken the trash out. Heather went to the dresser, picked up the journal, and sat down on the trunk at the foot of the bed to read. She was still reading when Ben came back in and startled her.

"Sorry, I didn't know you were in here. Have you found anything in the other journals yet?"

"No, you?"

"No. Not one hint that I could find. I'm about to give up on thinking we would have such luck as a link to the past. Well, other than the granddaughter of Rhea that I met."

"Oh, right, I had almost forgotten about her. Did you ever contact her that we may have found something?"

"No, Sara and Randall were pretty adamant that I didn't."

"True. You still have Rhea's contact information, though, right?"

"Of course. If nothing else, this family has taught me to save things. I mean, look at what saving things in the family has led us to?"

"Yes, confusion, questions, more unknowns."

"And don't forget love, caring, kindness, giving, and thinking of others first. Not to mention the truth."

"Okay, you've got me there." If Ben was talking, Heather had stopped listening.

"Ben, look!" She turned the journal toward him so he could see. "Read this."

Bella Rose—such a perfect name for this place. It is perfect with the rose bushes in full bloom lining the entrance lane and the beauty all around. The only thing I would have tried to add would be 'love.' This place is full of love, just like my adoptive mother told me it was. You see, Bella Rose, I was born here, according to her. She wouldn't give me many details, only that my birth mother stayed here just as I was born. She told me that my birth mother gave me up for adoption right after I was born because she could not care for me. I needed to see this place for myself. I wanted to meet the people who helped my mother, but I know they are now gone. I wanted to thank them. Not only for taking care of my mother (I don't know what happened to her) but also for finding my adoptive mother and family for me. I could not have asked for a better family.

I knew from a child that I was adopted; it was never kept from me. But, I was also not told of the legalities and never told who my birthing parents were. I understand my father may never have been a part of the situation, but I know my mother was here.

If I could ever find her, I would like to thank her. So whoever reads this, if you happen to know who my mother is, can you tell her my name is Dianna, and my birth date is June 18, 1955.

Thank you for keeping this place running after all these years. My adoptive mother is not in good health, but I think she would like to meet my birth mother as well, just to thank her for not giving up on me before it was time.

I hope to be back someday soon.

Dianna

"Oh my!" We found one! Now to find out more of her information and see if we can find her birth mother."

"Ben, I know you are glad we found one, but how in the world are we going to find her mother? Do we have a record of who stayed here back then? We have some of the letters, but who says any of those letters is from her mother."

"Spoilsport. We need to keep this one. I'll take it and make a copy of it in the office and be right back." Heather walked to the office and came right back, leaving the copy she made in a special file in the office.

"Okay, time to finish cleaning and call it a day. We can look more tomorrow. I'm going to go find Sara and tell her what we found."

"That's okay; I'll finish cleaning. Go share the news with Sara," Ben called out as she left the room.

Heather found her sister still sitting in the attic room.

"We found something," She announced as she entered the room. Sara jumped.

"Don't do that to me! You know I don't like surprises. Now, what did you find?"

"Ben and I found an entry from a lady named Dianna, born in 1955. She wrote that her adoptive mother told her that she was born here but adopted right after her birth. She was hoping to find the people who had helped her mother and would love to find her birth mother."

"That's a lot to know. Did you make a copy of that?"

"Of course. I put it on the desk in the office. Did you find anything new up here?"

"I've spent most of my time just sitting here and imagining what it would have been like here back then. So scary to have to hide in that room. Then I think about what the girls must have felt like being shown love and caring. Can you imagine being a teenager and going through that?"

"No. I'm glad we had loving parents. True, they had their troubles and not the perfect family life, but we knew our Mama and Daddy loved us."

"So true. I'd give anything to have them back so we could talk with them, to ask them more questions. Hear the truth from them instead of finding it all out through the will and letters and secret journals."

"I agree. Ben and I have vowed to each other not to keep any secrets from each other. Not worth it. Secrets can hurt people. We have been lucky that our family secrets have brought us closer together. I didn't know what we were missing while Andy was gone. He was gone so long we, or at least I, never thought we'd find him again. Let alone be close to him. God has been so good to us."

Sara hesitated and lowered her head. She hoped Heather didn't notice. She pretended to be looking at a letter. "Yes,

God has been good to us." She left it at that and didn't mention her brother nor the word secrets.

"Are you ready to call it a day?"

"I think I am. Too much thinking can wear you out." Sara laid the letter she was about to read on the desk and turned out the light. It was time to relax. She could read that letter the next time she came up.

The sisters left the attic and were laughing and walking arm in arm when they reached the kitchen.

"What have you two been doing?" Andy surprised them.

"Heck with us, what are you doing here? Everything alright?"

"Of course, why?"

"Because you have not been in this kitchen since your twins were born. At least not to cook. Look at you. You're cooking!"

"It was time to get back to life. A new life for sure. Karen will be over in a few minutes with the kids. They are big enough to start taking them places. At least this far. I'm not sure about being out in public yet. We don't want them getting sick. We were at the doctor earlier today."

"What did the doctor have to say?"

"She gave us the all-clear. Babies are up to date on shots and stuff. They are both healthy and growing the way they should be. She was very pleased."

"Such good news. You've done well, little brother."

"Thanks, Sis. We could not have done it without you. You saved us a few times there towards the end. You calmed Karen down. You calmed my nerves as well, I'll admit. I owe you one, Sis. I owe you one too, Sara."

Sara looked at Andy when he said that. She didn't say a word. Just looked. Yes, he did owe her one.

"Hello, all. I come bearing gifts. Namely River and Ryan." Karen announced when she came into the kitchen. Immediately all attention went to the little ones who were asleep in their carriers.

"Of course, they are asleep. I hardly ever see them awake." Sara said as she peeked in on them.

"You need to be at our house in the middle of the night; You'd see them awake then."

Sara laughed. "No, thank you. Unless you need me—you know I'd be there in a minute if you ever needed me."

"I know. Each one of you would be. You all have been wonderful to me and us. I love this family. Makes me miss mine. I wish they had lived to see these two."

"Speaking of family. When are Larry and Grace coming to see River and Ryan?"

"Larry called the other day. Grace just had surgery, nothing major. As soon as the doctor says she can travel this far, they will be down."

"Good. They need to see their grandchildren. It will be good to see them too."

"I hope they can visit for a while. We send photos of the kids, but I know it's not even close to seeing them in person." Andy said. "Now, who's ready for dinner?"

Everyone sat on the stools at the island where Andy had set their places for them. All they had to do was sit and enjoy the meal he had prepared. They were getting spoiled again. Randall and Rachelle had both joined them at the last minute. Randall had been at work, and Rachelle had been in town talking with the residents.

"Rachelle, were you able to find out anything in town yet?" Sara asked as she began to eat.

"No, not really. Some told me they knew Rose and Robert but either didn't seem to know much about the truth we've learned or were not willing to say. I didn't give away any information as I wanted to hear it from them and not influence them. I think if I start telling what we found out, there will be more rumors than we need, and then we will never know for sure if anyone knows more than we do."

"Good thinking."

"I did some searching while I was in the office. So far, I have found nothing about adoptions reported during that time frame that would be associated with this area."

"Have you found any adoption information?"

"Only across the border in North Carolina. One agency was forced to close because of some illegal transactions. I followed that information, but it didn't lead here."

"Okay. I was hoping. Maybe what our grandparents did was truly secretive. Granddaddy must have done an excellent job for those girls and families. Trouble is now we are finding people who want answers."

"We may never be able to provide that. Unfortunately." Randall said.

"I know. We have found some connections or what we think are connections, but nothing definite. More searching and putting letter against letter is needed and will take time. We will continue to search. I'm not giving up."

"Don't let it take up your whole life—any of you. You can't let it. I understand your desire to help these people. Heck, it shows how helping others runs in your family. I just don't want it to ruin your lives."

"How would it ruin our lives?"

"By becoming all-consuming. You all have other things to occupy your time. Twins, event planning, the manor to run." He then looked at Sara, "And a new husband who hasn't had a full honeymoon yet."

"Stop." Sara looked at him and grinned. "Our honeymoon is every day. We don't have to go away to have a honeymoon."

Everyone looked away and pretended not to hear the newlyweds talk of such things.

Chapter Fifteen

Everyone had taken Randall's advice and stepped away from their searching. He had been right. Life did go on, and some things may be better left alone.

Ben could not let it go. He held his thoughts to himself for a while, then talked with Heather one night as they were about to drift off to sleep. He told her he could not get the fact out of his mind that a lady named Rhea had sent her granddaughter to visit Bella Rose. He confided that the granddaughter had sent him an email asking if he had found anything further about when her grandmother had been here. He said he had not responded yet, because he was hoping to have a positive answer.

"Why does it bother you so much?"

"I don't know. Maybe it is that we are keeping a secret that could be the truth about Rhea's family. I think she has a right to know."

"Let it go, Ben. Or talk to Sara and see what she says. We have held off our search for a while; maybe it is time to start searching again. Now get some sleep."

"I will try. Good night. Thanks for listening. I love you." Ben continued to lay on his back—wide awake.

"I love you, too. Sweet dreams." Heather rolled away from him and closed her eyes to sleep.

Ben woke up in a sweat early the next morning. His mind was in a fog. A dream that lingered. The dream was of a lady reaching for a baby and another person handing the child over. He remembered feeling the pressure of being held tight. The sounds of car tires as they spun away. He remembered a long drive, the feeling of being surrounded by a room full of people and being handed from one person to another. The images kept returning, and he tried to see what was around him, but something was over his eyes. He forced his eyes open to his reality. He got up, washed his face with cold water, and then went to make coffee and sit in the dark. He tried to relive the nightmare and search for more details. There were none. He tried to remember what he had eaten before going to bed—nothing out of the ordinary.

Heather woke up and found Ben sitting in the dark in their kitchen. She turned the light on and saw that he had been crying. She sat by his side and held his hand.

"What's wrong? Are you feeling okay?"

"I had a nightmare."

"And that led you to tears?"

"For some reason, yes."

"What was your dream?"

"More of a nightmare. Dreams are pleasant. This was depressing. I think you may be right; we need to either let this search go, or I seriously need to find answers."

"Okay. But what was your dream/nightmare?"

Ben took a sip of his now cold coffee then set the mug down on the end table. He turned his head and looked at Heather. "You know I'm adopted, right?"

"Yes."

"Well, I think all this news of the adoptions, the girls in trouble, the secrets, the hidden room, the mystery is playing with me and my adoption. I dreamed about a lady taking a child away from another person. Then about being held almost too tightly. Next, the baby was being passed from one person to the next in a large room. I felt the child trying to see things, but a blanket covered its eyes and body. I, or the baby rather, struggled to get loose, but there was no escape. It was too tiny."

"Alright, what did you have to eat before you went to bed?"

"Not a thing. You were with me all evening; we didn't eat anything late."

"I think it is time we talk to Sara. You can't live like this. Maybe we should call Joe so you can talk to him about it."

"I thought about that, but that would mean I'd have to let the secrets out about Bella Rose."

"True." Heather leaned back in her chair. Enough was enough. Randall had his point of no need to rush into any of their searching, but was he right? "Let's go talk to Sara after breakfast. It's time to make this a priority and find the answers."

"Thank you for not thinking I'm crazy."

"You are not crazy. You are traumatized by all of this. You are too close to it. None of us gave any thought to how it might affect you. I can see that it has."

"I was fine until I talked with the one guest. I've not been able to get it out of my mind since."

Heather poured them each a fresh cup of coffee. It took only two sips of coffee before they heard their boys running into the kitchen to join them. They were full of giggles and ready for action. Oh, to wake up with that energy, Heather thought as she picked up Maddex and hugged Marc simultaneously. Marc had gotten too big to pick up anymore. Maddex was almost too big. Time was flying by.

Heather made breakfast for her family before they took the boys with them to find Sara. They found her sitting with Rachelle in the office at the manor. Heather asked if they could talk to Sara alone and asked Rachelle if she would mind watching the boys for a few minutes. Heather and Ben closed the door after Rachelle left with the boys. Sara knew something serious was up. She closed the file she had been reading and laid it aside.

"What's going on? Something wrong?"

"No, yes, maybe." Heather blurted out.

Sara raised her eyebrows and sat up in her seat, leaning her elbows on the desk and locking her fingers together. They had her full attention. "Talk to me."

Heather and Ben looked at each other before Heather spoke. "We have an issue with the hold put on the search for answers in the adoption history of the manor. I think we need to pursue it and make it a priority."

"Why?"

Ben took over where Heather had stopped. This topic affected him personally. "Sara, you know I was adopted."

"Yes, I know."

"You also know we have a connection between a recent guest and one of the girls that stayed here. We think she is the grandmother of our guest."

"We don't know if those two are a true connection."

"Yes, I know we have no proof. However, I honestly think the two are connected. I don't know what it is that makes me so strong in my belief, but I have not been able to put that out of my mind since finding that possibility." Ben stood up and started to pace. "I had a nightmare last night. One that woke me up in a sweat."

Sara sat quietly as Ben continued. "I dreamed of a child given to a lady who wrapped the child in a blanket and her rushing away with it in her arms. Then I remember hearing the sound of screeching tires. Then the child was passed from one person to another in a large room. The child tried to see what was around, but the blanket covered its eyes. The blanket was so tight it was hard to move. It was a baby. I don't know what it means, but when I woke up, I was damp from sweat and having a hard time breathing." He looked at Heather. He had not told her that part. He was glad she didn't react to that additional information.

"And you think this dream is connected to the adoption history here at the manor? Or do you think this has to do with your adoption?"

"I don't know for sure. I realize that knowing I cannot find my birth mother because of the sealed records has me wanting to help those who might be able to have the connection, if there is one, and if the parties involved both want to find their true family."

Sara sat in silence, as did Heather and Ben for a few moments. She was thinking. Who should she follow? Her husband, who was an attorney? Or her brother-in-law and sister? It wasn't that easy. Although it was easy—she knew she wanted to continue the search.

"Okay, tell you what. You find the letters from, who was it, Rhea, and find out all you can to connect them. Once you have as much truth to connect those two, let me know. Heather, I want you to see how many other letters and journal entries have connections. It is time to set all of this to rest. Or to carry out our desire of bringing these people together. Some of those young mothers may have already passed away. They would have been older than Mama. I know she died rather young, but so do a lot of people." Sara stood up, walked around to the front of the desk, and hugged both of them in a group hug. "Let's do this." Even she felt relief as they broke apart their hug.

"Thank you, Sis," Heather said.

"You're welcome." She said, then added, "I will come up with something to tell Randall. I hope he understands."

"He has to. If he loves you, he will." Heather said as she and Ben walked out arm in arm. They located their boys playing in the great room where Rachelle was watching them.

"You two look happy. I hope the meeting went well?"

"Yes, it did. We'll let Sara fill you in." They called for their boys to pick up their toys and told them it was time to go home.

"That went easier than I thought it would," Ben said as they reached their house.

"I know. I think Sara was ready to keep looking. She just didn't want to go against Randall. Young love, you know."

Ben laughed. "Yep. Randall and Sara need to learn, 'Yes Dear' works both ways."

"What do you mean?"

"You don't know? Typically, when a woman asks her husband to do something, he will look her in the eye and say, 'Yes, Dear.' Then he walks away and does whatever he wants. Well, men have to learn that it works the other way around too. Women do the same thing."

"We do not!"

"Well, you should. Did you do what you wanted when you were single, or did you do what someone else told you to do? As an adult living on your own, not when you were a teen."

"I did what I wanted. When I got married, that changed because we worked together to do things. It isn't that I did things just because you asked me to or because I thought I had to."

"I'm glad, and I like that, but I would be alright if once in a while you looked at me and said, 'Yes, Dear' and then did what you wanted."

"Yes, Dear." Heather laughed as she walked away.

"Very funny. Now can we go find those letters we need?"

"Yes, Dear." Heather walked over to him and kissed him. "I love you."

They grabbed some toys for the boys and headed back to the manor to find the letters.

Two hours later, they had what they needed. They had the letter from Rhea, and Ben had found the record of when Rhea had stayed there. So they had approximate dates for when the adoption would have taken place. What they didn't have was who that baby was. Rhea was the grandmother of their guest. Ben had never asked the guest if her mother or father was the connection between them. And they didn't know if that person was the adopted baby or one of the other two children Rhea had. It was time to find out.

Ben went into the office and showed Sara what he had found. She took the liberty to tell Ben to contact the guest and tell her when Rhea had been there. But cautioned him to inquire about her parent since Rhea had mentioned that she had had two other children in her letter. Plus, to be careful because the guest may not know why Rhea had been there.

Ben considered all that and even made notes. He told Sara he was going to talk with Heather first then contact the guest.

He found Heather and brought up the fact that the guest may not know why Rhea was there.

"This is true. Rhea only knew her grandmother was here because there was trouble at home. I think you should first ask if it was her mother or father as the connection to Rhea. Then let her know you have the dates she was here. Then ask if there is a way to get in touch with Rhea. Rhea may not want the granddaughter knowing about the adoption."

"If she didn't want her to know, why would she ever tell her about the manor?"

"Good question. Maybe I'll ask if she had found out why her grandmother was here."

"I can do that. Why is this suddenly all so complicated?"

Ben went to the computer to send the guest a message. Simply to tell her he had some information and a few questions. He had to look up her name on the registration records to ensure he had the right email address and name. Her name was Laura.

He finished the note to Laura and hit send. And waited.

Heather found him still sitting at the computer thirty minutes later. "What are you waiting for?"

"Waiting for an answer."

"You do realize it may take a while."

"I know. I was just hoping Laura would be sitting at her computer waiting."

"It's been a while since they were here; she may have even forgotten about it."

"I doubt it; she called a while ago to ask for an update."

"You're right. I am the one who forgot." She laughed.

Ben left the computer to play with his boys before they put them down for a nap.

As soon as the boys were down for their nap, Ben checked his email. He yelled for Heather to look! He had a long email from Laura.

Hi Ben,

Thank you for contacting me. Let me answer your questions. Yes, yes, and mother. LOL

Now let me explain. When I was there for a visit, I did not know why Grandma had been there. After I got back home, I told my mother, Diane, I had come there for a visit and spoke with you about grandma telling us to visit. Mom was shocked that I had visited and asked me if I had learned anything while there. I told her all I had learned was that you might be able to tell me when grandma had been there. Otherwise, I had not learned anything.

Then she sat me down and told me her story. And here is the story she told me.

Grandma was there because she was unmarried and pregnant, and her mother sent her there to have her baby. My mother also told me that Grandma gave that child up for adoption.

Grandma later got married and had two more children; Diane was one of them.

So if you are concerned about telling me about the adoption of her first child, don't worry. I already know. I don't know if it was a girl or a boy. Grandma never said.

I still would like to know when she was there and any other details you can tell me.

We talked with Grandma and told her I was there. She asked if I had found any information about her. When I told her I had not, she didn't give me any more information either. Mom says that she always wanted to find out more when she first found out about an older child being in the family. She said her mom, Rhea, would not tell her, saying that all the details were secret and sealed. We would love to know more if we can.

Thanks for all your help. Hope to hear from you soon.

Laura.

Ben was relieved that Laura at least knew some of the truth. And yet, now he was confused. He had assumed that the adopted baby would have been Laura's parent. Now the adoptive baby would have been her aunt or uncle.

He looked at Heather. "Now what?" We have the dates Rhea was here, but that's about it."

"Wait. We do have more. Do you remember reading the journal that we found from Grandmama?"

"Some, why?"

"Grandmama wrote about a girl that came here, the girl the ex-boyfriend was after. They hid her, and Grandmama lied and told the boy she was not there. That girl's name was Rhea."

"Yes, and?"

"And, Grandmama went on to write that Rhea had a boy that was the first, or one of the first, I don't remember, but she had a boy that was adopted out. She wrote that Rhea wanted to hold her child and name him before he was adopted."

"Yes, I remember. So, this girl had a boy that she named. Now we have more information we can give to Laura. It may not be much, but it's a start." And the Rhea that Grandmamma wrote about may not be the same Rhea."

"Let me get that journal and find the details so you can relate them correctly."

"Okay, I'll watch the boys nap." Ben smiled and leaned back in his chair. He felt good that he could help them find out about their family. Then he thought maybe it was too much. What if the girl, now a grandmother, didn't want anyone to know or didn't want to remember. But hadn't her letter said she wanted to know who her child was? And had she not said she hoped to meet him again one day?

Heather came back with the journal. "Here we go. Now let's put all the pieces together. Rhea B had a boy that she named Benjamin Thomas, then gave him up for adoption. Rhea then went on with her life, got married, had two other children – a boy and a girl. The girl has a child named Laura. So now we are trying to figure out who adopted Benjamin Thomas, or who he is and where he is now."

"Yes."

"What are we missing?"

"The date of birth."

"Which we have a rough idea about for the dates that Rhea was here at the manor. "

And that date is—November 1954." Heather answered.

Good, now let me make some better sense of all this and send Laura a message. If we could only find this Benjamin person, it would be wonderful!"

"Well, Rhea is in her late seventies. Benjamin would be in his mid-sixties like Mama. He would be two years older than Mama. Maybe someday we will find him. For now, let

Laura know what we do know. From that, maybe they can trace it as well."

Ben sat down and wrote Laura a message with the information they had. He also told her they had a letter Rhea had written to copy and send to her snail mail.

As he was writing the message, he mentally made another connection. One he had never come to mind. He stood up and went to find Heather, who was just getting the boys up from their nap.

"Heather. I think I know who that baby boy is! Was." He corrected himself.

"What are you talking about?"

"Heather – sit down."

"But the boys," Heather started to protest.

"The boys can play for a few minutes. This idea could be a significant breakthrough."

"Ben, what is it?" She sat down.

"I know who that baby boy is!"

"You said that already. Who is it? And how do you know?"

"Rhea's firstborn son.... has to be my adoptive father— David!"

Chapter Sixteen

Ben had decisions to make. He had known he was adopted. He always wondered why his father never spoke of grandparents. It would be interesting to hear his reasons. He still wished he could find his birth parents. Maybe his father would like to reconnect with his mother. He spent nearly a week fighting with himself about what to do and then just picked up the phone to call his parents. He was glad when David answered the phone but was suddenly unsure how to approach the subject. After a bit of small talk, he brought the subject up.

Their conversation lasted over an hour. It was filled with tears and confessions and ended with plans to get together, and Ben did his best to connect his father with Rhea.

Ben was still in tears when he got off the phone. Heather was by his side. They stood and hugged each other for a long time before Ben could tell her about the conversation. Although Ben wanted to tell everyone about his discovery, they had kept all of the information between the two of them until they knew for sure. Now Ben felt he knew for sure. Or felt ninety percent sure of the truth.

They gathered up the boys and headed to the manor for a dinner they had requested later that day. Andy was more than happy to make another one of his great dinners for everyone. Taking care of twin babies and cooking breakfast for the guests was one thing. Cooking dinner for his family was another. He loved to cook and to try new recipes using his family as testers.

After everyone gathered, dinner was served, Ben began to tell his story. He started with some background that most of them already knew and how he made the connection for Laura. He then told them of Heather connecting it more and them realizing who Rhea's children were. Both the one adopted out and the one she kept after she married.

"Heather noticed the name that Rhea had named her son before she gave him up for adoption. When we found the date that she was here, something just clicked. A little more research and a call to my father gave us the truth. My adoptive father is Rhea's son, David. Not the baby she gave away. David told me that when he was little, his family lived near here. He was still a baby when they moved away. Then he said that something had happened and he didn't remember much about his mother. His father never talked about what happened. But David was raised alone by his father. Then soon after David got married, they adopted me. David never mentioned much about his family, never mentioned any siblings. I thought he was an only child."

"So, you're telling me that one of the girls that Grandmama kept here and saved is your Grandmother?"

"Through adoption, yes. Since I am adopted, Rhea isn't a blood relative, but I feel the connection somehow. I felt something the moment I met Laura when she was here. It turns out she is my cousin. Her mother, Diane, and my adoptive father, David, are siblings. David doesn't remember much about his mother, saying his father raised him. But,"

"What a small world!" Sara said.

"I know! Now we need to figure out what to do. Do we pursue it and bring Rhea together with her son?"

"Does your father want to see her after all these years?"

"He told me he would love to."

"And from the letter that Rhea wrote to Grandmama, she eventually would like to be reconnected with her son. But we assumed she meant the one she gave away."

"Have you told Laura yet?"

"No, we wanted to tell all of you first. Now that we have this information, do we just keep it to ourselves, or do we try to reconnect Rhea to her family?"

"But, the son Rhea talked about reconnecting with is the one she gave up for adoption," Heather added.

"Maybe Rhea meant both when she wrote that letter but just made it seem like it was just her firstborn son. Maybe she didn't want the secret out that she had abandoned her family after she married and had more children. I wonder why she left them?" Ben was still full of unanswered questions.

"No more secrets!" Sara stood up. "I'm tired of all the secrets in this family. As far back as we have found, there have been secrets kept. We need to start being open and honest. If people can't handle the truth, that is on them. I would want to know the truth and deal with it from there. Some secrets may hurt, but life will be better when they come out or stop hiding them. It will be less stressful."

Andy sat in silence. His sister was right. Secrets had a way of placing a hole in your heart and your mind that stayed with you. He could tell his sister was talking about the old family secrets and his secret. The one he had asked her to keep.

"I guess that is our answer," Ben said and stood up. "I have a message to send."

"Ben?"

"Yes, dear?"

"You can sit and finish eating. This information will keep until after dinner."

Ben sat back down. "Yes, Dear." He said and winked at his wife. He still felt like doing what he wanted, but he would sit a bit longer.

After the family finished dinner Ben, Heather, and the boys went home. Ben was excited about what he had discovered and could not wait to tell Laura. He sat at his computer and typed up a long email to her. He had a response within an hour.

Andy was quiet when he and Karen took the twins home. When they got them to bed, Andy said he had to talk to Sara, then went outside and called her. As soon as she answered, he began to talk.

"Sara, I got your message loud and clear at dinner tonight, and you are right. We've had enough secrets. It has been eating at me for a while now. More than usual. I just don't know how to tell her." He took a breath which gave her a chance to reply.

"I know it will be difficult, but you have to. I'm not sure how much longer I can keep your secret, knowing how we all feel about the secrets this family has. The truth is, brother, your secret is minor compared to all the other ones this family has kept."

"What if she hates me when she finds out? What if it puts a wall between us?"

"And what if it brings all of us closer together?"

"Do you think it would?"

"It would break down the stress between you and me; I know that. And for everything we've been through since that day—it's worth having the truth come out. You may want to tell Karen first to prepare her for any of the 'what if's you fear occurring."

"Thanks, Sis. I will tell her, maybe. Then I will let you know when I am going to tell Heather."

"We can do it in Joe's office if you want. He can be a mediator for you. That might make it easier for everyone."

"That may be a good idea. Just you, me, Heather, and Joe?"

"Don't forget about Ben. And for that matter, as difficult as it may be, the whole family needs to know. Maybe not at first, but eventually. 'No Secrets,' remember?

"I'm not ready for that."

"I understand. I just realized Heather's not going to like Me much."

"Why?"

"Because I kept the secret all these years."

Andy was silent. His sister was right. Heather would not like either one of them.

"I'm so sorry, Sis."

"We will be okay. Our family has endured a lot. The truth coming out is going to be part of our healing and bringing our family closer together."

"Sis, can you call Joe for me? The whole family needs to hear it. I will tell Karen first to keep her reactions from interrupting those we receive from Heather and Ben.

"True. And yes, I will call Joe first thing in the morning. Now, go try to get some sleep."

"Thanks, Sis. I will try. Love you.

"Love you too, little brother. Bye"

"Good night"

Sara set her phone down. Life was about to get interesting – again. Why couldn't she have been born into a normal family?"

Heather, Ben, Karen, Andy, and Sara were sitting in Joe McBride's office a few days later. Heather and Ben had no clue why they were there. Sara had told them that she thought it would be best to have Joe's input on dealing with all the family secrets.

Joe leaned front, resting his elbows on his desk.

"It is so good to see all of you again. Nicole and I keep trying to find time to get away to visit Bella Rose, but life gets in the way." He took a deep breath and sat back in his chair.

"Enough about me. Let's get to why you all are here." He looked at each one of them.

"Secrets," Sara spoke up. "Family secrets. We've been discovering more about our family and Bella Rose. And what our family had been hiding for generations."

"Okay. Are these making you question who you are as a family?" Joe asked.

"No, they are just bringing up questions as to why so many secrets. And now that we know them, what do we do with them?"

Joe was about to speak when Andy stood up.

"That isn't the real reason we are here," he looked at Sara, who raised her eyebrows and then nodded her head.

Heather looked at Andy, confused.

Joe stayed silent.

"Heather, Ben, I am so sorry. There is no easy way to put this but just to blurt it all out the best I can." He turned to face Heather. "Heather, I am the reason you have those scars and a limp. It was me that night who ran you off the road and caused the accident." A tear escaped his eye as he sensed his sister's automatic reaction coming.

Andy raised his hand to stop what his sister may try to say. "Now, before you react, and this is no excuse for what I did, but I was drunk. I was so drunk that I did not know I had caused anyone to go off the road. I did not know I even had car damage until the next day and then had no idea how it had happened." He started to pace but continued talking.

"You see, I was supposed to meet Sara that night, but I chicken out. I was going to come home, but I guess I wasn't ready. I stopped for a drink to celebrate my decision to reconnect with my family. The first bad decision was to have a drink. The second was to allow others to talk me into having another drink and then another. The third mistake was getting in my car and driving. I knew I was drunk and would be a disgrace to the family for once again being a failure, so I just ran off – again.

"I didn't make the connection about your accident and that I was the cause of it until a while afterward when I

145

finally came home and found you scarred and with the limp. You all told me about the accident, but when Sara told me more about it, I realized I had been the cause. I was the reason for your accident. I couldn't tell you then. I had just come home, and we were starting our family over. The details of the will had us all so busy trying to figure it out that I couldn't risk ruining what Mama wanted. She wanted all of us together, and for the first time in nearly forever, we were."

He turned to look briefly at Sara. "I told Sara the truth when I realized it but swore her to secrecy. She kept it for me and to keep the family together. I only hope you can forgive me. I don't deserve it. I don't deserve this amazing family. But know that I love you all—no matter what you now think of me." He sat down. He felt spent. Telling the truth drained all his energy.

When Andy finished talking, the room was silent. Heather felt a pain in her leg that had not bothered her in nearly a year. Sara looked at Heather, waiting. Andy was crying, his head bent down, as he repeated how sorry he was. Even Joe was quiet, waiting for a reaction from Heather or even Ben. At least they had not yelled, screamed, or started a fight. That much was good.

Andy could not stand the silence. "Say something, Sis." He raised his tear-stained face to look briefly at her.

"I don't know what to say." She looked at Sara, who lowered her eyes. She couldn't even look at her sister for her feelings of guilt. "I think I'm more upset with you for keeping the secret."

"I understand. I don't blame you. I would be too. And I hated keeping it from you. I wanted to tell you or get Andy to tell you so often. I threw him hints time and time again over the years. Every time this family talked about secrets and Andy was around, I'd throw him a look. He was so afraid of how you would react. Then he felt it was too late. Then thought that it didn't matter anyway."

"But it did matter," Andy interjected. "It ate at me all the time."

Heather looked at Ben, searching for how to respond. He had nothing to offer his bride. Finally, she looked at Andy but didn't say anything. She felt her leg where her scars were. She thought back to that day. Back to when Andy did come home. Back to how her siblings were now altogether the way Mama had wanted them. Just like he said. How could she hate her little brother? How could she make him feel unwanted and unloved? They had lost him a few times early in their lives. She didn't want to lose him again. She stood up and walked over to Andy.

Kneeling in front of him as he just hung his head, she reached for his face and lifted it so she could look him in the eyes.

"Andy, Thank you. Thank you for telling me the truth. I know it was difficult for you. At first, I was angry. But the anger wasn't because of what you did. The anger was because you kept it from me. But, I quickly realized that God had a plan. He always has a plan for each of us. We don't always know why things happen. But we can accept them. That night changed my life. It brought me closer to my husband, although that took a while. In a way, it brought me closer to my family. I was thrilled when you came home and stayed. I still am. I'm proud of you, Andy. Now, let's put all of this behind us and get on with life. With no secrets!" She pulled at Andy's hands, making him stand up, and they hugged.

Sara joined in, and Ben, although still in a bit of a shock, joined in as well. Karen held Andy's hand as they all were crying.

Joe had been watching and listening without saying a word. He wished all of his clients could work out their issues that easily. "I am so glad you worked that out. I'm not sure you needed me, but it could have gone much worse. You have an amazing family. The love you show for each other is like no other I've seen."

"Thank you, Joe. Yes, it could have gone so differently. I'm glad it went well.

"We need to tell Rachelle, and eventually our children when they are old enough to understand.

Sara and Andy laughed. "Because," Sara started. "Our family is keeping no secrets." Andy finished.

"No, secrets. That's a tall order to follow."

"Yes, but we have found out that our family has had so many secrets over the last couple of generations that as a family, we have decided that there will be no more secrets between any of us."

"Like I said, a tall order. But, I wish you the best of luck."

"Thank you. Now, Joe, you and Nicole do need to come to visit us soon. We have a lot going on. Heather is now our event planner, so if you have an event coming up, you may want to give us a try."

"Thanks, Sara. I will keep that in mind."

"Time to go home, Sis," Heather said. " We have to pick up the boys from the sitter."

"We will meet you there. Thank you for, well, for being you." She hugged her sister and led them all out of the office. It was time to go home and start getting on with life without secrets.

Heather and Ben went to pick up their boys. Along the way, Ben asked Heather if she forgave her brother for what he did.

"Of course I do. Why do you ask?"

"I just wondered. I was having a hard time accepting it at first. I guess I was surprised, is all. I spent those years blaming myself for hurting you. Now I know it wasn't me. All the heartache I put you through back then. I took my guilt and pain out on you, and I didn't need to."

"Ben, we've been through all of this, years ago. We have moved on. At least I have. Haven't you?"

"Yes, I guess so. I thought I had. Now I have a new twist to that day. It may take me a few days to deal with it. That's all. I'll be fine. Let's get our boys." He ended their conversation as they pulled into the babysitter's driveway.

Chapter Seventeen

Ben had been emailing Laura for a few days discussing the latest information he had discovered. Laura responded with an email that she had talked with her mother, and they had called Rhea to tell her that they had found her son, David, and a grandson named Ben that David had adopted. Laura wrote that Rhea was quiet about the news at first but then said she was happy he had been found. She said she was glad her son had become a good man, especially that he had the heart to adopt a child. Rhea had added that she still hoped to find her firstborn son.

Knowing that Rhea was at least happy about the news, Ben was even more willing to meet her. The trick was in finding a place to meet. They lived so far away from each other, and Rhea didn't travel much since she was eighty years old, even though she was in fairly good health.

Laura said her grandmother was willing to travel to meet the family and visit the place that saved her life all those years ago. She had talked to her doctor, and he gave her clearance to travel by plane. Her only concern was affording the ticket, so Laura and Diane paid for her round-trip ticket.

Ben was thrilled. He told Heather what Laura had said in her last email. Now it was just a case of setting a time for her to make the trip. Heather reminded him that they needed to tell Sara and the rest of the family. He nodded his head. She was right. Here the family had just had a big meeting about not keeping secrets, and he had a big one. But he wanted to make sure it all would work out in his defense, and that connection was real. Ben told Heather that they would tell them the next day. Once they all knew they would come up with a time for Rhea to visit.

The next day, Ben was the one who called a family meeting. He had never done this before. It had always been Sara who called them. When Ben called for one, no one thought anything of it. They were not concerned but were curious. Ben just snickered when they asked him why. He kiddingly, but truthfully simultaneously, told them he had a good secret to share.

When they met later, Ben was ready, complete with copies of all the emails printed out. Everyone was quiet as they waited. Secrets were not allowed anymore, so they did not know what to expect.

Ben began by reminding them of finding the connection between Laura and Rhea. He then told them that he had done more research and found an even closer connection.

"It was Heather who made the connection. We were looking at the names and the dates, and it suddenly hit her. I was confused at first. David had never said anything about his family, and I had never asked. I assumed they were all gone by the time I entered their lives.

"What made you think Rhea's son was his father?"

"Mainly the birth date, but also the name she gave him. I remember my father talking about a Benjamin Thomas. At first, when I heard what Rhea had named her son, I thought that it was my father, but when I talked to David, he said no, that he was her son. But she had left the family when he was little. And he had had nothing to do with her since.

"Wow, that is quite a discovery," Sara said. Her mind was thinking. Life, no matter whose it is, has secrets.

"Once we straightened that out, I sent a message to Laura. Long story short, Rhea wants to come to visit and to see the place that saved her life all those years ago."

"That is wonderful!" We can set her up in our best room here unless you want her to stay with you. That would maybe be better. She could have more time with you."

"I think we will ask her which one she wants. She may want to stay here even though the new expansion wasn't here when she was. Or she may be daunted by the idea of staying here because of the bad part of the memories."

"Good idea. Just let us know. When does Rhea want to come?"

"We haven't set a date yet. I told Laura I wanted to talk with all of you first. She said her grandmother was open for any time as long as the weather was nice so she could fly."

"Anytime works for us as well. So just pick an open date. Heather, check your event calendar for an open weekend or week."

"I already have, and I have available dates in about two weeks."

"Perfect. That will give us time to clean a bit more and maybe even clean up the attic and secret room, so it is welcoming and beautiful. We don't know what it all looked like when she was here, but if the secret room was dreary, we want to brighten it up and make it a more positive room. And the garden will be in full bloom for her to see from that window!"

"Perfect! Thank you so much. This means a lot to me. I still wish I knew who my birth parents are or were, but this is almost as amazing."

"Yes, it is. And to have the connection of your family with our family even before you met Heather. What are the chances of that happening when you didn't live in this area when you met. Like I've said before, 'small world.'"

Ben could not wait to let Laura know that they had a date for Rhea to visit.

Arrangements were made for Rhea's flight and stay. The attic and secret room were cleaned and improved with new paint on the walls, wooden floors cleaned, and new curtains on the window in each room. The projects had been on their list of things to do, which gave them a good reason to get them done.

Heather and Ben sat their boys down and did their best to explain who was coming and why. Maddex was still too young to understand more than a new Grandma was coming. Marc, who was about to start school in the fall, had it figured out quickly. His response was priceless.

"So you were picked by your Mommy and Daddy as well as by God?"

"That's one way to look at it, I guess."

"Was I adopted, too?"

"No, God gave us you."

"Do you love me as much?"

"Of course, why?"

"Well, God sent me to you. You had to take me. Your Mommy and Daddy picked you. They could have picked someone else."

"Yes. We love you just as much, Marc. We love Maddex as much too."

"Okay, cool," was Marc's last comment as he got up and ran off to play with Maddex following close behind.

Rhea arrived at the airport where Ben and Heather, and the boys were waiting for her. She was thrilled when she saw them. The boys held up two signs with her name written on one and "Great Grandma" on the other. Seeing those made her feel welcome.

When they were in the SUV, Marc watched her. His young mind was busy.

"Grandma?" he asked.

Rhea didn't respond at first.

"Excuse me, Grandma?" He said as he touched her arm.

"Yes, little one?"

"I've been thinking about what you did. Mommy and Daddy told me, and I think you are special."

"You do?"

"Sure, you worked with God."

"I did? How did I do that?"

"You helped Him give a baby to a good family."

Everyone was silent for a moment.

"I guess I did, Marc. I never thought about it that way. You are pretty smart to figure that out."

Ben thought about that and smiled. "Out of the mouths of children."

"I'd say you are raising him right," Rhea said. "Keep up the good work."

"Thank you. We are doing the best we can."

As they turned off the main road onto the lane with the sign at the bottom, "Rose Lane," Rhea caught her breath.

"This is beautiful! Look at all the roses!"

"They are because of my Great Grandma. My other one." Marc explained.

"I knew your Great Grandma."

"You did?"

"I sure did. She was like a Mama to me for a little while."

"Did you live here?"

"I did for a while, yes."

"Marc, we told you that."

"I know, but now I'm having a conversation with Ms. Rhea. I mean Great Grandma."

Everyone was quiet – again. Marc had such good manners, most of the time. They were unsure where all this was coming from, and it was hard to keep a straight face when all they wanted to do was laugh at what he was saying. Almost like he was a grown-up, not a little boy just about to start school.

"I appreciate that, young man. I like having a conversation with you." Rhea said.

As soon as they rounded the last curve in the lane, Bella Rose Manor came into view, and Rhea caught her breath again. It looked so different from when she was there. It was beautiful.

"You all have made this such a beautiful place."

"It was our parents who built the main manor. We added other buildings you can't see from here. We will give you the complete tour later.

Ben parked the car, and they helped Rhea walk up the stairs. Not that she needed help. They were finding out she had a lot of energy and spunk for her age and was quite capable of handling them on her own. Ben was hoping they could keep up with her.

As they opened the door, the rest of the family greeted them with a warm welcome that Rhea thoroughly enjoyed. She was busy taking in everyone and what they were saying and looking around at this wonderful place. She looked to the left of the living room and knew that that was the area she knew best. A shiver ran down her back.

After introducing everyone, they walked her to the kitchen. She hesitated at the doorway.

"Are you alright, Rhea?" Ben asked.

"Yes, I'm fine. It's just this is part of what I remember. I'll be okay, don't you worry about me." She stepped into the kitchen.

"You have made some great changes here. Thank you."

"Why thank us? I'm curious." Sara responded. She thought it odd for her to say thank you.

"I have my memories of the time I was here. Not all of them are good memories. Some I have spent my life trying to forget. The changes you have made will help me with that. I will remember how it looks now instead of what it was like when I was here. I'm not saying it was bad. Not at all. Rose and Robert did their best to make this place of love, acceptance, and joy. It was other circumstances that brought the bad memories. Everyone who was here will have that mixture inside them."

"I'm so glad you like the changes," Sara said. She now understood what Rhea meant and was so glad they had changed the attic and secret room. Hopefully, Rhea would like the changes.

Andy and Karen had set the dining room table for everyone to eat dinner. The family usually ate at the kitchen island, but they had a guest who deserved the dining room table.

"You didn't have to go to so much trouble for just me." She said when she saw all the food served.

"Oh, this is normal," Andy said with a wink.

"No, it's not. Close, but not the norm for us."

"Sometimes there's more," Karen added. She had put the twins in the playpen, and they were still sleeping. Still so little but growing.

"I'm sure. Just wait until those two little ones start eating regular food. You will be making a lot more food, especially when they are all teenagers." She laughed and joined the rest of them, who were filling their plates with food.

The dinner conversation was just general talk about her flight, the kids, and minimal mentioning of Bella Rose. No one knew how to approach the subject of her time there. They weren't sure if she wanted to talk about it so soon.

When Andy brought out the dessert, Rhea was the one who brought up the subject. "I'm sure you want to hear about my time here. And I will gladly tell you all about it, later. For now, I just want to enjoy getting to know all of you and especially Ben and Heather. But even before that, let me just say, Andy, this chocolate cake is amazing!"

"We are blessed to have a certified chef in our family. He spoils us."

"Yes, he does, but we also get to be his food testers when he tries a new dish."

"I'm sure even those are good."

"Most of them. There have been a few that we rejected over the years."

"Well, this one passes with flying colors."

Chapter Eighteen

After dinner that first night, Rhea blessed them with stories of her time there and afterward. They were amazed to learn things about their grandparents that they had not known. Such as how Rose took in any girl who came to the door but would not let any boy beyond the front porch. Rhea said that Rose did not trust any male. Other than Robert, of course. She said that after Rose heard some of the stories from the girls, she became determined to be there for the girls to show them love and understanding. Rhea told them that Rose did not judge the girls at all for their condition. Most of the girls had just made mistakes. A couple of them had been abused or raped. The girls either ran away on their own, or their own families had turned them away. Rose took time to talk with them, listen to them and offer solid advice. They asked Rhea how she knew all of this since she was one of the first girls to come there. She said she stayed in the area for a while and had stayed in touch with Rose. She said that in time, some of the girls got in touch with her.

"I was one of Rose's successes, I guess. She contacted me at one point soon after I had returned to my own home and asked if I would be willing to have the girls contact me for encouragement. I told her I would be honored."

"How were you able to return to your home?"

"Well, once my baby, Benjamin Thomas, was born and given for adoption, I stayed on here for a little bit. I learned a lot from Rose and Robert. I contacted my parents after the baby was born, and we had some long talks. I told them I wanted to come home and finish school. They agreed. It was difficult at first—the tension between us. But my Mom came around first and listened to my story and how I had changed while I was here. Eventually, Daddy was able to accept me for who I was. I think there was always some tension, but life as a whole was good. I met a wonderful boy after I got back. We started as friends, and it grew over time. He knew what I had been through, knew about the baby, and loved me anyway. He was patient with me when I would have my 'moments.' We got married and had two children of our own. Life was good."

"Wow," Sara said. "I can't imagine how life was back then for you and the other girls. I'm so proud of my grandparents. They were so brave."

"Yes, they were. They took in girls who were runaways. Nowadays, the police would be searching for them and breaking down the door to search. In a way, it was easier back then."

"It still was a difficult time for you. I'm so glad you survived and thrived through it and because of it." Ben said.

"So am I, Ben. So am I". Rhea smiled at Ben. "And to be able to come here and meet the family of Rose and Robert completes the circle. I am looking forward to seeing more of this place and the area. But for now, I am a bit tired and could use some rest."

They had not realized how late it was. Time had just flown by during their conversation.

"Let me show you to your room. We got so engrossed in talking we haven't even shown you the guest room. But, you do have a choice. You can stay here in the manor in one of the guest rooms, or you can stay with us in our house." Heather said. "Rachelle has her apartment just off the back of the kitchen so that you won't be alone in this place, but you are our only guest for a few days."

"I think I would like to stay with you and get to know you more."

"That works for us. The boys will love it."

"Then let's get you settled in over there. It's close so that we just walk back and forth."

"I like that your whole family lives on this property. Not many families live close to each other anymore, including my own. I am glad computers came along because I can now stay in touch more. Phones are nice and, well, that is another topic for another time. All the inventions since I was little. Amazing, and some scary." Rhea stood and turned to the rest of the family. "Good night, everyone. Thank you so much for this opportunity. You are all so loving. Just like Rose and Robert were."

Ben and Heather gathered their boys, who had fallen asleep, and walked Rhea to their home. Ben was smiling the whole time. He may not be a blood relative to Rhea, but he felt a close bond. Family isn't always blood. It was a choice. It was like Marc had said—people working with God to form the perfect family.

During Rhea's stay, the family got to know her and loved her. She was so open about her life, the good and the bad.

The day after she arrived, she told them she wanted to see the rest of the house. She said she was ready to see where she spent the time in her life that made all the difference.

So as not to overwhelm her, she just wanted Ben to take her. He was the one who needed to see her and hear her story. Even though he wasn't blood to her, in her heart, he was.

Ben walked with her to the third floor and opened the door to the attic room. He told her they never knew what to call that room because it was more of an attic, but it was on the third floor along with the room opposite where Heather had her decorating supplies. Rhea told him that Rose always called it the 'upper room' because she didn't know what else to call it. She told him that the room on the opposite side was used for storage as far as she could remember. She said that Rose kept spare clothes and other things in there that the girls may need. Most of the girls didn't have much more than the clothes on their backs when they came. The ones brought by their mothers had a few more things, but not much. Ben had never even given that a thought.

As they entered the 'upper room,' Rhea smiled. She had no idea what to expect other than what she could remember what it looked like. This room was beautiful.

"You did a beautiful job redoing this room. I don't remember all the details of this room, but it certainly wasn't this."

"Thank you. It was rather drab and outdated when we found it."

"Found it? You mean you didn't know this room was here?"

Ben laughed. "If you only knew. Yes, and no. We knew the room was here, but we could not get into it for a while. It was locked, and we didn't have the key." He made it as simple as he could to keep it believable. Even the truth was hard to believe.

"What a shame. I'm sure it was worth the wait. Did Rose keep a lot of things in here?"

"Not so much her, but Susan did. We found letters and journals in here from when the manor belonged to her and Glen."

"Susan was your mother-in-law. Rose and Robert's daughter, right?"

"Yes, their only child. She inherited this place when they died. And when Susan and Glen both died, the place was willed to their three children; Sara, Heather, and Andy."

"I can tell that it has worked out well for the family. You all work well together?"

"Yes, we do. This family is like no other I've ever heard of."

"You are blessed."

Rhea walked around the room, looking at what was still inside. She recognized the desk and even the bed. But Rhea said the file cabinet was new. She went to the window and touched the curtains. She separated them and looked outside. Ben just let her be and didn't interrupt her thoughts. He knew it was an emotional time for her.

Rhea was reflecting on her childhood. She remembered feeling loved here. She remembered feeling afraid when her ex-boyfriend tried to break in and find her. She could still hear the argument if she closed her eyes. She had spent her life trying to forget that day. As she looked outside, she saw the garden and smiled. It was different from when she had been there, but she remembered the smile it put on her face and the other girls when they looked at it. She also remembered working in the garden to pull the weeds, plant new flowers, and pick the roses for vases inside the kitchen. This room brought back good memories as well as the difficult ones. She smiled as she turned. She was a survivor. She still was lost in her thoughts and hadn't said a word for a while. Ben continued to let her be.

She came to the door of the secret room and finally spoke again. "You opened up the secret door. I like that. I used to have to bend down to get inside. The first time Rose pushed me inside, I saw the door and thought the whole room was going to be tiny. Robert had just built it after I got here, and once I stepped inside, I felt so safe." She walked through the door. She stopped short and closed her eyes. Going inside was more difficult than she thought it would be. After all these years, it brought back the bad feelings. She took a deep breath and opened her eyes. She took another step inside and began to look around. A smile came to her.

The way she remembered it was nothing like it was now. Now it looked like a small, sweet room that any child or teen would love to have. Light curtains of pinks and purples hung in front of the window but only diffused the light without blocking it out, giving the room a soft glow of light. A twin bed, a real twin bed, not just a cot, was set up with beautiful pink, purple, and off-white quilt cover along with matching throw pillows. The dresser had fresh flowers in a delicate clear glass vase on top, a card table and folding chair in the back, and a short two-drawer bookcase with several books lining the shelves. They had transformed the room well.

"You've done well, Ben. All the changes here help the healing. I wish all the girls could come back and see this. I have spent my life reliving my time here. I could picture this room in every detail in my sleep, I think. Now I have a better vision to remember."

She walked to the window to look out at the garden. "Were you the one who reworked the garden?"

"Yes, we never noticed it until we found this room and opened it up. Someone had boarded up the window, so it was dark when we first found it and came in. I took down the board and looked out to find only the outline of where the garden had been. From the ground, we had just thought it was rocks set around. From up here, I could make out that it used to be a garden. So I restored it and added to it. Now the boys spend time playing there in their private playground."

"I am quite proud of you, son," Rhea said, still standing near the window. You've done well."

Ben caught that she called him 'son' and wasn't sure if he should remind her that he was her grandson or if she just used that term in general. He let it go for now. But he silently hoped she was not a bit delusional. That would be heartbreaking.

"Are you ready to go back downstairs?"

"Yes, I think I am. I may want to come back on my own before I go back home, but for now, I am ready. Thank you for doing all of this."

"It was nothing." Ben said as he led her out of the secret room and the 'upper room' and walked her down to the first floor.

They could smell fresh baked cookies as they reached the first floor. Andy was making his famous cookies because this was a special occasion. These were the cookies he usually made just for holidays.

As Rhea entered the kitchen, she lifted her head, raising her nose to take in the incredible aroma. "What is that delicious smell?"

"Those are Andy's special chocolate chip cookies. He only makes those on holidays and for very special occasions."

"What holiday is it? Did I miss a holiday?"

Ben laughed. "No, You, Grandma, are the special occasion."

"I am? I'm nothing special."

"Oh, yes, you are. You are very special. And I am so glad we were able to meet." Ben put his arms around her and hugged her. They walked together to the kitchen island where a plate of fresh, out-of-the-oven cookies sat, waiting.

Rhea reached for one, and as she tasted it, Ben could see her savoring the flavors that matched the aroma she had inhaled. "These are amazing!" She slowly finished the cookie, enjoying every single bite without saying another word.

Ben was smiling as he watched his Grandmother enjoying the simple pleasures of life in a place that once was her only safe haven. A haven where she found love but also witnessed the greatest fear she may have ever witnessed. The fear of her ex-boyfriend. In his mind, he smiled even bigger as he knew that the love she found here overpowered any fear she may have had.

Rhea noticed his smile, and when she had finished the cookie, she asked him why he was smiling.

"I was just enjoying watching you enjoy that cookie."

"It was more than that. I may be old, but I can still read people's looks pretty well. I got good at it quickly as a young child."

He didn't doubt her one bit. "You're right. I was thinking of how you are here enjoying a simple cookie at a place that at one time was your only safe place and also the place where you witnessed what was most likely your greatest fear."

164

"Oh, I never had my biggest fear here. No." She shook her head, her eyes drifting back in time. "No, that fear came before I came here. I was so afraid when I found out I was pregnant and knew I had to tell my parents. I already knew what they would do to me. I put off telling them for as long as I could. Then it was almost too late. Well, it was too late for what my boyfriend wanted me to do."

"What did he want you to do?"

"When I first told him I was going to have his baby, he just thought I was talking about our future. When he realized I meant that I was already 'with child,' he told me to go off and find a way to get rid of it."

"He wanted you to have an abortion?" Ben was surprised.

"Oh, yes. I told him I was too far along for that. That was when he told me to have good luck with my parents, and he bid me goodbye. He walked out of my life. I never saw him after that until he tried to break in here. Somehow he found out where I was. I assumed my mother slipped up, and he overheard it. I don't know. But when my parents found out my condition and that I was so far along, they brought me here and dropped me off. I'm not sure how they found this place. Considering it is so far away, and it wasn't what Bella Rose Manor was at the time."

"I have been wondering how the girls found out about this place. Especially since it did not begin as a place for wayward girls."

"I don't know either. But many of us found our way here. And I'm so grateful. My life could have been completely different. I quit thinking about 'what ifs' a long time ago. Those thoughts are a waste of time and energy. Life is too short for that." She reached for a second cookie. "Don't let me take another one of these! They are addictive!"

Ben just smiled at her. He admired how positive she was. With all that she had been through, she looked at life like no one else he knew. He liked her attitude.

Chapter Nineteen

All too soon, it was time for Rhea to return home. Her visit had opened their eyes to many things, not only about Bella Rose Manor and their family background but about life in general. Except for her ex-boyfriend, she didn't have a negative word to say about anyone. And she told them that she had even forgiven him in the last few years. She said she never saw him again after he attempted to find her, but said at one time she heard that he lived alone somewhere in the backcountry of Alaska, living off the land. The last she heard was that he had gotten killed in a freak accident. She didn't tell them any details. If she did know them, she wasn't sharing.

As she was preparing to leave, she gathered the family together one last time. She said she wanted to share one last thing before she left.

Everyone gathered in the great room where they could sit comfortably.

Rhea raised out of her chair when she saw everyone she wanted to talk to was there. She had a message to give them.

"I want to tell all of you that my stay here has been one of the highlights of my life. My recent stay with all of you." she clarified, as she didn't want them to think she was talking about when she was a child here. "You have shown me that love, caring, compassion, understanding, and your attitudes would make Rose and Robert proud. I never knew your Mama and Daddy, so I don't know what they were like, but I do know that they raised you in a way that your grandparents would be proud of." She then looked at Ben. "Ben, you may not be a blood relative, but in my book, you are one special person. Whoever gave you up for adoption missed out."

She looked around the room at each one. Her look made them feel, in a good way, that she was looking into their souls. Her eyes were full of compassion, love, and caring. "I want to thank you all for letting me come into your lives so I could find closure in mine. The first time I held my firstborn child was also my last. I gave a part of my heart away that day. I didn't know where my child was going. I didn't know if he would be loved as much as I had instantly loved him. I had emotions I didn't know existed, nor did I understand them. All I knew was that Rose and Robert were there for me. They showed me love. They supported my decision to give my son to another family. I trusted them to do the best and right for him. I still worried about him. For the rest of my life, I never knew what had happened to him. It took me several years to open my heart to love someone." She stopped to take a breath. Revealing her past was still difficult.

She smiled and continued. "But I did. I found love in a man I met near my hometown. We had two children and a wonderful life together. He often comforted me when I would cry. I could not even tell him why for the longest time. Yet, he loved me. When I finally opened up to him and told him my story, he stood by me. He held me. He told me I needed to share my story with our children. But before they were old enough, our marriage hit a rocky road, and I had to leave. Sadly, I also left my children. I knew he would take better care of them. Due to that action, I missed out on getting to know them as they grew. I have reconnected with my daughter, but not my son. Not the one who raised you, Ben."

"Years later, I told Diane about this place. I didn't tell her any details, just that I had spent time here and if she ever had the chance that she should visit. I didn't tell her the details because I knew that our life here was a secret to the rest of the world. I didn't know if the people who owned this place knew the history. I wasn't even sure this place was still here. When Laura called to tell me she was here, my heart jumped. I knew then that I needed to see if I could find my son. I say all that to simply say, Thank you."

Rhea had talked her way into tears. Ben reached around her shoulders and held her close.

"I am so glad you are here. You have given us so many answers that we didn't even know we had questions. We didn't know several things you told us about the secret room or what Rose and Robert did to help so many girls, how they risked their lives to help each of you. We are blessed to have you here and to be a part of our lives."

"Rhea, please stay in touch with us and let us know how you are doing. And know that you are welcome back here anytime. I'm sure Ben and Heather and the boys are going to stay in touch. After all, they now have a wonderful Grandma and Great Grandma in their lives."

"Thank you all. I will stay in touch. And when I think of more stories, I will share them with you. Please feel free to call me and ask me about anything. I know you still have more letters or journals to go through that you found in the secret room that Heather mentioned. I hope they tell more great stories about this place."

Ben looked at the clock. It was time to take Rhea to the airport. He hated to see her go but knew it was time. Marc had asked if he could go to the airport with them, and Ben and Rhea both said that was a great idea.

Rhea said her goodbyes to everyone while Ben carried her luggage to the car. Marc climbed into his car seat and waited for them. It was all small talk until they got to the airport. There Marc, in his young wisdom, reached up to hug Rhea goodbye. "Thank you, Great-Grandma. Thank you for working with God when you were a little girl. I hope I get to work with Him someday."

More tears. Again, out of the mouths of the children. Ben wiped his tear away as he carried her bags into the terminal. As Rhea was getting ready to board, Ben told her that David, his dad, wanted to reconnect with her. He told her that her son wanted to at least talk with her someday. He was not ready this time around.

Rhea said she understood. She thanked Ben for his efforts to join her family together, and his family. Although he was adopted into it, she felt he belonged.

Ben and Marc watched as she walked away a few minutes later to wait to board the plane. They stood at the windows so they could watch the plane take off into the sky after everyone was on board.

"I'm going to miss her, Daddy," Marc said as he watched the plane begin to taxi away. "I love Great-Grandma."

"I love her too, son."

They watched and waved as the plane took off. They didn't know when they would see her again, but they knew they would stay in touch and knew their hearts were fuller with her in their lives.

Back at the Manor, while Ben and Marc had taken Rhea to fly home, everyone was just lost in their thoughts. The last several days had been a whirlwind with Rhea, and they sat in silence.

Finally, Sara spoke. "Does anyone else feel drained? In a good way, but drained? Like we just had so much information given to us that we don't know how to sift through it all and make anything out of it?"

"I know I do. I never imagined half of what Rhea told us. It's hard to visualize all of that happening here." Heather said as she looked blankly at the floor. " It's almost like it was all a dream."

"I know what you mean. Maybe it was too much all at once. We were used to searching for answers when we had time, then Rhea came into our lives and filled in a lot of the blanks like a water faucet opened at high pressure. Did anyone take notes while she told us all those stories?"

"I wrote some of it down," Rachelle said. "But, you are right, she had a lot of information. It was like she had it all bottled up inside of her all these years and finally had someplace to let it all out."

"That's exactly what it was. She said she told her husband, but I think she still needed to tell the ones who had helped her. It must be such a relief to her to have that closure. After holding in all those secrets for so long."

"I know that feeling," Andy said as he looked at Heather. "It's best when you can get the truth out."

Heather smiled.

Just then, they heard Ben and Marc coming in the front door.

"Guess what, Mommy?" Marc was jumping up and down.

"What?" Heather asked, reaching for her son.

"We watched Great Grandma take off on a big jet! It was huge! But, you know what else?"

"What?" Heather held him still.

I thanked her for working with God and told her that someday I wanted to work with God too."

Heather wrapped her arms around him and gave Marc a full-body hug. "That would be awesome!" She wiped a tear from her eye.

Everyone had been gathered around the kitchen island when Ben and Marc came home. Andy was messing with a pile of papers, Karen was busy rocking the twins in their little cradles, Sara and Randall were chatting, Rachelle was looking at the notes she had taken while Rhea had been there, and Heather had been playing with Maddex. Life looked like it had gotten back to normal already.

While Sara and Randall were chatting, Sara thought about how life had changed once again with Rhea's visit. What was their next step? What should they do now? How do they move forward? Or do they just let it all go and box up the letters and journals? "No, we have to read the rest of the letters."

"What?" Randall asked, tilting his head and raising his eyebrows. "Where did that come from?"

"Sorry, I guess I answered out loud what I was thinking about."

Everyone was listening to her now.

"Of course, we have to read the rest of the letters. Why was that even a question?" Heather asked. She may have been playing with Maddex, but she had learned to hear everything around her while she dealt with two kids. It paid off. She had also learned to tune out things when she didn't want people to know she heard them. A talent she was sure all mothers learned.

"I was just wondering. I know we found out a lot in the upper room and then from Rhea, but I think the letters in the 'upper room,' as Rhea told us it was called, deal with something different than hiding the girls. I think when Mama and Daddy ran the manor, it was more just a bed and breakfast like it is now."

"I would agree with you, Sis. I don't remember anything else but regular guests. I do remember a lot of the guests being singles when we were little. Do you think there is something to that?"

Sara thought back to her memories. She, too, remembered a lot of singles being there. Most were also young, from what she recalled. "I wonder if there was something to that. It certainly wasn't a time when it was fashionable to be single, out on your own. It was a time in life when a woman's goal was to find the right man and get married. Women went to college in pursuit of receiving their MRS."

"MRS?" Andy asked

"Married status," Heather answered. "If a woman was not married by the time she was thirty, she was considered an old maid, and people doubted she would get married."

"Ah. Yes. I forgot. Even in my travels as a teen, it was the men who worked. The woman stayed home having babies or busy raising the ones they had."

"So, when do we get back to the upper room?" Rachelle asked while she tidied up the papers she was organizing. "I hope to write out these notes and make some sense of them for you to have."

"What notes are those?" Sara asked.

"I was making notes while Rhea was here. I wasn't involved in all the conversations, but I wrote what I heard and noted what you talked about in your discussions with her."

"Thank you. I appreciate that. That gives me an idea. With all the letters and journals from the past, are any of us writing a current journal? Our kids and grandkids may want to know about our generation."

No one spoke up.

"I can do it." Rachelle offered. "I know I'm not a blood relative to this family nor connected to this place, but that gives me a slight advantage. I can write it as the outsider looking in."

"I do need to start one for my boys, so they know about growing up here. Who knows if they will ever read it, or care, or even live here when they grow up, but at least it would be there if they wanted to know."

I think I will start one for our twins as well. They will have to share the copy; I'm not writing one for each of them. I can just make two copies for them." Karen laughed.

"What's so funny?" Andy asked.

"I just thought what an awesome, embarrassing gift that would be to give their brides on their wedding days!"

"Oh, yes, how cruel. You must do it!" Andy chuckled and gave her a side hug.

"Okay." Sara stood up. She had a plan. Everyone looked at her. They knew she meant business.

"We're listening," Randall replied. He knew his wife was serious when she stood up to talk. He hoped everyone was prepared for what she may have on her mind. Even he was afraid.

"Okay. Here's the plan. We all get together and read the letters and the last couple of journals we found in the upper room. From there, we figure out what this place was like when our parents ran it. Then we work, with Rachelle's help, if she is willing to take charge of it, we work putting together "The Life and Times of Bella Rose." We can summarize all the details and make it easier for our kids and grandkids, and even the general public, to learn about this place. I think it has a place in local history."

"Adventurous task," Heather voiced her opinion

"Yes, it is, but if we don't get it started, we will continue to put it off, and it will never get done. Rachelle, are you willing to help out?"

"Of course. I already volunteered to write some of it anyway. I think it will be interesting. We need to go through more letters dealing with the girls staying here when Rose and Robert ran it. We have a few letters and journals and what Rhea told us, so we already have a lot. But I may be able to find more."

"Good. Randall, can you keep investigating if what they were doing was legal, and if not, what happens if we reveal the truth? Do we risk any restitution? Or will we be okay with telling our story?"

"I will look further into it. I don't think after all these years that it will be a legal issue. So at least I say go for it even if it is just for the family."

"Sis. What do you think about looking for more of the girls who were here? As we continue reading, we can make a list of those who sounded like they would want to come back, or at least get in touch with Rose and Robert, and then we can search for them."

"Do you realize how long that would take? Plus, most are going to be Rhea's age, give or take a couple of years."

"True, but I think we could maybe find a couple more. Then we can invite the ladies to come here as we did with Rhea." Heather was becoming more excited about it the more she thought about it.

"I wouldn't get your hopes up. We may be better off searching for those who have written the letters and journals in the upper room. The time Mama and Daddy ran it."

"True. Then again, maybe we could find the kids or grandkids of the ones who were here when Rhea was here."

"That would be even more difficult. But, you can try. I just don't want you to be disappointed."

"I can at least try."

"For now, we get some rest. It has been a very busy week physically and mentally."

"That it has," Ben agreed. He had been on his toes all week with Rhea. She had been a delight, but he swore she had more energy than any of them did.

Chapter Twenty

Once again, Bella Rose was back to what was considered normal. Many years ago, the family learned that there was no such thing as normal for them, even when it was just a single house of newlyweds who had no plans to do more than starting a family and enjoying life.

Rachelle buried herself in reading the letters everyone else had already read to decide what would work best in her writing. She wanted to include them all, believing they played a major role in the history of this family. She also continued to help Sara with the paperwork and business end of the Manor.

The girls were busy gathering the letters that remained in the upper room and reading them. They each had a couple of the last journals they were reading. They were small journals, not the ones that span a full year, with each page a new day's event. They were composition notebooks with guest's entries. At first, the girls thought they would be like the ones they left in the current guests' rooms that each guest could write in. When they took a closer look, each page was the writing of one person. For some reason, whoever had them had used them as their short diary and then left them there. Sara found this not odd; it was interesting. Maybe they contained some important information that could explain what was happening while she was growing up there.

Sara and Heather had lived there all their lives, but when they were little, they didn't pay attention to much of anything other than having other kids to play with from time to time. As they grew older, they did help out with the work such as cleaning and helping their Grandmama cook. These memories were during the time that they vaguely remember their Mama being away.

When Sara showed Heather the journals and told her what she thought they were, it intrigued her as well. They each took a couple of them home with them and set about to read them. They both figured it would take a few nights to get through them.

The next morning when they all met for breakfast, they looked at each other and shook their heads while snickering.

"I take it you didn't sleep either?"

"Not at all, and it wasn't the boys keeping me up. They are long past not sleeping and getting me up every two hours to eat. It was the journals. Is that why you have those dark circles under your eyes?"

"You found me out. I opened the first one, and that was it. I never even made it to bed. Randall found me on the sofa this morning. I had fallen asleep at some point with the journal on my lap. It was still opened to the page I was reading, and I was immediately lost in the reading again when I picked it up. Randall brought me a cup of fresh coffee, which was cold by the time I took my first sip."

"Wow, Sis, you had it worse than I did. No wonder your dark circles are darker than mine."

"Thanks. I guess I'll have to find my concealer and some makeup today."

"Not for my sake. I'm fine with you just the way you are. So what did you find out in your journal?"

"Well, I found out that this young girl spent about six weeks here. On her own."

"Oh?"

"Yes, at first, I thought maybe she was from our grandmother's time and not Mama's time, but the date on it was right for the time we were kids. She most likely wasn't much older than we are."

"Interesting."

"Well, as I read what she wrote, I was surprised. It seems that during that time, Mama and Daddy took in kids that had no place to go. Not that she was pregnant, just that for whatever reason, their parents sent them packing. This particular one was here because, according to her, she had quit school because she didn't get along with her teachers or her classmates. She was a victim of bullying before it was a term commonly used and dealt with. Back then, if you were a victim of bullying, you fought it out and got over it. But for her, when she fought back, she got kicked out of school, and her parents didn't know what to do with her. No other school was in the area, and the family refused to move. So they sent her on her way. She was supposed to find her way to an aunt but stumbled across this place on her way, and once she was here, she never left. She wrote that Susan and Glen took her in as if she was their own. She was given a private room and soon learned to pitch in and help clean and cook. She wasn't there very long, maybe a few months, but she fell in love with the place. She wrote that she would love to come back someday to visit if not stay and help."

"Did she go into any details as to why she stayed so long? Or what she did that got her to leave?"

"That's the interesting part. She says that Susan and Glen worked with her and sent her to school while she was here. She liked the school and liked being here, but one day her father showed up and told Susan and Glen that this girl's grandmother had died and needed to come home. She wrote in the notebook that she was promised the bullying had stopped at her other school, so she agreed to go home. She missed her family but didn't like how they treated others. Plus, she doubted the bullying had stopped."

"Sounds almost like she wasn't sure what home would be like when she got there."

"I know. She left the journal here when she left, and there is a lot more that she wrote about, but she knew she would have to leave the journal here as her father would not allow such a thing in their house. She wrote that she would be okay at school with the bullying but was more afraid of what her father would do to her if she spoke out of turn, did something wrong, or just about anything to irritate him."

"I feel so sorry for her. I hope she was okay after she went home."

"I hope so too. Too bad there was no way for her to continue writing the journal. Odd really that she left it here."

"Not so odd. She would get into trouble if her father found it. She wanted someone to find it and either treasure it or trace it to her home and make sure she was alright and still alive. She could not imagine life being good again."

"Oh, no. So not only was she bullied at school, she was not treated well at home either."

"Sadly, no. I wonder if she was able to make something of her life?"

"See, that's what I'm talking about—finding these former guests. I know she would be a little older than we are, so she should still be alive."

"That is true. Why don't you get on the computer and search for these people as we read their letters and journals? Now that we have a name and date, it may be fairly easy to find these people."

"Of course, we have the issue of her last name."

"Yes, but there are programs on the internet that allow you to find people so much easier than the old paper trails."

"We can start our search when we finish reading everything. I don't want to look for one and ignore the others. I think it would be easier to do them all at once. I know we may not find all of them for whatever reason, but we can at least try."

"I agree. Maybe Randall can help us by telling us where to search. I'm sure he will have a few ideas as well as resources we can utilize."

"So what was written in the journal you read?"

"Mine was from a girl as well. I figure she was almost an adult when she was here. She wrote about running away from home when she was sixteen, and after trying the New York scene for a short time, she was broke and had no place to go. She met a girl in New York who told her about this place being a safe haven for young girls. The girl told her that her mother had been here once and said if she ever needed a place to stay to check this place out. She wrote of spending hours on the road and hitchhiking along the road until a truck driver picked her up in his eighteen-wheeler. She said she was scared at first, but it was her only option, so she took it and prayed for safety. The horror stories over the years about truck drivers and motorcyclists had taught her to distrust both. She said her mother would have had a fit had she known she was in the cab of a diesel truck with a strange man and a full-size bed in the cab."

"I can only imagine what she must have felt. She must have had a lot of faith to overcome her distrust. Does it say that she arrived at the Manor on that truck?"

"No, she goes on to write that he could not get her further than the interstate highway, but he told her how to find her way here. He told her to stop anywhere in town and ask if she got lost. It seems everyone knew where the manor was."

"Good to know the Manor was well known back then. Of course, we knew it was. Do you remember it ever being empty?"

"Not that I know of. Maybe during January like it is now, but I don't remember all the details about back then. Heck, we didn't remember these girls being here."

"Well, maybe we remember them being here but never knew their stories. We were preteens at that time. Do preteens pay that much attention?"

"You're right. Do you think we will be able to find many of these guests?"

"I don't know. It may be a waste of time, but I want to pursue it anyway. Even if just for our satisfaction of knowing more about our family."

"I agree. Did you get to read the second journal?"

"That was the one I was reading when I fell asleep. I will finish it tonight."

"Are you making notes while you read?"

"No, I'm just reading. That is a good idea about the notes. Hey, don't forget we can get the guest register books in the attic, I mean, upper room, so we can maybe find contact information on these girls. It may not lead us to where they are now, but it may give us a clue. Any help we can get to find these people."

"And what are we going to do when we find them?"

"We are going to plan a party. And that, dear Sister, is where you are the expert. So you might as well start making notes for a party as well."

Chapter Twenty-One

Life has a way of interrupting the plans one has for life and what they want to have happen. The same was the case for Bella Rose Manor. It seemed she had her own plans and wasn't ready.

Sara and Heather had the letters and journals to read that involved Bella Rose. They also had the land to deal with that their father had left them. They had almost forgotten about an appointment they had made for a meeting with the attorney in West Tennessee. The attorney called Sara to remind her the week before. Sara told Heather they would have to take a slight break in what they were doing since they had to travel across the state to meet with him. They had papers to sign since the people had agreed to purchase the land from them. Heather and Ben made arrangements with the babysitter to watch the boys. Ben could take care of his boys most of the time, but the babysitter was on call if he had to work and could not have the kids around. She was a retired lady who loved watching their children.

The day came for Sara and Heather to take their road trip. They had never gone on a road trip together, so they both thought it would be fun. And for the most part, it was fun. Traffic held them up a few times, but it gave them time to chat. No other family, no interruptions, no opinions from other people, just sisters being alone for hours for the first time—ever.

Their conversations ranged from childhood to marriage, babies, and then to the manor itself and all the family secrets. The topics led them to imagine what the attorney had to tell them about their Dad and why he had the land. None of their assumptions were close to reality.

As soon as they arrived at the attorney's office, he walked them into his office. They were surprised they didn't have to wait, but it was a small town, and they did have an appointment.

It was late in the day, and the girls had made hotel reservations in the next town. They had debated checking in there first, then changed their minds when it was running late, which may have made them late for the meeting. If it was one thing Sara had learned from Randall, it was not to be late for your appointment with an attorney. Even with a small-town attorney.

After Sara introduced Heather to the attorney, he didn't waste time with small talk. He was direct and to the point.

"Thank you, ladies, for coming all this way. I know it takes you away from your work there, so I do appreciate your time. As you know, your father purchased this land many years ago when it was just that, land. There was nothing here. He talked about building a house and then selling the rest off in lots for others to build houses on. He did build one small house and was talking with others that lived nearby about his plans. That was when the idea came to create a small town. So he began to set the wheels in motion to do that. There were issues with some of the land and what could and could not be done with it. This required legal changes by the county. These also took a while. Eventually, this building was built as the center of town and became the court house, small jail, and the church." He looked at Heather, "Like we said, small town."

Heather smiled but didn't say anything.

He continued, "After the first couple of buildings were built, Glen got called away on other business. He didn't live here much, just used it as a vacation home. Glen told us it was his getaway place. Said he traveled for a living making investments, which was why he had bought the land. As an investment into my future is what Glen called it. Then one day, he stopped coming. He called me and had me draw up some legal papers for his will of this land. He told me he had a regular will that took care of everything else in his life, but he confided in me that no one in his family knew about this land. He told me that it had been a secret even from his wife. He said that he bought it as a surprise for her and then their marriage fell apart. He kept the land and kept the secret."

"So our Mama never knew about this land?"

"No, not that I know of."

"So what did his will say?" Heather asked.

"Well, that was the strange one. Glen had me compose it that the land should remain in his name for five years after he died. I asked him why the five years, and he told me that it would take that long for his family to deal with his other will. I just shook my head at him and wrote what he wanted."

"If you knew what our Mama's will said, you would understand. He must have known how Mama was going to write hers, even then." Sara shook her head. What a family they had.

"So, the will said that you hold it for five years and then contact us with options of what to do with it?"

"Yes."

"I do have a question. Why did he leave it to just the two of us? We do have a younger brother. Why not include him?" Sara thought she knew why but wasn't going to say anything.

"I didn't know at first that there was a younger brother involved. When he bought the land, he said his family was just starting and that he had two little girls. Then when his marriage broke up, he didn't come here very often; we also didn't stay in touch very often. The land sort of took care of itself. It wasn't going anywhere."

"When he came in to sign the will, he told me about your younger brother and the long story." The attorney sat back in his chair.

"He told me that he and Susan, your mother, had reconnected. I was happy for him. I also noticed when I told him that I was happy for him that his face changed slightly. He then went on to tell me that Susan had another child that came along with the 'deal,' as he called it. He told me that he wasn't sure how to handle raising a child she had had out of wedlock, even though it was while they divorced. Glen understood that she had every right to have another life and even another child. He told about his remarriage and that she had passed away a few years after they married. He wanted the land to stay a secret from his whole family until he was gone. He said he wanted to be sure his girls, you two, had something to call your own when the time came. Said he was afraid Susan would give the boy more than you girls. Or at least that things would be divided between the three of you when it should be just the two of you if it were coming from him and Susan."

"He told you that he didn't know how to deal with Andy in his life?"

"That he did. I was shocked at first. That way of thinking wasn't the man I had known for so many years. The old man would have given the shirt off his back for anyone. I never took him as a man who would hold a grudge. But, there he was, sitting in my office spilling his guts out to me about his feelings. I'm an attorney; I deal in legal things, facts, not feelings. I was a bit uncomfortable with all he was sharing. I was also his friend, though, so I listened. I filed it away and never told anyone. Not even my wife. She would have hated him for what he was doing."

"I hate him for it," Sara said. "He never did get close to Andy. Not once. I never dreamed Daddy would go to those extremes to exclude him from the family."

"Unreal," was all Heather could say.

"Where are those papers for us to sign? I don't even want to see this land he owned."

"Heather, we do need to talk about it. But maybe you are right. Let's just sign the papers and take the money. I'm not sure what I want to do with the money either. I feel like it's tainted somehow."

"The money is good." The Attorney said.

"I know the money is good; it's the story that is sad and a bit hateful. Maybe tainted isn't the right word for it."

The attorney opened the file cabinet near his desk and pulled out a small file. He pulled out the papers for the girls to sign. He had another copy and read some of it to them to completely understand what they were signing. When all the papers were signed, and they had copies of everything, the girls stood. Heather immediately headed for the door.

"Thank you, sir." Sara reached across the desk to shake his hand. "You have been so helpful. I appreciate your honesty in telling us the truth about our father and his dealings here. I wish you all the best with this town and whatever you eventually do with it."

"You are welcome. I am sorry the story wasn't a pleasant one for you to hear. I do hope it turns into something positive for you and your sister."

"And our family. We plan to share this with all of them. He may have wanted it to just be for the two of us, but we are family." Heather added as she opened the door. Sara could see how hurt Heather was.

They said their goodbyes and walked to Sara's car.

They were silent as Sara drove along the country roads to reach the interstate highway. Each lost in their thoughts. Neither one knew what to say. Each had mixed emotions.

It was after Sara had driven five miles along the interstate that she spoke.

"Here's the exit for the hotel. Time to call it a night, get some rest and start out early in the morning."

After they settled into their room and had something to eat at the restaurant next door, they finally talked about the money and the news they had heard.

"What are we going to do?"

"About the money?"

"That, and do we tell the truth to Andy and why he mitted from this land deal?"

"I'm not sure what to do with the money. But I do know that we have to tell Andy the truth. Remember what we have all just been through. About how keeping secrets in this family, well, you know."

"Yes, I was thinking the same thing. We need to tell Andy. I just hate that, once again, Daddy put a wall up between him and Andy. Andy has dealt with that wall all his life."

"I know. I often wish life could have been different for him. Then I think that if it had been any different, everything would be different as we know it now. And I don't think that difference could have been any better than it is now. I love the family we have become."

"I do too. I, too, wish we had suffered less stress to get here, but we certainly can't change anything about the past and how it was. We just work at making the present and the future better. For all of us."

"And we are doing what we can to do that. Maybe now that this chapter in our life has ended, we can get on to the better ones."

"I think once we finish going through the letters and journals and finding as many of those girls as we can that it may not only be time for a new chapter, but a completely new book."

Heather laughed. "I've never heard of life starting over in a new book. But I like that. I agree. In the meantime, we have to deal with the current chapters."

"Yes, and the first thing is telling the family the new-found truth about Daddy."

"That won't be easy."

"No, it won't, but I think our family has become open and willing to hear the honesty from us. Once we hear it, we learn to deal with it. What helps is we have all stuck together on all of it."

"Odd as it sounds and as hard as it was to figure out what the heck Mama was doing when she wrote her will the way she did, somehow Mama knew what she was doing. She may not have known how to bring the family together when she was alive, but she did know how to do it in her death."

"I wonder if any of that had to do with her not being able to be the way she wanted to be when she was married?"

"What do you mean?"

"I wonder if some of what she didn't do was because of what Glen didn't want her to do?"

"I'm not sure where you are going with that? Do you think he was controlling? She always seemed to do what she wanted to do."

"Yes, but maybe she wanted to do more, and we just don't know about it."

"You're digging too deep, Sister. Let it go."

"You're right. Too much thought into the past and the what if's that we can't control. And a different path I don't want to go down. I'll just let that idea go. Back to what is currently going on. We have enough to deal with there."

"Yes, we do. Time for another family meeting as soon as we get home. For now, let's get some rest. We have a long trip tomorrow."

Chapter Twenty-Two

The family gathered around the kitchen island. It was still the gathering place for family meetings. For them, this was as informal as it could get. The warmth of the family kitchen, even if it was the kitchen for the manor, the familiar kitchen still was where they all felt the closest. Somehow, even though they had remodeled it to fit their needs, they knew it was here where their mother and even their grandmother had cooked all the meals once the manor was built. It was filled with love for family and strangers alike.

Sara and Heather had talked a lot about what they would tell their family during their drive home just a few days earlier. Sitting here, looking at their family full of life, love, joy, happiness, they knew that what they had to share would most likely change at least some of that. They also knew that they had to share it, or the secret would eat at the two of them, eventually destroying what the family had finally become. Honest, trusting, and open.

They had postponed the inevitable due to everyone's previous appointments, including guests they had staying at Bella Rose.

Once everyone was seated, the boys were playing in the other room, and the twins playing in the playpen they had set up in the corner for them, Sara started the conversation.

"As you all know, Heather and I went to West Tennessee to deal with the land that Glen had." She tilted her head and shrugged her shoulders slightly. "The land none of us knew about until recently. Randall found out about it and took me there for our honeymoon of all things. He hoped it would be a wonderful surprise for me. And at first, it was—until we learned the details. Heather and I talked about our options, and we decided to sell the land and take the money."

Sara lifted the check from the file folder lying on the countertop in front of her. "I have the check in my hand. Now, before you get curious about how much we sold it for," she began.

"It's none of our business, is it?" Karen asked.

"I can see why you may think that, after all, Glen willed it to Heather and me. However, we talked on our way home. We certainly had enough hours for that. It's a long trip. Anyway, even on the way to sign the papers and get the check, our thoughts were to share the money. Yes, legally, it is just ours. But, to us, it belongs to all of us." Sara took a break from speaking. This next part was going to be the hard part. She looked at Heather, who took her hint and took over for her.

"You see. We went over there this time to sign the papers and get the check. We also had a lot of questions about it. One was why Glen owned the land to start with, the next was why he left it to just the two of us, and the third was his intentions when he bought it. What was the overall story? So we asked. The answers threw us. Glen bought the land as an investment when he and Mama first got married. He wanted to surprise her with it in later years. He was not at home all those times, he told her it dealt with investments, but he never explained those. I think she assumed it was just money dealings, stocks, that sort of thing. None of us thought about land. As we all know, Mama and Daddy got divorced, went their separate ways then reconnected. Glen held on to that land through it all. When he and Mama got back together, he contacted the attorney there and had a will drawn up addressing just the land."

"I didn't know you could do that," Ben said, looking at Randall.

191

"It is very rare, but there are times when a family reads a will they think is the only will out there, then they do find other wills. It does happen."

Heather looked at Sara, who gave her the nod to continue. "We sat and talked with the attorney for a couple of hours. He told us all the details he knew about Glen and the land."

Sara then spoke up. She looked at Andy as she began. This was going to be difficult. "When Mama and Glen got together again, Mama had Andy. As we all know, the relationship between Glen and Andy was never a good one. I think they both tried, but the love was just not there. Andy, I know you tried."

Andy nodded his head. His look was one of defeat even all these years later.

"Well, we found out that the reason Glen's will about the land was written the way it was, is because," she hesitated. "and I quote 'wanted his girls to have what they deserved' unquote. He told the attorney that he knew when it came his and Susan's times of death that everything else would be split three ways, but he wanted to make sure that the land he had purchased to be an investment for his family was just that, His family. He told the attorney that he had not even told Mama about the land and wasn't about to tell her after their divorce. Then when they reconnected, and she had another child by another man, he still wanted the land to just be for his girls. The attorney told us he tried to talk some sense into him and tell him that Andy was his child now too, that he was part of the family, but Glen would hear nothing of it. He said he felt betrayed."

"How could he feel betrayed? He went out and got remarried, had a child, and helped raise another woman's child. Did he think what Mama did was different?"

"Yes, he did. See, Glen had gotten remarried. He held it against Mama for not getting remarried first or at all to Andy's father."

192

"But he and Larry became good friends over the years! I don't get it." Andy said. "Why did that man hate me so much?" He stood to walk away but stayed and just paced the floor.

"I don't know, Andy. It doesn't make sense to us either. I think he did it for spite against Mama as well as you. It must have eaten at him over the years, though, as he never even told her about the land. Maybe he thought he would die first and that there would be enough time for her to learn of the land before her death. He was out for the last revenge. Little did he know that would not be the case."

"It is because we are better than that, that we are going to share this money with Andy as well." Sara turned to Andy. "You, little brother, are a part of us. You always have been. It doesn't matter who your father is. To us, the three of us are equal. We want to share it equally between the three of us. And each of us can do with it what we want. Or pool it together to use on Bella Rose. Or discuss other options.

Andy had tears running down his face as he walked over to Sara and hugged her, with Heather joining them. "Thank you, Sises."

They broke from their huddle hug after a few moments and dried the tears they were each shedding. Andy spoke. "I think we should use at least part of the money for Bella Rose. Build something in honor of Mama or something. We will get the last laugh over Glen. We will do something for Mama."

Everyone who had been just listening and taking it all in spoke their agreement. Then came the task of deciding on what to do.

Sara looked at Andy. "You are okay with this?"

"What's not to be?"

"Glen cut you out of his will in regards to that land. Heather and I were so worried you would be mad about that."

"Look, Sis, Glen and I never had a good relationship. We had very little of what one would call any relationship—ever. He never liked me being in the family. He always resented me. So for him, not including me made sense. He was looking out for you two, not me. He figured Mama would look out for me. He probably thought Larry would look out for me. And who knows, he may be right about that. But Larry is still with us, and we've never talked about that. I don't even know if he has a will or if I'm in it. It's not something you talk about very often. Anyway, to answer your concern, I am fine with it all. He may have tried to block me out of his life, but I have two loving and caring sisters who have loved me no matter how bad I try to mess up everything."

"You don't mess up everything," Heather said.

"Oh, right." He lowered his head and looked at her over imaginary glasses—and didn't say another word.

"Okay, maybe you messed up a few things, but we are past those times. All is good between us."

"Thank you, Sis."

"Have you thought about what to use the money for?" Randal broke the family's concentration to get it off all the mistakes Andy had made in his life.

"My first thought was to just put it into a fund for the Manor that we could use for repairs, upgrades, that sort of thing. It would give us a cushion for when things happen around here."

"And your next thought?"

"I've not had one yet. Anyone else?"

"I say we do something in memory of Mama," Andy said. "I'm not sure what yet. She has a marker at her grave. She loved to write. What could we do about that? She liked to cook. Loved her guests. Loved the lake in Pennsylvania."

"My suggestion is to put it in the bank in a special account until you can think of how to use it," Randall suggested, after no other ideas were brought up.

"That sounds like a good plan. I don't want the check just sitting around and maybe getting lost. The three of us can go to the bank in the morning and take care of that. When anyone has any ideas, let us know, and we can discuss them."

"Sounds good."

"I agree." All were in agreement.

"I need to get the twins to bed. Are you ready to head home, Andy?" Karen asked.

"Yes, I'm ready—time to take these precious ones home. I'm so glad they are both sleeping through the night now. Those first few months were torture." He said as he picked up River. Karen bent down to pick up Ryan. Both babies were sound asleep, but she knew that they would be awake for a while after they got home.

"Sure, they sleep all night, but they don't go to bed for the night until midnight." She gave Andy a loving but sarcastic look.

"At least they are not up every two hours anymore."

"True. And let's hope tonight isn't a step backward for them. They've been doing great."

"Good night, everyone. See you in the morning." Andy and Karen left to go home.

Rachelle said good night and went to her apartment. She still lived in the newest addition just off the kitchen. Handy for all the guests while giving her all the privacy needed. She loved it, but at times missed being completely on her own. There were times she wanted to move further away, but she loved the family she had here, which made it all perfect.

Ben went into the living room to gather the boys to go home. While he was gone, Sara and Heather talked for a few minutes. They were both surprised that Andy took it all so well. They had worried all the way home that this newest development in their family would put a wall between them. They were thrilled when Andy seemed just to take it as fact and a part of life.

"We are blessed." That was all Heather had to say before Ben, and two sleepy little boys joined them. "See you all in the morning."

"Love you, Sis. See you in the morning." Sara and Randall were the only two left in the kitchen. Sara reached for Randall's hand. "Time for us to go home as well. I am so relieved that this latest news went so well."

"You have an amazing family, Sara. I've seen families fall apart and never talk to each other again over far less drama. How do you all do it?"

"We choose to face facts, deal with whatever we get faced with, and move on. Lord knows we've been through a lot. And lately to find out so much more about our family. It truly is a God thing. If it were not for our faith, our belief that things happen for a reason, and our ability to lean on each other, I'm not sure if we would have survived these last few years." Randall put his arm around her shoulder, and together they walked to their home.

Sara awakened in the middle of the night by a dream. She opened her eyes and saw the slightest stream of light coming in through the slit of an open curtain as the moon shone into the room. She quickly closed her eyes to return to her dream. She wanted to find out how it ended. But the dream was gone. She could only relive what had woken her up. Maybe that was enough.

She tried to go back to sleep but just tossed and turned, which woke Randall. He asked her if she was alright, and she just shook her head.

"I just had a bad dream. Now I can't sleep."

"What was the dream? Do you remember it?"

"Not really. Part of it was about a little girl with no shoes on."

"That's a start. Anything else?" Randall was holding her in his arms as they were sitting up on the bed.

" She was dirty and sitting in a corner. She looked scared. The room was dark and small."

"Maybe you were dreaming about one of the girls in the secret room."

Sara turned her head to look at him. Her eyes were shifting side to side. Her thoughts were reaching back to try to see more details of the dream. She closed her eyes. Nothing more came to her. She broke away from his arms and swung her feet over her side of the bed. As she stood, she replied to his comment. "Maybe." She took a few steps, then turned to look back at him. "Why would I dream about that?"

"I don't know. Something about it must be in the back of your mind."

"I was concentrating on Glen this past week instead of the girls and what the Manor was in its beginning. I'm not sure why the dream should show up now." She reached for her bathrobe and walked into the bathroom to take a shower. Her thoughts were still full of the vision in her mind.

After her shower, Randall met her in the bedroom with a fresh cup of coffee. "Are you okay now?"

"Yes, much better. Time to get this day started. I have to meet with Heather and Andy to go to the bank today. "You would think my dream would have been about the money or Glen, but nooo, I have to start something else to deal with."

"You can do your best to shake it from your mind. We already know about the girls and the secret room. I'd hate to think there is more to that room that we don't know about."

"I agree. We've had enough. Heather and Rachelle are searching for the girls to contact them and work on a reunion of some sort. That is if they want to come back. Some of the letters indicate that they do, but they were just girls when they wrote them. Many may have gone on with their lives and put their past behind them."

"I hope a few of them still want to come. It will be interesting to hear the stories of when they were here and to know what your grandparents did for them."

"And to hear what they made of their lives afterward."
I'm sure what happened to them as children played a part in
what they did with their lives."

"I can only imagine. I hope all of them were happy."

"Me too. I have to get going to meet Heather and Andy. I
will see you later today. Have a good day at work." Sara
refilled her coffee mug, poured it into her travel mug, gave
Randall a quick kiss, and went out the door.

Sara drove her car from her house to the manor since they
would drive from there into town. Her car was the only one
without two car seats in it for kids. Instead, her car became
a grown-up-family car. Heather and Andy were waiting for
her inside the manor. Both were ready to go.

"Good morning. Are you both ready for this?"

"Good morning. Yes, I'm ready. I've been thinking about
what to use it for, but nothing has come to mind."

"Good morning, Sis. I've not come up with anything
either. For now, the best place for it will be in the bank. Are
you okay, Sis? You look tired."

"I'm okay. I just had a bad dream. Not sure what to make
of it."

"What was the dream?"

"It was about a little girl with no shoes, rattled hair, sitting
in a dark room, crying."

"Sounds something like what the girls may have been like
when they came here when Grandmama and Granddaddy
operated Bella Rose. Maybe with what we've been finding
out about that room, it just sat on your mind while you slept."

"That's what Randall and I were thinking. We need to
finish reading the more current letters and keep searching for
all the girls and the guests. See what all we can find out about
them."

"I've been reading some, and so has Rachelle. I hope to
read more of them this afternoon when we get home. It's not
easy to find time with the two boys keeping me on my toes.
I will be glad, in a way, for Marc to be starting school this

fall. I was also thinking of getting Maddex involved with preschool."

"That is a good idea. I can't believe the boys are so big already. Where has the time gone?"

"I could tell you both where it has gone. We've been so busy with life, past and present, that they have grown up in front of us without our noticing. Look at my twins! They'll be in college soon." He laughed. "Not really, but I'm afraid if we don't slow down some and pay attention, they will be before we know it."

Sara parked the car when they reached the bank. As they neared the building, Sara noticed a little girl walking down the sidewalk with her head hung down. She smiled when she envisioned the girl walking home from school just a block away—then remembered that it was still morning. Heather and Andy were directing her to the bank, so she took her focus off the girl.

Inside they told the bank clerk what they wanted to do. She told them to have a seat, and she would get another teller to talk with them in the office about opening a special account.

They sat and waited.

It was finally their turn. Sara had forgotten how busy a bank was on a Monday morning.

"Hi, my name is Ms Davenport; how may I help you?" The teller began after they had all found seats in the cramped office.

Sara told Ms Davenport that the family had money they wanted to invest yet could use whenever they wanted. Ms Davenport asked several other questions about their intentions with the money so she could get a better understanding and would best know what to offer them. She suggested a few options, including dividing it up and putting some just into a savings account so they would have instant access to it. Other suggestions were a trust fund if they had a person in mind as a beneficiary. She brought up several other options, and by the time she finished, they were so confused they decided to take the information and do more research on it. For the time being, they put it all into a new savings account with all three of their names on it. They agreed that the money could not be touched by either of them individually but withdrawing any money would require all three signatures.

The teller tried to convince them to make it that only two signatures be needed. In case of someone's death, she explained. The word death caught them all off guard. They had enough dealing with death and the aftermath in their family. Because of that, they understood why she was suggesting it. They agreed that two could sign in the case of death as long as a death certificate was provided. The teller was reluctant about that as she knew if they needed the money in a hurry, it would strain them if one of them died and had to wait for the death certificate. But she agreed. Plus, she didn't know what other financial resources they had, so it was none of her business. It was just her business to make suggestions and follow what they wanted.

It took an hour, but finally, they were on their way home. The morning was gone. It was time for lunch. Instead of going home, they stopped at the Cafe in town and ate lunch. It had been a long time since they had gone out to eat. With everything happening—the babies being born and so much taking up their time, they almost forgot that eating out once in a while was fun.

While they waited for their meal and then ate, they talked about the kids and all the fun things they were doing. Even the twins were starting to pick up things, laugh, and develop personalities. Sara was happy for her siblings. She loved having her nephews and niece living so close that she could watch them grow every day.

Once they finished, Sara drove them all home. She called Randall and told him she was home and that everything had gone well at the bank. She also told him about the little girl she saw on the street.

"What do you think she was doing on the street in the middle of the morning?" She asked.

"Sara, it could be anything. She could have been sent home from school, but her mother was not home, so she walked. She could have had the day off school for some reason. Maybe she had to go home to get her homework she forgot. Anything."

"I guess you're right. I think my dream, nightmare, was getting to me. I'll see you tonight. I love you."

"I love you too. Now maybe you should get some rest."

"I will try," Sara said and hung up the phone.

Resting at the moment was the last thing on her mind. She wanted to go back to the upper room, even just to sit and feel the past. Sara called Rachelle and asked if she could handle all the paperwork and reservations for her. She told her she needed to spend time in the upper room. When Rachelle asked her why Sara said she wasn't sure why but felt she had to. Rachelle told her she could handle the day's work and added that if Sara wanted to talk, she could handle that too.

Sara thanked her and set out for the upper room, although she didn't know why. It was just calling her. That and the dream were pulling at her.

Chapter Twenty-Three

Sara continued to dream at least once a week about the little girl in the dark room. Her time in the upper room had not revealed much to her. The letters and journals they recovered from there had not given them much either. At least not yet.

She did her best to get on with daily life the way it was supposed to go, but everyone noticed a change in her—especially Randall. He tried to talk to her about it, but she brushed him off every time. Randall went to Heather to ask if she had noticed the change. She had. She told Randall that it all started when they found out about the secret land that Glen owned.

"I noticed something about both of you when you came back from there. You both have stopped calling him Dad or Daddy. You both now refer to him as Glen. Why is that?"

"I think because we saw a side of him we didn't like anymore. He wasn't the loving father we had loved as a child. He was now just this judgmental man in our lives. I don't think we did it consciously; it just happened. It also made it easier to talk about him as Andy saw him. He was never a Dad to him. He was Glen."

"Although I understand, it is sad. I'm wondering if all that has anything to do with how Sara seems to have changed."

"Most likely. My sister always admired him. Even after we realized how he was toward Andy, she still felt close to him. She doesn't talk about him much anymore. When we talk about that time in our lives or the upper room details, she just talks about what Mama did."

"I wonder if she would be willing to talk to Joe. He's always been good with this family. He knows a lot about us through the times we've talked with him. He may be able to get her to open up and get back to herself."

"Worth a shot. Do you want me to talk to her? Maybe if I approach her that I have not dealt well with Glen and how it changed everything and I want to talk to Joe, but would like her there with me? Think that would work?"

"That may work out the best. Are you having issues?"

"A little. Not as much as her. It would do us both good to talk with an outsider and get unbiased feedback. I'll talk to her later today."

"Thanks, Heather. You're the best."

Surprisingly Sara easily agreed to see Joe when Heather brought the subject up. Of course, she thought it was more to help her sister than it was about herself. In the week they had to wait to meet with Joe, Sara had the dream one more time. When the day came to see Joe, she was ready to open up and find out what was happening.

"Good to see the two of you." Joe greeted them in the waiting room of his office. Come on back, let's chat." He turned to his receptionist, "Hold my calls, please."

Sara and Heather sat on the sofa that was opposite Joe's desk. Joe pulled out the armchair next to his desk and sat facing them without the desk separating them. He leaned against the back of the chair so he wouldn't seem confrontational. He knew they were there just to talk about an issue that was bothering them. He was there just as a sounding board. He had known them long enough that it was just a matter of them not knowing how to voice their thoughts with ease. He knew some of his patients had problems once in a while and just needed a safe place to talk. This was one of them.

"So, Ladies, how can I help you today? I hope all is well at the Manor and with the family."

"Yes, the family is physically fine," Sara said.

"It's mentally that the two of us are having problems," Heather added.

"What's going on? Let's talk about it."

Sara looked at Heather as she began to speak. "As you know, our family isn't your typical family. We have been through a lot. Dealt with a lot of secrets and mysteries of the family and the Manor."

"Yes, I'm aware. You all have handled it quite well."

"Well, now we have another one. And this one has negatively affected how I think about my father."

"Glen? What happened?"

"I'll be as brief as I can be, but it takes some background." She hesitated just long enough to gather her thoughts.

"When Randall and I got married, he surprised me with our honeymoon destination. I was hoping for someplace romantic and wonderful. Instead, he took me to West Tennessee to a small unincorporated town that he had found was owned by my, our, father." Sara tilted her head toward Heather.

Joe's facial expression must have changed because Sara stopped before proceeding with her story.

"Yes, our father, Glen, owned property we didn't know about." Heather filled in.

"When I found out about it, I was confused as you look," Sara said as she pointed to Joe. "We found out Glen owned the property that had become a rural town, of sorts. He left it to Heather and me in a separate will. The will stated that we could do whatever we wanted with it. We could keep it, develop it, keep it as it is, or sell it to the people that lived there."

"We chose to sell it to the people." Heather filled in.

"Okay, so what is the issue?"

"It is the reason he had the land, his original purpose, and his ultimate decision. He had originally bought it as an investment for Mama. He hung on to it to gain value and then planned to present it to her on one of their anniversaries, or at least sometime later. As you know, they ended up in a divorce. During that time, he developed a section of it by starting a town. It has a courthouse building that is also the town's church and other offices. There are a few families that live there. And a small store. It is not incorporated, so no rules or regulations for taxes or whatever except for the county government aspect. Then when Glen and Mama got back together and remarried, instead of telling her about the land, he kept it a secret from her and had a will drawn up. The will read that the land was to go to us, just Heather and I, but not until five years after his death."

"That is why we never knew about it until recently. The attorney there contacted Randall. How he knew which attorney to call, I don't know."

"True, I never did ask Randall how that attorney knew who to contact. Oh, well. That doesn't matter." Sara then wondered if it did matter but pushed that thought out of her mind. That wasn't the current issue.

"So, you find out that Glen has this land that he willed to the two of you, that he kept secret from your Mama. I still don't see a real issue. Keep going."

"The issue comes in the reason he gave it just to us and not Andy. When he and our mother reconnected, he didn't like that she had a child with another man. He spent his life resenting Andy. They never got along. Even though he had remarried and had a child, it was the fact that Mama had a child out of wedlock that bothered him. I don't know why that should make a difference, but maybe back then, it did. Glen left the story with the attorney that he was giving the land to just the two of us because he knew that the three of us would inherit a lot when he and Mama died. But he wanted to be sure that the two of us had more. Glen wanted us to have what we deserved, adding that Andy didn't deserve any of it. He didn't think Mama deserved any of it either, and that is why he never even told her about it. I'm angry with him. My whole attitude toward him has changed. And I don't even feel the same about Bella Rose because somehow I feel he wasn't true to Mama. I feel, I don't know, like the whole family is tainted?"

"Wow, that is quite a tale. I understand why you may feel that way. Heather, how do you feel about it?"

"I feel the same way. Maybe not as strong as Sara does, but I feel hurt. I feel like he should have included Andy. He should have told Mama, shared with her. She certainly shared Bella Rose with him. She took him into it and made him part owner. She didn't have to do that. It had been left to her, but she had him added onto the title. She included him in everything. He kept secrets. We are finding out so many secrets of our family and even the history of Bella Rose. We have agreed between all of us that there will be no more secrets. Now, this."

"Does Andy know about the land and the inheritance?"

"Yes, of course. Heather and I talked at length about what to do. We have sold the land to the people who live there and taken the money. We told Andy about the land and the money from the sale. The three of us have put the money in a separate account in the bank. We want to do something special with it in memory of our Mama."

"Does Andy know the whole story?"

"Oh, yes, we had a family meeting. Everyone in our family at Bella Rose knows all the details. Like we said, no secrets."

"How does Andy feel about it?"

"He seems fine with it. He told us that he and Glen never did get along, so Glen's actions don't surprise him. He is thrilled that we have included him in the inheritance, and he was the one that suggested we do something special with it."

"So, Andy is or seems fine with it. You are the ones who are having issues."

"Yes, I know I am. My opinion of Glen has changed. I used to think he was this wonderful man. I mean, look what he helped Mama do with the manor and running it? He was great to her. At least we thought he was."

"Okay. I understand why you may feel that way. I don't have an easy answer for you. Sorry. What he did is going to be a case of acceptance. You cannot change the past. You cannot change what he did, nor the reasons he did it. What you can change you already have. You have included Andy in your family. You have turned what you saw as a negative and turned it into a positive." Joe chuckled.

"What's so funny?"

"Friend to friend, not a doctor to a patient?"

"Yes, what are you thinking, as a friend?"

"I think your actions are a way of showing Glen that he has no control over you. What you have done could be your way of telling Glen, good try, but that's not how this family works."

Sara sat and thought about that. She looked at Heather and knew she was thinking about it as well.

"I like that." It will take concentrating on that for a while."

"Yes, you will. You will still have negative feelings from time to time, but it will help to start looking at Glen's actions differently. And that is the doctor talking. The doctor liked what the 'friend' said." Joe said. "Although not all patients would appreciate it if the doctor had come up with that. I knew you would."

Sara and Heather just sat there for a few minutes before Heather spoke. "Do you think we can change our attitude towards Glen?"

"I think so. I will do my best to appreciate what Glen did for Mama and Bella Rose but add the gotcha thought when thinking about the land he kept secret. When we do decide what to use the money for, I think that will help too. It will be his money helping Mama, the lady he tried to keep in the dark."

"That is a good way to deal with it. Use it wisely for a good cause." Joe said.

"Thank you, Joe. You are always so helpful. I'm so glad you are a part of our lives."

"I'm grateful as well. For everything you have done for our family and me." Heather said, thinking about the first time he met them. He and his wife Nicole had been the ones who stopped to help when she, Ben, and Marc had been in that accident. She was forever grateful. Also thankful that he had saved her marriage. Joe was good at his job.

Sara and Heather left Joe's office with a new way of looking at their family and about life in general. They talked on the way home but kept snickering. Then they would repeat how Joe told them to react to what Glen had done. Joe was right. They could not change the past. They could only deal with what they were given, the way they were given it, and turn that around for the betterment of all their family. It would be a good thing. No thanks to Glen. Well, many thanks to Glen, but not what he had intended.

They were both laughing and having a good sister's day by the time they arrived home. Once they were inside, they made themselves lunch and discussed how best to use the money. None of the ideas went further than bringing the idea up. Each one was rejected for one reason or another.

Andy soon joined them. He had come in to make dessert for the guests when they came back from their day trips. The girls joined in as the three of them talked.

They discussed a trust fund for all the kids, Except Sara, who had no children, yet, so they didn't think that was fair. They thought of just a fund to take care of Bella Rose, but they already had enough for that. Another expansion? What else did they need? Nothing. They had the main manor where guests stayed, complete with the living room, kitchen, dining room. They had the chapel and the reception hall. They even had a gazebo. The view of the mountains was beautiful. They had a hiking trail. The landscaping and gardens were perfect. They had no other ideas.

"I conclude we leave it where it is now," Sara said after nothing had been decided.

"I agree. Whatever we use it for has to be special and in memory of Mama, at least part of it anyway."

"Yes, something that Mama would have wanted."

They finished making and taste testing the dessert, and then each went their separate ways.

Rachelle had been busy with the journals and letters that everyone had already read. She was doing her best to pull the most important letters and excerpts from the journals to make the Bella Rose History book. She had found several letters where the girls had written a desire to come back someday. She put their names on a list along with any information, dates, names they may have mentioned, and any contact information. After she had three of them listed, she figuratively kicked herself. She took the note pages to her computer and started a spreadsheet. She should have thought of that when she started making notes. Maybe by writing the information again, something would come to her. She knew that the way she was formulating the details, the program would capture identical information. It would also be easier to see any of the similarities.

Chapter Twenty-Four

Sara told Randall about her conversation with her siblings. She said that they had not found any use for the money from the sale of the property. She told him some of the suggestions, including a trust fund for the kids, but added that Andy said that wasn't fair because we had no children. Plus, they all agreed at least part of the money needed to be used for something in memory of their Mama.

Randall looked at Sara and suggested they could change the 'no kids' situation. His eyes were flirty, and he had a sheepish grin on his face.

Sara laughed. "I don't think so."

"And just why not?"

"Randall, we're in our forties. I don't want to be sixty years old, and our child still be in high school. I don't want to risk the possible problems of pregnancy this late in life."

Randall sat back and didn't respond.

"What's wrong?" Sara stopped what she was doing and looked at him. She realized she had hit a nerve.

"I guess we never talked of having kids before we got married. I never gave it a thought that you would not want to have children. You are so great with your nephews and niece."

"It's not that I don't want them. I just don't want to go through being pregnant and all the risk factors at my age. I had resigned myself to the fact of not being a mother a long time ago." Sara shrugged her shoulders. "Of course, I never thought I'd get married again either."

"See, you can change your mind! There's hope."

"No, there isn't. Sorry."

Randall's heart sank. He had always wanted kids.

Yes, he was in his forties, but to him, that didn't matter. He had never thought about twenty years down the road and the age he would be when his child may still be so young. Maybe Sara was right. They were too old to have a baby of their own. His eyes lit up, and he sat forward. "How about adoption?"

Sara had been watching him and experiencing the silence between them. It was making her uncomfortable. They had never disagreed on anything major. She had to refocus when she heard him speak. "What?"

"How about adoption? We could adopt an older child."

"Adoption?"

"Yes. We could adopt an older child. Look what your grandparents did for those girls. It's almost like it's in your genes."

"They didn't adopt any kids."

"No, but they found homes for the babies who needed a place to be loved."

"That is such a sweet way to put it."

"What is?"

"'A place to be loved.' So often, you hear of families, usually with foster parents, being in it for the money. So many nightmare stories."

"You are so right. So when do you want to start the adoption process?"

Sara drew in a breath. She shook her head. She had not given this much thought until now. He was right, though. They could adopt an older child who needed a place to be loved. They certainly had the love to give and the complete family who would love the child. "Let me sleep on it."

"Okay. I will ask you about it in the morning." Randall went to her and helped her stand up so he could hug her. "I love you. No matter what you decide." He kissed her forehead. "You will make a wonderful mother."

"Don't push it. I may decide against it, you know."

"I doubt it. You have too much love to give." He let her go and went to the kitchen.

The next morning Sara woke up from a similar dream she had once before. She had attributed the other one to the discussion about the girls her grandparents took in. This time she decided it was because she and Randall had discussed adopting an older child. But why was the dream about a little girl that looked so homeless, dirty, and sad? Was this the little girl that they would adopt? And where would they find her?

She told Randall about her dream and her thoughts. "Could it be God's plan for us to find this girl?"

"Your dream always has her coming to the house."

"Yes, but are we just waiting for her to show up? And if she does, then what do we do? We can't just keep her as my grandparents did."

"No, but we can investigate the situation and contact the authorities and go from there."

"But once the authorities get involved, well, I've heard too many negative stories with horrible outcomes. They end up in foster care, and you know what we discussed last night about foster care and loving a child. They usually don't go together."

"I know. But for now, we move forward with our plans to adopt. I say we contact an agency today and find out what we have to do."

"I want to talk to the family first. I can't just spring it on them, and one day we meet at the kitchen island and suddenly introduce a child as our child. They deserve to know what we are considering. Remember – no secrets."

"Oh, good. That means no secrets when it comes to Christmas either!" Randall winked.

"Christmas is totally different. It is the only time of year that a person can 'hold back the truth.'"

"Nice safe way to say it's the only time of year a person can lie and get away with it around here."

"Yes." She smiled.

"I will be spending the day at the Manor. Do you mind if I talk to the gang while you're at work? Or do you want me to wait?"

"I know you. You had better tell them. They will know something is going on with you, and you are no good at keeping secrets."

"I beg to differ on me not being good at it, but you are right. I do not think I can keep a straight face this time. To be honest, I'm getting excited about it."

Randall wrapped his arms around her as he faced her before he turned to head to work. "I am so glad you came around on the topic of having kids."

"I've not changed my mind on having them, just about how to have them. I love the idea of adopting one, but not of being pregnant."

"Does that mean we stop practicing?" He winked.

Sara blushed and just shook her head as she carefully broke away from him. "No, we can always practice."

He started to walk back to her with those flirty eyes looking at her.

"Just not now!" She laughed. "You have to get to work."

"If you insist."

"Someone has to earn the money; we have a child on the way! I hope."

"I love you, Ms Sara."

"I love you too, Mr. Randall."

After Randall left for work, Sara went to the Manor. Everyone in the family was there working already. Marc and Maddex were busy playing, River and Ryan played in the play pen with their toys. They were growing so fast. Sara just watched them all for a few minutes before she wandered around to find everyone.

"Coffee break." She told each one when she found them. They all knew that meant 'meeting at the island.'

"Good morning all. I hope you all slept well and are ready for a busy day."

Everyone just looked at her. They knew something was up when she called for a coffee break. Now she was extra cheerful. Their faces all asked the same question, 'what was going on.'

"We're fine," Andy responded. "What's going on? You have me curious."

"Me too. You are not this cheerful this early."

"Hey, yes I, okay, maybe not. But I have a reason to be today."

"Okay, so spill it. Did we inherit more money? Land? A new car? What?"

"Very funny, Heather. No, we didn't inherit anything – this time." Sara took a sip of her coffee before she continued. She was having fun keeping them in suspense.

"Do you remember not too long ago the dream I had about the little girl showing up at the front door?"

"The one you said was dirty and sad? Sure."

"Well, I had that dream again last night."

"And that is why you called the meeting?"

"No, silly. But that does bring us to our topic. Randall and I were talking about that dream, the first one, and then we got talking about us not having kids, and that is one reason why we have decided not to use the trust fund on the kids, because Andy said it wouldn't be fair to me. We all agreed to that. And the money sits in the bank until we all come together on an idea for it. Randall and I got talking about him and me having kids. I told him I did not want any."

Everyone in the room looked at her. They were unsure where she was going with this, but they never thought she would not want kids.

"What do you mean you don't want kids?" Karen asked. "Kids are wonderful!"

"They are also a handful at times," Heather added.

"So, truthfully, I do not want to go through the pregnancy part. I do not want to grow old while my baby is still a child. I know you all have little ones, but you are also younger than I am. By the time my child is about to graduate, I'll be retired."

"Sis, I don't think you get to retire from this place. We are in it for life." Andy interjected.

"Good point. What I'm saying is, I do not want to go through all of that. I have no desire to go through the pregnancy process. I've watched you two go through it. I admire you both, but it is not for me. I resigned myself when I got divorced that I would never remarry and never have children. I did find love again and am so glad to be married, but I still felt I'd never become a mother."

"But you are so good with kids." Heather interrupted.

"Thank you. Randall said the same thing. However, that alone is not enough for me to want to go through childbirth."

"You never know what God has planned for you." Again Heather voiced her opinion.

"I understand that. Which is what I'm here to discuss— my dream. I think it is a sign. At first, I thought it was just a nightmare after reading the letters and journals and finding out what they did for those girls. Some of those girls had nothing when they came here. When I had that dream again, it was right after Randall and I had talked about having kids and adopting. Well. I have jumped ahead." She took a breath and looked at each one.

"Randall and I have decided to look into adoption! She smiled. It felt like such a relief to say those words. She had not realized the effect it had on her.

"I think that is wonderful! A new baby in the family!" Andy said.

"No, no." Sara held her hand up. "We want to adopt an older child."

"Older?"

215

"Yes, like that girl in my dream."

Everyone sat in silence.

Finally, Rachelle spoke. "I think it is a wonderful idea. Older children often get left in orphanages because most people want to adopt the newborn babies."

"Do you have someone selected yet?"

"No. Randall wanted to start our search today, but I told him I wanted to let all of you know first."

"We are all behind you," Andy said as he looked around for everyone to confirm his comment.

"Yes, we are definitely behind you."

Everyone stood and gathered around Sara and gave her a big family hug.

"Let us know if there is anything we can do to help."

"I will. I would say I may need help with babysitting, but the child may be the one doing the babysitting."

"Now, there's a thought." Heather laughed.

"Do you want a boy or a girl?"

"I am leaning toward a girl because of the dream and because of all the girls our grandparents helped."

After the family meeting, Rachelle asked if she could talk with Sara privately. She sounded serious, and Sara hoped nothing was wrong. When they were in the office, Sara asked her what was wrong.

"Not a thing is wrong. It might be wonderful news."

"Okay, what is it?"

"Well, you want to adopt an older child, a girl, right?" she smiled as she asked.

"Yes, we do." She looked at Rachelle and winked. "You are too old to adopt. Besides, you are a big part of this family already."

"Very funny! I am not talking about me."

"You know someone?"

"I think I do."

Chapter Twenty-Five

Gayle stood with her head hung down. Her shoulders slouched. Her straight dark hair was down to her waist. When she finally looked up, her blue eyes were filled with sadness. Randall and Sara took one look at her through the window and fell in love. This little girl needed a home.

This day had taken a while to become a reality. They had talked with the adoption agency several months earlier about their desires. They had gone through all the red tape, all the home visits, all the paperwork, all the tests. The family had also gone through all the interviews required. It was just a matter of time for the right child to become available. They were waiting to become foster parents as they had learned that was the first step to adopting. They told the Adoption Agency that they only wanted one child. A girl. An older girl. Preteen age.

Each day Sara woke up hoping and praying that would be the day they got a phone call. Each night Sara went to bed praying for God to give them the child He wanted them to love. Randall could see the heartache his wife was putting herself through. He was just about ready to suggest they halt the process and give up. He told Sara he was concerned about her. She told him she was fine, just anxious. So he held her a little tighter each night, called her more often each day just to tell her he loved her.

Early one morning, the phone rang before Randall left for work. He answered it, expecting it to be one of Sara's family. Instead, he was brought to full attention when he heard it was the adoption agency. Sara noticed his reaction and rushed to his side. She instantly knew it was the adoption agency.

"Yes, I see. That's wonderful. Yes, we can be there this afternoon. First thing after lunch. Yes. Thank you." Randall hung up the phone as he pulled Sara into his arms.

"Yes?"

"She says she thinks she has a match for us."

"And?"

"And we get to meet her right after lunch today."

"And?"

"And what? All she said was she has a girl that may fit us."

"You didn't ask for details?" Sara pulled away from him and looked with pleading eyes. She wanted to know all about this child before she went to see her.

"You heard my side of the conversation. I just told you what the caseworker said." He realized he should have asked maybe a few more questions. He hung his head. "Sorry. I can call her back if you want. Or you can call her."

"No, I don't want to sound too anxious or demanding. Maybe it is best if we don't know more until we talk to the case worker and meet the girl. You did say it was a girl, right?"

"Yes. She is a girl. That is all I know."

"Okay. I will try to contain myself for the next few," Sara looked at the clock on the wall. "Several hours."

Sara took a deep breath letting out her frustration. She stepped over to the coffee maker and poured herself a cup of coffee. Suddenly it hit her. She picked up the coffee mug and noticed her hand was shaking.

"Why are you shaking?" Randall asked when he saw her try to hold the mug.

"Now I'm excited! I have to clean the house! I have to..."

"Sara, my dear." Randall took hold of her arm and guided her to the kitchen table. "First, drink your coffee. Then take one step at a time. I will stay home with you if you like, to help clean or whatever you think you have to do."

"No, you go to work. I'll be fine." She took a sip of coffee. Oddly it calmed her. "I will get the house in order, talk to the family and meet you at the agency."

"What if I come to pick you up? That way, we have just one car, so if we are a good match, we can bring her home together."

"Car! I hope she doesn't need a car seat! Did we think to ask about that?"

"No. I never thought of that. I'm sure if she was that young that the case manager would have said something."

"Okay. Good. Now, get ready for work. I'll be fine."

Randall left for work soon after they ended their conversation. On his way in, he realized that he was excited as well. He was not sure how much work he would get done in the next few hours. He had his assistant rearrange his clients or have them just come in to talk with her if it was something that she could handle without him.

By noon the house was spotless. The entire family was excited. They could not wait to meet this child. Sara told them that they hadn't even met her yet. And that it might be a day or two before they introduced her to all of them—if this child was the one for them. She had a gut feeling about her, though. And it all depended on the girl's situation and how she reacted to meeting several new people at once, so soon after being in a new home. She told them she would let them know and asked them to pray for everything to work out the way it was supposed to. They were all leaving it up to God and knew this could be His answer.

A few minutes before noon Randall came home. They ate a quick lunch and headed out to meet the person who could become their daughter.

When they arrived, the caseworker took them to a small room where they could watch the little girl through a one-way window. They watched through the glass partition as the little girl named Gayle Marie was reading a book and tapping her foot on the floor while she waited. She seemed quiet and shy. There were other children in the room, but she was engrossed in her book. Maybe it was just that she knew she would be meeting a new family soon. At least she didn't seem agitated or angry. Sara was afraid that the child would have anger issues. A negative thought hit Sara as she watched the child. Maybe they have her sedated. She shook her head and threw that idea out. That would not make sense. When Gayle stood up and looked so sad, that was when their hearts filled with love, and they knew she was the one for them.

The case manager was telling them about Gayle. She was eleven years old. Her parents had died in a drug-related tragedy. With no other relatives, she had spent the last six months with a foster family, but that was not working out. The family already had six foster children and felt Gayle needed to be in a smaller family. They saw the potential in her, but they could not give her the love and attention she needed to blossom. They had hoped another, smaller family could take her in or that someone would want to adopt her.

When her foster family returned her, the case manager immediately thought of Sara and Randall. She thought it would be a perfect match.

"We know that Gayle does well in school, usually. The teachers report that she has not been herself this year, but that is understandable. Gayle needs a family who will be there for her. Nurture her and have the patience to deal with her. Since she lost her parents at such a young age and has no other living relatives, she is lost. She has a few friends, but none that would be considered a best friend. The teachers say it is almost like she closed the door on everyone. She won't let anyone in."

"I can understand that. Poor girl has lost the only two people she knew who loved her, cared for her, and took care of her. She doesn't want to let anyone else in because she is afraid they will leave her as well." Sara chimed in her thoughts.

"Wow!" the case manager sat up straighter. " Do you have a psychology degree? You have a good knowledge of this situation."

"No. I've been to one a few times. He is also a friend of the family. To me, that just makes sense. Why risk losing again and going through that pain when you don't have to. By not opening your heart, you don't feel the pain as much if someone disappoints you or leaves."

The case manager looked at Randall and smiled. She pointed to Sara. "I think we have found the perfect match for Gayle." She smiled at Sara. You, young lady, will make a wonderful mother." She stood up from her seat behind her desk. "Are you two ready to meet your daughter?"

"Potential daughter," Randall said with caution. "Once we meet, we may not be the perfect match for a family either of you two is hoping for."

"Oh, I have a feeling." The case manager said as she led them to the door to her office.

A short walk down the hall and life was about to change – again. Sara smiled inwardly. Yes, she thought, life was about to change. She was about to become a mother. She glanced at Randall. Reaching for his arm, she tugged on him gently. He stopped and looked down at her. His eyes held a bit of fear. "What is it?"

"Are you ready to become a Daddy?"

Randall smiled. "I've been ready." He said, lowering his head to place a kiss on her forehead. "I was born ready."

Sara smiled and nodded her head. She looked at the case manager, who had also stopped, afraid that they had changed their mind without even meeting Gayle. Sara gave her a slight nod. The Case Manager reached the door and stopped. The three of them looked at each other in silence. No last-minute tips and no suggestions. Those had all been said over the months of their search. It was now time. The case manager opened the door to the client's waiting room.

The case manager walked in first, followed by Sara and then Randall. The case manager spoke.

"Gayle, this is Mr. and Mrs. Williams. Sara and Randall. They have come to meet you.

"Hello, Gayle," Sara said quietly. She suddenly didn't know how to act or what to say.

"Hi, Gayle, it's so nice to meet you. Your case manager has told us about you." Randall said as he walked closer to her. Sara followed. There was a sofa positioned across from the armchair Gayle was sitting in with her book.

"What book are you reading?" Sara asked as they all sat down on the sofa.

"Charlotte's Web." My Mom used to read it to me when I was little."

"I love that book too. Who is your favorite character? Charlotte or Wilbur?"

"Charlotte. She's kind."

"Yes, she is. She likes to make people and Wilbur smile."

Gayle closed the book but first placed an old bookmark into the opened page so she would not lose her place in the story. She raised her head and finally took her first look at Sara and Randall. "Are you going to adopt me?" She asked timidly.

Sara and Randall looked at the Case manager. They didn't know how to respond. They didn't want to say yes and disappoint her if they decided not to and didn't want to say no. That would make this meeting meaningless.

The Case manager answered for them. "Sara and Randall are here to meet you. I've talked with them and told them a lot about you. I wanted the three of you to meet and see if you liked each other before making any decisions. But, they are interested. And they are looking for a girl your age that they can love and welcome into their home and lives.

"What if we don't get along?"

"Then we may need to find another family for you. But, let's all talk so you can get to know them."

"Okay. Can I ask questions?"

"Sure you may." Sara was glad for that opening. At least she knew the girl was curious about them.

"Why do you want a kid instead of a baby?"

Wow, right to the point. Sara liked her already. "That is a long story and one I already have a feeling you will get to know someday. We want an older child because we know so many kids lack the love they deserve when they need it the most. They feel hurt, sad, maybe even rejected. We want to be able to give our love to a child that needs a family to love. One who can feel at home with us. One that will become part of our family as if they were our own."

"I had a Mom and Dad. Once. I don't know about calling anyone else Mom or Dad."

"That is okay. We know you had parents that you loved very much. We don't want to take those memories away from you. They will always be a part of you. You will always carry them with you in your heart. My parents are gone too, but I still love them and hold them dear to my heart."

Gayle took in what Sara had said. She just stared at them for a few moments then lowered her head again. She had lost all trust in people after her parents had died and left her alone. Her parents had told her they would always be there for her, and now they were gone. The lady who took her in first after that later took her to this place. She had told Gayle she would be there for her. Now this couple was here to take her away yet again. She looked at Sara again. This lady was smiling at her. She was reaching out her hand. She wasn't pushy like the last one had been. She looked at the man. He stood by the lady's side. He had a smile on his face as well. He took a step forward.

"Gayle, we would love to have you live with us. We know you have been through a lot, and we will do our best to help you through all of that. What you have been through is more than most people ever have to go through, and you are so young to have that in your thoughts. Let us give you support, comfort, and love. A place to just be the girl you are and to experience the joys you deserve."

There was that word. The one that Gayle had only trusted to hear from her parents. She loved her parents and didn't think she could love anyone else. She doubted anyone else could love her. But here were these strangers telling her they would love her. Maybe it would be alright to go with them. It wasn't like she had a choice. She had not had a choice with the last family. She looked at the case manager and raised her eyebrows. Without words, she asked if this was the right thing to do. The case manager saw her look and nodded her head, just enough to let Gayle know she had her approval.

Gayle then turned to Sara and Randall, and for the first time in days, she smiled. She slowly reached out her hand to Sara. Sara gently took it in hers and helped her up from her chair. Gayle stood up but resisted the hug she knew was coming. She was willing to go with these people, just not ready for that much closeness. Sara understood her resistance and did not force the hug. Randall reached around and put his hand on Gayle's shoulder. A gentle touch to show his love for his new family.

The case manager was smiling as she walked to the door of the visitation room.

"Let's go into the office and finish the paperwork so the three of you can go home."

"Yes, let's," Sara said. The three of them left the room, with Gayle leading them. She had not let go of Sara's hand. That was a good sign. Randall followed behind the two women now in his life. The smile on his face grew inside and on his face—this was a beautiful day. His life was about to change into something he had wanted for so long.

Gayle went with one of the other case managers back to her room to finish packing her belongings. She didn't have much to pack as she didn't have a lot of belongings.

Everything she once had was lost in the transition of being moved out of the only home she knew into a waiting house, then to her first foster home, and then to this place. She missed her things. Maybe this family could get them for her. She didn't know that all her things were in a storage room in the back of the agency.

Sara and Randall were signing the last papers when Gayle walked back to the office, this time with her suitcase. As she opened the door, she heard the case manager say, "We will bring the rest of her belongings out to your home in a day or two."

'Rest of her belongings'? Had Gayle heard right? She didn't react except in her mind. She didn't want to get too excited, only to be disappointed. Maybe the belongings were for someone else. She wasn't the only child there.

Sara and Randall stood and turned to see Gayle waiting behind them. They both smiled. "Are you ready to go home?" Randall asked.

Gayle just nodded her head. She was hesitant and unsure. Others had hurt her so many times before that she didn't trust that this would be her new forever home. She would have to wait and see.

"Gayle?" the case manager called to her. "I want you to know that it has been such a delight to have you here with us. We will stay in touch. If there is anything you need, know that you can call me. Sara and Randall have my phone number. I know you will be happy with Sara and Randall. They are good people." The case manager reached out to hug Gayle. Gayle just leaned into her embrace but didn't return the emotion nor the physical motions. The case manager understood. She knew Gayle had been through a lot. All the children she dealt with had been, but Gayle had a special place in her heart. So young, so pretty, so sad, but so much love hidden. She prayed that one day she could open her heart and love again.

Randall drove the car around to the front entrance to pick up Sara and Gayle. He put Gayle's suitcase in the back of the SUV and opened the door for her. Gayle climbed in and buckled the seat belt. Sara climbed into the front seat and adjusted her seat to make sure Gayle had enough leg room. Gayle may have only been eleven, but she was a tall eleven-year-old.

As Randall drove onto the main highway, Sara was thrilled. A new way of living was about to begin for all of them. She hoped and prayed they could give Gayle all the love she needed. She reached over to hold Randall's hand. The look between them was of pure joy and love. Gayle noticed but kept her observation to herself. She looked out her window, pretending she had not seen anything. She smiled a short smile. Her eyes were watering. Maybe, just maybe—this may work. Gayle settled in as she continued to look outside.

Chapter Twenty-Six

Gayle watched as the city view she was familiar with changed into the look of the countryside. She was finding herself enjoying the view. Gayle had to admit to her young self that she had seen enough of the city. She had been raised in the country and had not realized how much she missed it. She could feel herself enjoying it, but as soon as she did, it reminded her of her parents, and she felt a tear fall from her eye. Just one—slid down her right cheek. She reached up to wipe it off before it reached her chin. She didn't want to cry anymore. She wanted to be happy. She wanted her parents back. She wanted to go home—to her home. Instead, she felt the car turn left. She looked out the other window and saw a row of rose bushes and other flowers she didn't recognize. Not all of them were in bloom, but she had a feeling they would all be beautiful. Some of them reminded her of the flowers in her mother's garden. She waited for another tear. But felt a smile growing instead. She quickly wiped that from her face too. She didn't want Sara and Randall to think she was happy.

Randall drove past the manor and pulled up to the front of their house. The house that now would be a real home. One with a real family. He smiled as he got out and walked to Gayle's door to open it for her. Before he reached it, she had opened it and gotten out on her own. Sara had opened her door as well and stood with Gayle. Randall took one look at the two of them side by side. Beauty. Love. Family.

"Welcome to your new home, Gayle. Let's go inside and get comfortable." Randall got her suitcase out of the back of the SUV, then followed his two ladies to the front door. They waited for Randall to open the door for them, which he did, then stepped aside to let the ladies inside first. His father had taught him to be a gentleman to all women, no matter what age they were. Young children or older ladies all deserved a man's respect and courtesy. He was not a chauvinist by any means.

Gayle looked around. Her first glimpse at her new home. She had made up her mind not to like this place. It, like the other one, would only be temporary. She did her best not to be impressed. It was just a house. A place to live. A place to, to what? To wait for another shoe to drop? Another disappointment to come into her life? She didn't know. As she looked around and followed Sara from room to room, she found herself liking what she saw. Then Sara opened the door to one more room.

"Here is your room. We've painted it and decorated it the way we thought you might like, but if you want to change things, we can talk about it."

Gayle walked in and looked around. The walls were a very pale pink. The double bed had a white wooden headboard. Throw pillows rested on top of the bed pillows with a coordinating comforter. The dresser and nightstand matched the design and white color of the bed's headboard. There was a natural wooden trunk at the foot of the bed. The curtains covering the single window were floral, a mixture of pinks, white, yellows, and green. A rocking chair occupied the space just to the left of the window.

Further to the left was another door. Gayle carefully pushed it open. Her own bathroom! She couldn't help but smile.

"Do you like it?" Sara asked. She could not tell in Gayle's silence. With Gayle facing away from her, Sara had not seen her smile.

Gayle turned, wiping the smile from her face so Sara could not see it. "I like it." She said quietly with little emotion. She hung her head just a bit to better hide her eyes.

"I'm glad. As I said, we can change things if you want. This is your room. We do want you to keep it clean and neat, but we will work together on that until you learn your way around here." Sara then changed the subject. "Are you hungry?"

"Yes," Gayle said with more enthusiasm than expected and more emotion than she had in her response about her room.

"That's my girl. Let's go see what Randall may be cooking." She reached for Gayle's hand. Gayle held out her hand and let Sara wrap her fingers around her hand.

Randall was in the kitchen making grilled cheese sandwiches. "Something simple just to hold us over until supper time. I hope you like grilled cheese."

"I do. Do you have any mustard to dip it in?"

"Mustard?"

"Yes. My Mom always ate hers by dipping it in mustard. And pickles. I need pickles."

"We have those as well." Sara opened the refrigerator. Gayle could see inside. She had never seen a refrigerator so full of food.

"Wow! Is all that for just us?"

Sara turned and noticed where Gayle was looking. "Yes, just for us. We didn't know what you liked, so I think we have a bit of everything in here.' She laughed. "We will talk about what you like to eat and take it from there."

Gayle walked closer to get a better look. The refrigerator beeped when she got too close. She jumped back. "What's that? An alarm?"

"No. well, sort of. It indicates that the door has been open too long. Not that we have to close it. It just thinks we left the door open and walked away."

"Then close it. Can we open it again?"

"Of course." Sara closed the door and reopened it. "See, now it will be silent for a few moments."

'Lunch is served." Randall said as he set the plates on the table. Each plate had a grilled cheese sandwich cut corner to corner like every child likes their sandwich cut. He watched Gayle as she waited to sit. "You may sit at the head of the table if you want. Reserved today for a very special person--you." Gayle pulled out the chair and sat down.

Sara sat to her left around the side of the table, and Randall sat to her right. As she picked up her sandwich, she noticed both Sara and Randall had reached out their hands to her and had bowed their heads. Gayle put her sandwich down and looked from one to the other. She slowly reached over and held each of their outstretched hands. She waited. Randall began to speak in a low tone.

"Thank you, Jesus, for this precious day. Thank you for the blessings of answering our prayers and bringing Gayle into our home and our lives. Bless her and all that she does. Bless our new family. Thank you for this food, too. Lord. Bless it to nourish us and give us the strength we need. Be with us for the rest of today. Amen."

Gayle let loose of their hands and waited. Sara picked up her sandwich and took a bite, then reached for the mustard. "Let's see what this tastes like.' She squirted some mustard onto her plate. Then reached over and squirted some on Gayle's plate. "Like that?" She asked to make sure she had done it the correct way.

"Perfect." Gayle picked up her sandwich and dipped the one corner into the mustard. Then she took a big bite. "Yep, perfect," she said with a full mouth that gave way to a smile.

Randall took the hint and put some on his plate as well. "To new family traditions." He said as he raised his mustard-dipped sandwich in the air like someone would do with a glass of champagne when they make a toast. The girls joined in and raised their already bitten sandwiches into the air. They all broke into laughter. It was the first time Gayle had laughed in a long time. Sara was overjoyed at the sound of Gayle's laugh.

The phone rang as they finished up the lunch mess Randall had made on the kitchen counter and put the dishes in the dishwasher. Sara walked over to the counter to answer it. "Hello. Yes, we are home. No. I'm not sure she is ready for that yet."

Gayle listened. She wasn't sure what 'she wasn't ready for yet' meant and hoped the conversation wasn't even about her. Her smile faded as she looked over at Sara.

"Yes, let us have some time at the house, and I'll call you later. Yes, that may work. Just dessert. Yes. Love you too, Sis. Bye."

Sara hung up the phone. She looked at Randall but didn't say anything. He read her mind. He wasn't sure Gayle was ready to meet a large family either.

"Shall we go sit in the living room and talk?"

"Who was that on the phone?" Gayle asked instead of answering the question. She knew the question was more of a statement anyway and what she said would not matter whether they went to the living room or not.

Sara looked at Randall. She hesitated until she read what was in Randall's eyes. He was right. No secrets. Family rule. This rule included her new family.

"That was my sister on the phone."

"Does she live nearby?"

"Yes, very close." Sara smiled. "Do you want me to tell you about your new family?" She reached for Gayle's hand and led her to the window seating with the view of the mountain.

"Wow! Look at that view!" Gayle gasped as she sat down. She sat sideways with her leg under her so she could look outside. Sara noticed how the young girl sat. It was the same way she used to sit when she was younger.

Randall sat in the armchair next to the window.

"Do you have a big family?" Gayle asked. "I always wanted to have a little sister. Or brother. But I never got one. I don't have any other family either." She lowered her head. She remembered how alone she had felt just yesterday.

"Yes, we have a big family. They are your family now too."

"No, they aren't. I'm just your foster kid."

"Gayle," Randall said as he leaned closer to her and touched her knee. "You are our foster child only because it is the step we have to take before adopting you." He sat back just a bit. He hoped that had not come out too fast. They had not told her yet about adopting her. So she had been right in her comment. She thought she was just a foster kid.

"Really?" Gayle's eyes lit up with hope. "But what if you don't like me?"

"Don't like you? How is that possible? Who else could we find that likes mustard with their grilled cheese sandwiches? You are perfect!"

"Really?" Gayle said cheerfully.

"Yes.

"So tell me about your, our, family."

Sara was amazed at how fast Gayle had changed since bringing her home with them. It had only been a few hours. She was sure in time the shoe would drop, or her dream would end. She pinched herself. Yep, that hurt. She was not dreaming.

"Our family is a little big. It's also a little complicated. Let me tell you the easy part. In time you will learn the more complicated portion."

"Trust me, it's complicated, but also interesting and a whole lot of fun. I'm glad I joined the family several years ago. I would not trade them for anyone else." Randall warned Gayle.

"Okay. I have a sister and a brother. My sister, Heather, is married to Ben, and they have two boys, Marc and

Maddex. My brother, Andy, is married to Karen, and they have twins, River and Ryan."

"River?" That's her name?" Gayle was all ears when she realized there were other children in the family.

"Yes, Her name is River. Not sure how they came up with that name."

"It has to do with the lake." Randall reminded her.

"Lake? There is a lake around here?" Gayle asked.

"No. Yes, there are lakes around here, but her name came from one in Pennsylvania."

Gayle just looked at Sara, confused.

"I told you it was complicated, now back to the regular easy stuff.

"Together, my siblings and I own the manor we drove past on our way here. Our grandparents started this place, and it has grown over the years to what it is now. We all work at the manor. Well, all except Randall. He is an attorney in town." Sara took a breath so Gayle could try and keep it all straight. Sara continued after a moment. "Andy is the chef at the manor. Heather is the event coordinator. Karen helps Andy, but right now is busy with the twins. Ben takes care of the maintenance and the landscaping here at the manor."

"What is the manor?"

"The manor is a place for people to come and stay while they are on vacation. It's like a hotel, but they get a more personal touch with, in our case, Andy making them breakfast. He also makes a lot of snacks and desserts for them to enjoy when they come back at the end of the day when they are out and about sightseeing."

"So, there are a lot of strangers staying with you there?"

"Yes, I guess that is one way to look at it. We do our best to select who stays with us. We are not as big as a hotel, so we get to know the people who stay here. Several of them return because they like us and consider us as part of their family."

"That makes you have a Really big family."

"Yes, it does," Sara smiled.

"I like that," Gayle said as she leaned back against the side wall. She was taking in all the information Sara was telling her. She was thinking she was going to like it here. Lots of family, breakfast, snacks, and dessert? How could it be so bad?

"When do I get to meet them?"

Sara laughed. "That, young lady, is what Heather, your Aunt Heather, wanted to know. She is so anxious to meet you."

"Can we go now?"

"Not so fast. I told Heather we would be there after supper. Just in time for dessert."

"Is Andy, I mean," she thought for a moment. "Uncle Andy making the dessert?"

"Yes, yes he is. Just for you."

"Just so that you know. I like mustard. But not with my dessert." They all laughed.

"That is good to know. I will make sure Andy doesn't put mustard in any of the desserts." Sara said as she looked at Randall and smiled. She knew the ice between her family had been broken.

"We also have a lady by the name of Rachelle at the manor. While she isn't a blood relative, she is very close to our family."

"Is she adopted too?" Gayle asked.

"No, not like that. Rachelle is more like a sister to me. You can call her Rachelle or even Aunt Rachelle if you like. She helps me operate the place doing a lot of the paperwork and office work."

"Does she have any kids?"

"No, no kids, and she is not married. She lives alone in the back of the manor."

"Okay."

"I think that is all of us." Not a real big family, but big enough. And the best part is they all live on this property!"

"They all live here?" Gayle motioned with her hands at the house.

"Not all in this house. But all live within walking distance of here. We are a close family, and we all live close to Bella Rose Manor."

"Is that the name of this place?"

"Yes, it was named after my grandmother, Rose."

"And Bella means beautiful."

"Yes, yes it does." She was surprised that Gayle knew that. "How did you know that?"

"One of the kids I used to go to school with was named Bella."

"Lucky girl."

"I guess so." she shrugged her shoulders. She then stood up and started to walk around, looking at the decorations. Sara took that as a sign that the family discussion was over for the moment. She and Randall just sat and watched as Gayle explored.

The smell of chocolate met them at the door as they entered the manor through the kitchen entrance. The entire family had gathered around the room to meet Gayle. They stopped talking as they watched Sara and Randall walk in with their new little girl walking between them.

"Hi everyone. Andy, this place smells wonderful! Everyone, we would like you to meet our newest family member, Gayle. Gayle. this is everyone."

One by one, they all said hello and said who they were. Gayle said hi to each one. When everyone had finished introducing themselves, Randall told her that there would be a test later. She looked up at him in a panic. "Just kidding. It doesn't matter what you call them, but I have learned never to call them late for a meal. They don't like that name." He winked at his daughter.

Karen was busy pouring glasses of milk for the kids and coffee for the adults. Gayle had made herself at home – with her new cousins Marc and Maddex. She joined them on the floor playing with them and their toys. The adults looked at them and smiled as they looked around at each other. Heather walked over to Sara and gave her a shoulder hug as they watched their kids playing together.

Andy pulled the latest tray of chocolate chip cookies from the oven. He turned and set the cookie sheet on the cooling tray and then lifted them one by one onto another cooling tray. He then picked up a plate he had already filled with an earlier batch.

"Time for chocolate goodness!" He called in a raised voice so the kids could hear him above their noise of playing. Gayle and Marc raced each other to the island and grabbed stools next to each other. Maddex followed close behind and raised his hands so someone could lift him. Ben picked him up and sat him on the other side of Gayle.

Life was looking good.

Chapter Twenty-Seven

During the next few months, Gayle quickly adapted to her new family. She got along well with all of her cousins as she grew to call them and loved to hold the twins, helping to feed them and rock them to sleep. Gayle was only eleven but sometimes felt much older. All the same, she still loved being the little girl for as long as she could be.

Sara and Randall took Gayle shopping to buy her new clothes, toys, games, and craft supplies. They didn't know what she liked to do the most, and she didn't either, so they tried several things. She didn't know what she liked because life had not been the best for her. Her parents didn't have much. For most of Gayle's time as a small child, she remembered sitting in her room, reading and pretending. She would get lost in the books she read. The ones she borrowed from the school library only because her family could not afford to buy her any. When Sara found that out, she ordered a bookcase and several books for her. She had Ben come over one day after the bookcase had arrived so he could assemble it. He also brought paint and painted her name on a sign that he hung on the wall above the bookcase. The sign read: "Gayle's Library." When Gayle came home from school that day, she had a new book from school to read. Sara smiled and took her into her room and showed her the new addition. Gayle stood in awe at the case, the books, and the sign.

"For me?" she asked

"Just for you," Sara replied, smiling as she watched the excitement in her daughter's eyes.

"Not only that, there are notepads, pens, and pencils on the one shelf so you can write stories or draw pictures. You can create your own world. Someday maybe you will be an author, and another child will have your book in their bookcase to read and take them away to a far-off land."

"Do you think so?" Gayle asked as she picked up the blank notebook. She held it close to her chest. "This is amazing! Thank you." She went to Sara, and with the notepad between them, she gave her a big hug. "I love you," Gayle whispered. It was just loud enough for Sara to hear. "I love you, too, little one."

When Randall came home from the office, Gayle barely let him inside the door before grabbing his arm and dragging him into her room. He glanced back at Sara, who just smiled. A big, loving smile. This little girl would soon officially be theirs.

After Gayle and Randall emerged from her room, Sara told them that it was time to chat. Gayle's expression immediately changed. Chatting or talking was not a good thing in her mind. She was getting somewhat used to it being in a more positive environment with this family, but those words always made her afraid that something bad had happened or was about to happen.

"What do we need to chat about?" Randall asked.

Sara just tilted her head towards Gayle. Gayle noticed the silent movement but didn't say a word. She didn't want to jinx it. She lowered her eyes and looked at the floor. Her shoulders sank. She could feel the tears welling up inside her. Here it comes. They are sending me back. But why buy me a bookcase and books and a notepad? She raised her eyes and, with a look of hope, looked at Sara and then Randall.

"Oh, yes. We do. Do you think it could wait until after dinner? I'm starving," he winked at Sara.

"NO!" Gayle burst out. "If it is something bad, I don't even want to hear it." She started to walk away.

"Gayle," Sara called after her. "Come here. Let's sit in the living room." Sara reached for her hand with her left hand, and with her right hand, she reached for Randall's hand.

Gayle and Randall walked with her to the living room. Sara led Gayle to the seat at the window where they had first sat when she came home with them. Randall sat again in the side chair.

"Gayle, do you remember the first time you sat here?"

"Yes, it was when you brought me home, here."

"Do you remember how you felt? What you thought about the view?"

"I felt welcomed. I loved the view. I still do. I think at one time I told you I could live here forever." She looked at Sara with pleading eyes.

"That's right. Do you remember what we told you about being our foster child when you said that we would only keep you for a while and then give you back as the other family had done?"

She heaved a sigh and shrugged her shoulders. "Yes." She lowered her eyes and turned to look at the view she loved. She wanted to remember the view. She felt it was going to be her last time to see it. She didn't want to cry.

"What we said was true. We wanted to adopt you."

"Wanted? As in past tense?" Gayle whipped her head around. She felt the urge to run.

Sara reached for her hand to hold her in place. Randall reached behind him and pulled out something that had been hiding. He handed it to Gayle.

"This is for you. We wanted you to have it, so you know how we felt from that first day we met you."

Gayle slowly took it from him. She looked at Randall and then at Sara. Her eyes were squinted. Her forehead wrinkled as it told of her concern and questions.

"Open it," Sara said, doing her best to keep a straight face.

Gayle lifted it. She turned it over. All she could tell was that it was a box. She carefully took the white bow off the top, then slowly separated the tape from the paper. She had been raised to save wrapping paper and was doing her best to save this paper as well. It was rather pretty paper, pink with multicolored flowers.

She finally had all the paper off and looked at the wooden box. It had her first name carved on the top. White roses adorned the box above and below her name. Below the flowers, to the right of her first name, it said *Williams*. She rubbed her fingers over the engraved letters. She looked up at Sara. Her eyes were full of hope. Was this what she thought it was?

"Open it," Sara instructed her.

Gayle opened it. Inside was a framed document. Gayle lifted it out of the box as she read it. She could not read it all before her eyes filled with tears. It was her official Certificate of adoption. Her name was written in fancy cursive handwriting. Below her name, it stated that she was adopted into the Williams family by Randall and Sara Williams. Gayle wrapped her arms around Sara—her new Mom. She reached for Randall, who came over and knelt beside them. The three stayed there for a long time, wrapped in each other's arms—Mom, Dad, and daughter.

Several minutes later, they separated; each was wiping their eyes while smiles overtook their faces. Joy and love had filled their hearts and flooded over into the room.

"And now, we have a special dinner waiting for us at the manor," Sara said as she helped Randall up from his kneeling position. Gayle grabbed his other arm to help her Dad up. By the time he stood up on his own, they were all laughing.

"Thanks, girls. I'm getting too old to do that."

Half an hour later, they joined the rest of the family at the manor. The dining room had been decorated with balloons, streamers, a welcome to the family sign, the table set as if it were a holiday celebration. Which, in a way, it was. This day would be celebrated as the day Gayle officially joined the family. It would be the day her life changed.

When they entered the dining room, the whole family shouted out. "Welcome to the family!" and tossed confetti in Gayle's direction. She took a bow and thanked them repeatedly.

Dinner was grilled cheese sandwiches with mustard on the side and sliced dill pickles. Andy had also made fresh-cut french fries, sweet potato fries, and a salad for those who wanted one. When everyone finished eating, Andy retreated into the kitchen along with Karen. Together they returned with a chocolate cake complete with chocolate chip cookies hanging out from the bottom and sparklers lit on top. They sang 'welcome to the family' to the tune of Happy Birthday. Gayle just shook her head and laughed at her new family. She loved all the attention.

Sara and Randall just watched their little girl as they ate cake, cookies, and ice cream. They had not stopped smiling since they gave her the box. They felt so blessed. Sara was glad she had decided to adopt instead of having her own child. This, yes, this family picture she was watching was perfect. She could feel the pride her Grandmama would have in her. It felt like the circle of the family was now complete.

Rachelle, who had been quiet most of the night, lifted her glass of water and got everyone's attention. "I would like to give a toast to the family." She looked around at everyone as they raised their glasses to join her. "To this wonderful family. A family who loves without question. A family that brings a warmth and a sense of belonging to everyone, whether we are blood or not. A family who continues to amaze me in all they do for their family members and others. May this just be the beginning of a wonderful new beginning for Gayle. May we all continue to share this unconditional love that began so many years ago."

"To love. To family. To our future." Heather added. Everyone clinked their glasses with one another. Gayle was laughing as she had never seen anything like that before and thought it was great to cling the glasses and make a lot of noise.

Later that night, after everyone had gone home, Gayle asked Sara and Randall if it was alright if she called them Mom and Dad. The question nearly brought them to tears. They hugged her simultaneously and said they would be honored to be called Mom and Dad.

They went to bed that night as a new, complete family. Sara felt a love she had never known. It was an amazing feeling. As she was drifting off to sleep, she thought about her Grandmama and Granddaddy. She understood now why they took in those lost girls. She knew why they risked their lives for them. She also felt sad for the girls. They had experienced so much in their young lives. She thought the hardest part would have been to give up their babies. To be instantly in love with a newborn, just to give it away and never to see it again. She wondered if they ever forgot about that. She didn't think that was possible.

That night, after months of no dreams, she dreamed about that little girl again. She had on the same dress, same disheveled appearance, same everything. She woke up in a sweat. Who was this girl? She kept the dream to herself this time. There was no need to expand on it. She had Gayle. That was enough.

Chapter Twenty-Eight

The next thing on the agenda for the family was to register Marc for first grade and Gayle for fourth grade. Sara had already received her daughter's school records from her previous school. The records showed that she had been good in first grade, but her grades dropped in second grade, and the teacher's comment reflected some bad behavior. The teachers had excused the behavior by including that they expected it was due to losing her parents. Such a sad thing to have on your school records, Sara thought as she read over them. At least the teachers had passed her on to the next grade. She just hoped that it was not a case of passing her just for the sake of passing her, and it was because she had earned it. Time would tell. Sara suspected that she would have to spend a lot of time with her this school year to help her. She was looking forward to it.

Heather and Sara put the kids in Heather's SUV since it had the car seat for Marc and the four of them went to the school. They were going to meet the teachers, and the kids would go on a tour of the school, meet their teachers, and hopefully get a positive attitude for school. Marc said he was looking forward to it. He added that he wanted to get away from Maddex. 'He gets on my nerves,' were his exact words. They never did figure out where he heard such a comment to repeat. It was cute until they realized he literally had an attitude about his little brother when he said it. Heather and Ben were keeping an eye on him.

After they finished with the school event with the kids, they took them out for ice cream. They didn't go out to eat very often, so it was a big treat for all of them. Gayle said she wanted a big banana split. Marc just wanted a vanilla cone. Heather and Sara each ordered a milkshake.

When they got home, Rachelle was sitting at the island sipping coffee. In front of her lay a three-ring binder. It was closed, revealing a custom insert on the front. Sara and Heather sent the kids outside to play and joined her.

"What is this?" Sara asked as she sat and reached for the binder.

She saw the custom insert. "Really? You have it finished?"

"What finished?" Heather asked as she brought over two mugs of freshly poured coffee for her and Sara. She sat them down and looked at the binder. Even upside down, she could see what it said. "Wow!" She moved around to stand by Sara to look at it right side up with her sister.

"It is finished. At least for now. I put it into a binder so we can add to it over time or when we find out more information."

'Bella Rose – A Treasure of Love, Family, and Secrets.' Below the words, Rachelle had put a photo of the original Bella Rose home. The one that had been upgraded over the years and where Sara and her family now lived.

"This is beautiful."

I took all the letters you both have read, along with the journals, and wrote the story from them. I may have missed a few things, which is why it is in a binder. That makes it easy to add to or to edit and reprint as needed. Once we have it completed the way you want it, we can have it made into a real bound book if you want."

"You can do that?" Heather asked.

"Not me, but I'm sure I can find someone or some company who can."

Sara opened the binder and started flipping through the pages. She wasn't taking the time to read much of it but caught a few words here and there. As Sara continued to turn the pages, she saw that Rachelle included photos taken over the years. When she got to the end, she found where Rachelle had included the spread sheet of everyone's names and other information she had on each one. She then noticed a page with just names and addresses and phone numbers.

"What are these?" She asked as she pointed to the list of names, most of which she did not recognize.

"Those are the names of the girls who wrote letters and mentioned that they would love to come back here someday."

"Really? Do you think most of them are still alive?"

"I don't know for sure. The ones further down the list are the ones that wrote about their time here when your parents managed Bella Rose."

"Wait. We didn't read more than a few of those letters. How did you get that information?" Sara asked, looking in awe at Rachelle.

"I only have a few. And those are from a few letters that either one of you had already read. There are still plenty of letters to read from that time." She was quiet for a moment. "Have any of you read the journals that are in the current rooms?"

Sara and Heather looked at each other. They hung their heads, ashamed to admit that neither one had read any of them. "No," they said in unison. "I guess we should."

"How about if the two of you find the letters from the time your parents owned it and I read through the current journals?"

Sara shrugged her shoulders. "Sounds good to me."

"Me too. You're as close to a sister as we are going to have besides each other. I'm sure Andy won't mind."

"Okay. I will start to read the journals tomorrow. After my work on the binder and reading the ones I did read and include, it will be interesting to see how people have changed over the years."

"How do you mean?" Heather asked.

"Well, in the beginning, the letters were from girls who were unwed, lost, going through a very difficult time in their lives. That obviously changed with the guests your parents entertained. We have no indication that they took in lost and troubled girls, but it was still a difficult time in the world. And now life is so much better for folks. People come here on vacations and to have a good time."

"Very true. Life has changed over the generations. Now, if it would just slow down so we can read about them and catch up." Sara said. "Maybe when their kids go to school, we will have a bit more time."

"Ha!" Heather laughed. Once school starts, we get involved with the school functions, after-school events, homework, extra laundry....."

"Enough. I'm not ready for that."

"Too late, Sis. You're a Mama now. Your life has changed forever."

"And what a wonderful way for it to change." She smiled as she hid the fact about her dream still being there.

As she spoke, the back door opened, and three kids with mud on their shoes ran into the kitchen.

"WHOA!" Heather reached out her arm to stop them. They skidded to a stop. "Off with those shoes before you go any further." The three sat down on the floor, pushed off their shoes, letting them scatter wherever they landed, and ran into the living room to the toys in the corner.

"Still glad you became a Mom?" Heather asked Sara as she looked at the shoes and shook her head.

"Yep. Totally." Sara smiled as she bent to pick up all the shoes and put them by the door. Heather watched her and shook her head. She looked at Rachelle and quietly said, "She'll get over that real quick." They both were laughing when Sara rejoined them.

"What's so funny?"

"Oh, nothing," Heather said as she winked at Rachelle.

247

Sara just looked at the two of them and shook her head. She wondered what was so funny but didn't push it. She realized it might be better if she didn't know some things about kids just yet.

A week later, Sara was driving Gayle to school. She pulled up to the front of the school and parked her car. She reached the back door just as Gayle was climbing out. Sara touched her on the shoulder and told her to have a good day. Before they had left the house, she asked her daughter if she wanted to be walked to her classroom. Gayle had looked at her and told her she could figure it out. Sara felt a bit hurt but also knew that Gayle was an independent child. This independence could be a good thing or a bad thing.

"I love you, little one," Sara said as Gayle took a step away from her.

"I love you too, Mom. See you after school. You will be here, right?

"Of course!"

"Thank you. Be careful." Gayle said. She gave her a quick side hug and took off up the school steps. Gayle didn't look back although, she wanted to. Sara watched her until she had gone inside. Then she sat in her car and cried. Her little girl that she had known only a few months was growing up too fast. Being a mother was not an easy job. She smiled and wondered how Heather was doing. She'd find out when they meet for brunch later.

Heather had parked at the school and walked Marc into his class. They had to stand in line to wait for the classroom to be open. During that time, Marc stood by his Mama until he saw a boy he had met earlier on registration day. He looked at his Mama and then just walked away to stand by the other boy. Heather watched him and shook her head. Just then, the classroom door opened, and the teacher stood outside welcoming the students inside. Marc looked at his Mama and ran over to her and hugged her.

"I love you, kiddo. You have a good day in school. Behave."

"I love you too, Mama. Bye." He turned and walked into his classroom.

Heather slowly walked away. Once inside her car, she shook her head. My baby is growing up, she thought. She wanted to stay parked there if he needed her but knew that was the wrong thing to do. She started the car and drove towards town. She was meeting Sara for brunch and had an errand to run first.

"Hi Sis," Heather said when she met her at the cafe. She pulled out a chair and sat down. "How did it go with you dropping Gayle off at school?"

"For her, I think it went well." She lowered her head, shaking it slightly. "For me, not so well. I got back to the car and just sat there and bawled! Why would I cry?" Sara looked up at Heather.

"Because you just dropped off your little girl on her first day of school."

"It's not her first day."

"No, but it is *your* first day of school as her mother."

"I never realized how much I could love someone I barely know. Is this how you feel toward Marc and Maddex?"

"Yes. I shed a few tears as well this morning. Marc clung to me for several minutes until he saw a boy he had met at registration. Then he almost forgot about me when the classroom door opened. He did come back to hug me goodbye."

The waitress interrupted them to take their order. After she walked away, Heather continued.

"It was like a part of me broke off this morning. He now has a bit more independence. It's scary."

"I agree. I just hope Gayle makes some nice friends, being new to the school and all. She's been through a lot. I know I talked with the teacher, and she knows Gayle's story, so that

should help if there are any problems with the other kids."
But yes, it is scary."

"You know how some parents are so glad when the kids go back to school after the summer break? I wonder if we will be like them next year?"

The waitress brought their meals, and they began to eat. "We will see. I don't see it happening even next year. I want Gayle with me at all times, so she knows we are there for her."

"She knows."

"Are you sure? She hasn't been with us all that long."

"I can see it in her eyes. She has adapted quickly and very well. She loves playing with Marc and Maddex. And have you watched her with the twins? She loves them."

"I know. I just worry."

"Stop worrying. You'll get gray hair fast enough now that you are a mother."

Silently they finished eating—each in deep thoughts about their children who were growing up fast before their eyes.

As they were leaving, Sara said she would make a special treat for Gayle when she came home.

"You're going to make something? Not have Andy make it?"

"Very funny. I can cook. Okay, I can at least try to make something for her. When we have a brother and sister-in-law who are great at cooking and baking, it is hard to do something on our own that would top what they do. I don't want to pester them all the time to make me something. I need to show Gayle that I can make things too."

"I know what you mean. I have learned to make a lot of things on my own. Once the kids came along, we have more meals at home."

"Yes, so do we. That leaves Andy time to be with his family now too." Sara was silent with a big smile on her face.

"What's the smile about, Sis?"

"Us, all of us have kids now. It's the next generation for Bella Rose. Do you ever wonder who will stay and take over when we are too old?"

"No, not really. We will train them all as they grow up and see which one or ones take to it."

"Good idea. Well, I must get going. I guess everything is going well at school." Sara lifted her cell phone out of her pocket. "No phone calls yet."

"You're funny." Heather then pulled out her cell phone to see if she had a phone call or text message. "Here either. I think we are good. For the first day. See you later." She added as she put her cell phone back in her purse and walked away.

"See you later. Thanks for meeting me for brunch." She called out. She wasn't sure if Heather had heard her or not.

A few hours later, Sara was sitting back in her car waiting for her daughter to get out of school. She watched for Gayle as the front door opened and students piled out. Several minutes passed with no sign of her daughter, and Sara began to be concerned. Then she smiled as Gayle was bouncing down the steps with two other girls who looked her age.

Gayle headed toward the car and waved to the other girls who had turned to go to their own parent's cars.

"Hi, Mom!" Gayle said as she opened the door and sat in the back seat.

"Hi, Gayle. How was school?"

"It was great. I've already made friends with two girls in my class. They are adopted, like me, although they were adopted when they were babies."

"I'm glad you've made some friends. How about your teacher and classes? Do you like them? "

"Teacher is nice. She had us introduce ourselves to each other. Most have been going there since first grade, but there are about three of us that are new."

"Do you like your classes?"

"I guess. We didn't spend much time in each class today. It was more of a fun getting-to-know-each-other day. The hard part starts tomorrow."

"Hard part?"

" Classes, Learning stuff. Homework. The hard stuff."

Sara smiled as she drove out of the school parking lot and headed home. Sara was glad the first day went so well. She knew the bad days would come soon enough. They always did.

Chapter Twenty-Nine

The year was flying by. So much had happened that had changed their family. The manor had been at full occupancy all summer and had reservations set through to Christmas. People were calling to make reservations for the next year already. A few of the regulars had booked their next stay before they completed their current one.

Heather was building her client list and had already planned a couple of events. She had two more events scheduled for the year. She was learning as she went and hoped that the next year would find her with more special events.

Karen had gotten back to helping Andy in the kitchen and with baking her cakes. Andy was finally able to get back to the project he had started when Bella Rose first reopened. It had turned into a major project taking more time than he thought it would. Most of that was due to all the things going on with the family. Having twins wasn't easy. He had taken a break when Rachelle joined the family. Another break when Maddex was born. A big break when Karen got pregnant and had to take precautions not to lose them. And when the twins were born, he took time to help take care of them and Karen. He took Another break when Sara got married.

Now it was time to get back to the recipe book he had been developing. He had most of the recipes written out, photos taken, and foods had been taste-tested. Andy had even included comments on the recipe pages. And for those that benefited from them, he had written the backstories about the recipe. He had already contacted a local publisher who was waiting for the final edits before publishing.

He was hoping to at least have enough copies in hand for his family by Christmas. Thanksgiving would work well too. He could let them know how thankful he was to be a part of this family.

Karen had helped him with a portion of the book and knew he had stayed up late many nights, editing. She was so proud of him. After the babies had been born, he said he wanted to add recipes for baby food, but Karen told him that he could write a separate book for that. This book was all about the recipes and stories related to Bella Rose. He had agreed. That may be a separate book.

The phone rang early one morning, and Andy answered.

"Hey, buddy. How are you?"

"I'm fine. Who is this?"

"This is John, your publisher."

"Oh, I didn't recognize your voice. What's going on?"

"I was wondering if you have your book ready for me to see. I have a few days open that we can work on it and get it out there."

Andy cleared his head. Finishing the book had not been on his mind yet that day.

"I am just about done. It needs a good cover, but otherwise, I think I'm ready."

"Good. Why don't you come over later this morning, and we can work on the cover and the layout for it?"

"Sure. That would be great. As soon as I finish breakfast at Bella Rose, I'll come over."

"Great. See you later."

Andy hung up the phone and scratched his head.

"Who was that?" Karen asked as she carried River into the living room.

"That was John, my publisher. He wants me to come in later this morning to work out the final details."

"That's great!" Karen sat River down next to Ryan, who was already playing on the floor. They had not started to walk yet, but they were crawling around and starting to get into everything they could reach.

"Will you be alright on your own with the twins?"

"Of course. I'll be fine. You need to go. That book won't publish itself."

"Don't I know it. It's been a long time in the making."

"Yes, it has."

"Did you get that last page finished?"

"Yes, I did that just the other night. It wasn't easy. How do you bring a cookbook to a close? Especially one like mine?"

"Your book is unique. But it is also what your family will love, and all the guests have been asking for."

"Maybe if we get it done on time, it can be for sale for Christmas!" Andy was getting more excited. "Or maybe I should wait to make it public and see how the family likes it first."

"Stop second-guessing yourself. It's a great cookbook. See what your publisher has to say about it, including the timing, and take it from there. If it has to wait, so be it."

Andy went over to Karen and kissed her. 'You're the best." He rose and looked at the clock. "I have to go; guests will want breakfast." He bent down and kissed River and then Ryan. "I love you." He said to Karen as he walked out.

"Love you too." She said as the door closed. And she did love him. So much. He had changed her life dramatically and all for the better.

Andy was making breakfast for all the guests when Rachelle came in.

"Good morning."

"Good morning. You look like you could use some coffee."

"Yes, Please." Rachelle lay her head in her hands on the island. "I didn't sleep well last night. Been staying up late working on the Bella Rose Book."

"I thought you had it done."

"I did, sort of. Then Sara, Heather, and I read more letters from when your Mom and Glen owned it. So I've been adding and rearranging some of it."

'Writing a book isn't easy."

"It's not a book, but you're right. Speaking of which, how is your cookbook coming along?"

"Funny you should ask. I am meeting with the publisher later this morning." Andy turned from the stove and smiled.

"That's amazing! Do the girls know?"

"No, and can you keep it a secret from them?"

"A secret?" She looked at him with raised eyebrows.

"Oh, come on. This is a good secret. It won't be a secret for long. You know that."

"Okay. I will be quiet about it."

The door opened at that moment. "Quiet about what?"

Rachelle and Andy looked at each other. Andy kept his cool. "A special dessert I'm going to make for later this week."

"Something new?"

"You'll just have to wait and see. I'm sure you will like it, though."

"I am sure we will. We have not found anything you make that we don't like. Well, maybe," Sara's voice trailed off.

"What? What don't you like?" Andy turned, sincerely concerned there was something that people didn't like.

"Well, to be honest." She hesitated, making him sweat.

"What?"

"I honestly have not found anything I don't like yet." She laughed.

"You are so mean!" He wished he had some whipped cream to throw in her face. She was lucky.

"I love seeing you worry."

"No, you don't."

"You're right. I don't. But that was fun."

"So, what are you up to today?"

"Nothing much. I was going to work on my special recipe. I have to get some stuff this morning, but I'll be back early this afternoon. I should have the dessert ready by dinner time." Andy looked at Rachelle. His eyes told her he had no idea what he was going to make for dessert.

"I look forward to it," Rachelle said with a hint of sarcasm. "It should be interesting."

Sara heard that last comment but let it go. She thought Rachelle's choice of words was interesting. Sara wondered if Rachelle was in on what the dessert was. But she didn't pry. She had to get her daughter to school

"Got to run, guys. Time to get Gayle to school." Sara left with a mug of coffee in her hand to take along. She had forgotten what she had gone there to get. But coffee was always a good reason.

"That was a close one," Andy said after Sara left. "Time to drop the subject before someone else comes in. Besides, breakfast is ready to serve. Do you want to help?"

"Sure." Rachelle grabbed the plates to set the table. A couple of the guests were just coming in from the hallway where their rooms were.

"Such a lovely day today." One of them said.

"Yes, it is. Do you have plans for the day?" she asked.

"We are headed just downtown. We went through Cades Cove yesterday."

"Did you enjoy your trip?"

"We sure did. We were lucky to see a mama bear and her two cubs. They were all up the tree, but we stopped and watched them climb down and follow their mama. Luckily they walked away from us."

" Few people get to see that. You were blessed." Rachelle finished setting the table.

"Breakfast is on its way. Help yourself to some coffee." The coffee carafe sat in the center of the table. "Coffee is hot and fresh. I think Andy said he made the Vanilla bean flavor today."

"Perfect. Andy is such a great chef. Does he hire out?"

"No, at least not that I know of."

"I'd love to have a copy of some of his recipes. They are amazing." the lady said.

"I will let him know." Just then, Andy came into the dining room with breakfast. Rachelle turned. "Or you can ask him yourself." She walked back into the kitchen.

"Ask me what?"

"My wife was just saying she would love to have a copy of some of your recipes."

Andy laughed. "Your wish may be coming true soon." He placed the scrambled eggs on the table and then set the dish of pastries next to it. "I am working on a cookbook to sell."

" Where do I sign up to order one?" The lady asked.

"I don't have a list, but I guess I will have to start one. Remind me before you leave. I will have a place for people to sign up for email notifications."

"How exciting! I can't wait."

Andy turned and walked back into the kitchen as the couples were seated and starting to fill their plates and enjoy breakfast.

"Can't wait for what?" Another guest asked.

"Andy's cookbook to be published."

"He has a cookbook? I was wondering how to get his recipes. Where do we sign up?"

"He is making a sign-up sheet for us. Just let him know you want to be notified when it is available. I'm sure he will have them for sale here as well when they are available."

"I'll sign up!"

Andy could not help overhearing the ladies talk about his cookbook. He could not wait to meet with his publisher in just a few hours.

When he entered his publisher's office, Andy had the new recipes in hand and a printout of an idea for the cover. It was a small local company, but it was perfect. He could not imagine his cookbook being available worldwide. He had written it for the locals and guests at Bella Rose. He didn't know why anyone else would want it. It was tasting the food that made the demand for the book. Going to a local company made the best sense.

"Come on in, Andy. Good to see you." Mr. Jacobs motioned for him to come in and have a seat. Andy sat across from Mr. Jacobs's desk. "How have you been?"

"Busy. Between work at Bella Rose, new twins, and trying to get this book done. I don't have much spare time."

"I guess not. Hopefully, you will have more time to relax now that the book is finished."

"That would be nice. But I don't think I will be relaxing for another twenty years old. Not with twins to raise." Andy laughed.

Mr. Jacobs laughed. "You are so right. I have three children, so I understand just a little. I"m sure twins are a little more intense."

"Right now, they are still tiny. Not even a year old, so not even walking yet. I can only imagine the trouble they will get into once they start walking."

"Definitely. Safeguard everything."

"Karen already has done that. We installed gates once they started to crawl. We moved things out of the lower cabinets, plugged the electrical outlets. The works. I'm surprised she didn't lock the refrigerator." Andy smiled.

"That comes when they become teenagers." Mr. Jacobs pulled out the file on Andy. "So, what do you have new for me?"

"I have a rough sketch for the front cover, as well as two new recipes to add. I hope that is okay."

"Sure. Cookbooks are easy to edit; that's why I like publishing them. The market for them may be small, but it allows me to enjoy life more. I prefer that to overstressing all the time."

"I don't blame you. I'm glad you are local and small. It makes it more personal."

"Yes. More like a family." Mr. Jacobs looked at Andy's sketch. "This looks great. Do you want it left as a sketch, or do you want my art department to take it from here and work with it?"

"What do you suggest?"

"To be honest, I would leave it the way it is. It gives the feeling of nostalgia, and I think, at least for this first cookbook, that is what you want to show. The history of Bella Rose. The beginnings. The roots. The original."

"First cookbook?" Andy interjected.

Mr. Jacobs chuckled. "Yes, first. I'm sure you will have another one. In time."

"Wow." Andy rubbed his hand over the back of his head. "I never gave a second one a thought. I thought this would be it."

"You still create new dishes, right?"

"Of course."

"Your guests love them?"

"Yes,"

"Second cookbook, in the making."

"I thought I was going to have time to relax. You said I would."

"I lied." He winked at Andy. "You said you wouldn't relax until the twins were twenty anyway."

"Very funny. So, we keep the cover as the sketch, add the two new recipes, and then what?"

"I send it to my editing staff to put it all together. The editors ensure that if a recipe takes two pages, those pages are in the right order. They will check for any typos. Then they will put it together in a mock book form. I will have you come back to approve it, and then I send it off for printing."

"How long will that take?"

"That will take about four weeks. Why?"

"I was wondering if it would be out in time for Christmas this year, that's all."

Mr. Jacobs looked at the calendar even though he knew full well what day it was. "It will be cutting it close. But I think we can make it. It depends on what the editors find and how many corrections it needs, but yes, I think we can do it." He hesitated to say the next thing on his mind, but he was only joking. "Of course, my fee goes up some if we rush it."

"Figures. How much more?"

"I'm just messing with you—no extra cost. Now, if it was December first and you wanted it by Christmas, I'd add quite a bit to my fee and everyone else's cut."

"I would not do that to you. So how much do I owe you so far?"

"Not a dime. Once it is all done, I simply get a percentage of the sales." He handed Andy the contract to look over again. They had discussed all the fees, percentages, and details before. Now it was just a matter of signing the paper, the contract granting Mr. Jacob's permission to format, print sample copies, and publish for the masses. It included that Andy would be available for local autograph sessions at the local book store and that Andy would do some of the marketing for his book. Such were the drawbacks of a small town and a small publishing company. The author had to do more than just write it. Andy was ready for whatever else he needed to do for his recipe book. People had requested it for long enough. It was time to respond. He read over the contract again just to be sure he understood everything. This endeavor was a big step for him. He reached for the pen Mr. Jacobs was offering him. He took a deep breath, signed his name on the bottom line, dated it, and handed the contract and the pen back to Mr. Jacobs.

"There. Done. I feel such a weight lifted off of me."

"Of course you do. Now it's all on me." Mr. Jacobs lowered his shoulders as if taking on more weight.

Andy stood and reached out to shake his hand.

"Thank you so much for working with me on this. It has been a labor of love. It took a lot longer to do than I thought it would, but life had a way of interrupting just about everything from time to time. Weddings, babies, trips, family changes—it's been quite a ride over the last several years. I hope now things will calm down for a while."

"I hope for your sake and for your family that they do too." Mr. Jacobs walked Andy to the door. "Have a wonderful day. Now go home and let your family know they have a published author to contend with."

"I'm not published yet." Andy shook his hand as he took a step out of the office.

"Close enough. Go celebrate."

"Thanks." Andy left the room, and as he left the building, he could not control the smile he had on his face. 'Published author. Who could have ever guessed?'

Chapter Thirty

Rachelle had been busy working in her area of the office. Sara had been so busy with Gayle that it left Rachelle in charge of just about everything related to the manor. It worked out very well for Rachelle as it also gave her time and access to everything that she was working on for the family. A secret. Yes, she knew about the family history and secrets, but there does come a time when a good secret is fine to keep.

Sara, Heather, and Rachelle had been reading the last of the letters and the journals they had found in the upper room. They had made copies of them and added notes and underlined important statements on the copies for Rachelle to use in the book. They all knew about the book. What they didn't know was the other project she was creating. She was doing her best to contact as many of the former guests as she could. Her focus was on finding the girls there when Rose and Robert took in the girls. She knew they would be hard to locate if she could find any of them at all. Some of them could already be dead. At the least, they would be grown, with new lives and families. And even if in their letters back to Rose they had mentioned wanting to return someday, she knew that as time went on and their lives changed, they may have changed their minds. They may be keeping secrets from their new families.

There was one that she was able to find. In addition to them finding Rhea, she had found one of the last girls to stay at the manor during that time. Her name was Mrs. Baker. She was in her late-seventies, close to Rhea's age. She had moved on with her life, but she was now alone. Her husband had passed, her children had grown and moved away. When Rachelle found her, she was hesitant to talk at first, but the more she listened to Rachelle, and the more she thought back to the positive side of her life as a little lost girl, the more she opened up. Rachelle asked her if she wanted to come to visit. Initially, she said no, that she was too old to make the trip. It wasn't that she lived that far away; she just didn't drive anymore and didn't like flying or taking the bus. Rachelle was disappointed that she couldn't make it. Then Rachelle had an idea.

"Mrs. Baker, how about if I come to get you?"

"Oh, sweety, that's too far for you to come. I couldn't ask you to do that."

"Mrs. Baker, you are not asking me; I am offering."

"Well, can I think about it?"

"Sure. You have my cell phone number. You can call anytime, even if it is just to talk. I'm here."

"Thank you. You are so kind. Your Grandparents were so kind to me when I was a little girl. I was so scared, but they took me in. They found a home for my baby, too." She was repeating herself, but Rachelle listened as if it were the first time she had heard this story from her.

As Rachelle thought back to her conversation with Mrs. Baker a month earlier and, while adding her story to the book's ending, her cell phone rang. It was Mrs. Baker.

"Rachelle?"

"Yes, this is she."

"This is Mrs. Baker. Is it too late to take you up on your offer?"

"Not at all!" Rachelle forgot everything she was doing and broke into a huge smile. She swung around in her office chair and found it hard not to stand up and dance.

"When would be a good time? So I can let the home know I will be traveling."

Rachelle had not thought about when a good time would be. It was almost Thanksgiving, and then it would be Christmas. It will be the new year before there may be a *good* time. Then she thought.

"How about for Thanksgiving?"

"Are you sure? Won't that interfere with your family time?"

"Mrs. Baker, you are family. I'm more concerned that it will interfere with your family time."

"Oh, Dear, my family has not spent a holiday with me in years. They are all too busy with their own families and work."

"Then it is set. I will make arrangements to leave here the Sunday before, pick you up, and we can be back here to surprise the family on Wednesday."

"Surprise the family? You mean they don't know about me?"

Rachelle laughed. "Mrs. Baker, I will tell you all about this family when I pick you up. But, to answer your question, no, they don't know I've found you nor that we have been in touch. They certainly don't know you are coming to visit."

Mrs. Baker laughed. "Alrighty then. I will let them know here at the Home so they can get me ready. And Rachelle? Please, call me Ginny."

"Yes, ma'am, Ginny. I will see you in about a week."

"I am looking forward to it. Oh, to see that place again. I hope I can handle it."

"I will be by your side as much as you want me to be. You will love the place; and this family."

"If the rest are anything like you have been and like Rose and Robert were, I know I will. Goodbye, dear."

"Goodbye, Mrs. ....Ginny," Rachelle corrected herself. She waited until Ginny hung up the phone. Her mind was reeling. How was she going to pull this off? What secret story could she make up?

Time to make some phone calls.

First, Rachelle had to go for a walk. Away from Bella Rose. She had to hide her smile. If she could pull this surprise off, it would be amazing. And it would be a great ending to the year. It may even be better than whatever was planned for Christmas this year. Although it being the first Christmas with Gayle would be a big deal as well.

"Gayle," Rachelle said her name out loud. How much did Gayle know about the history of Bella Rose? She had not been with them for that long. Would bringing Ginny there for Thanksgiving confuse her? Take away from her first Thanksgiving? Was her plan of surprise a good one? She started to second guess herself. She got up and headed for her car to drive to town to take a walk.

Sara and Gayle were headed up the lane after school. They passed Rachelle on her way down. Luckily for Rachelle, Sara just waved at her as they passed. Her smile had not faded, and she knew Sara would sense something was up.

Her walk took her to the antique shops in town. She noticed a few things and wondered how many of them Ginny had owned in her younger days. She would make it a point to bring her here to shop, or at least look around. What was the town like back then? Did the girls ever get a chance to come to town? She became overwhelmed with questions. Then she smiled. She and Ginny would have a lot to talk about on their road trip. She smiled again. She decided it was a good plan.

Andy had approved the final revision to the cookbook within days of his publisher bringing it to him. The cover looked amazing. A pencil sketch of what the kitchen at Bella Rose Manor looked like years ago. The old bean pot, an oil lamp, an old rolling pin, a cookie jar with the lid off. Chocolate Chip cookies on a white plate. All on the counter of an old-timey kitchen complete with a potbelly stove. It was perfect. He had come up with the new design at the last minute and rushed it to Mr. Jacobs, hoping it would be in time. He was very pleased with the results.

The title, *The Sweet Side of Bella Rose, Stories of the Kitchen* Compiled by Andy Fairchild, was a long title, but that in itself told the story. If you read between the lines, you knew there was another side to Bella Rose.

Andy waited patiently to hear that the books were ready. He knew it would be cutting it close to have them in time for Christmas, but he was hoping.

Rachelle wasn't sure how to pull off her secret until a couple of days after last speaking with Ginny. Rachelle saw Gayle come home from school with Sara, which reminded her of her own childhood.

'That's it! That should work,' she thought to herself. She didn't realize she was smiling until Sara spotted her.

"Nice smile. Do you have good news?"

"What?" Rachelle asked.

"I said you have a nice smile."

"Oh, sorry, I had something on my mind."

"Something good, I presume?"

"Well, it could be. If I can make it work."

"What's up? Something I can help with?"

"No. Not really. It's just that I got a phone call from an old friend, and she wants me to come for a visit."

"So, go. We can cover for you. When do you want to go?"

"That's just it. She wants me to come to see her just before Thanksgiving."

"Oh. That is a little different." Sara thought for a moment. "Will you be back for Thanksgiving?"

"I'm sure I will," Rachelle said.

"Then go. Enjoy time with your friend."

"Are you sure?"

"Yes. When was the last time you had any time off from here?"

Rachelle thought but didn't reply.

"Exactly," Sara answered.

Rachelle arrived at the Assisted Living Home where Ginny lived by mid-afternoon on the Sunday before Thanksgiving. She had made arrangements to spend the night in one of the guest rooms they kept for overnight family visitors. Then she and Ginny were going to head out first thing in the morning to get back to East Tennessee.

As soon as she opened the door, she heard music. A few people were singing, someone was playing piano, and someone else was playing the guitar. It brought a smile to her face after such a long drive. She walked to the double doors that were open and stood there watching and listening. As she stepped inside the room, she noticed a couple dancing. Maybe they were just holding each other up as close as they were. But, they were smiling, and it warmed her heart.

A nurse spotted her and walked over to her.

"May I help you?" she asked.

Rachelle read her name tag before she replied.

"Hi, Judy. I'm Rachelle Connors, and I'm here for ...

"Ms Ginny!" Judy smiled. You are all she has talked about for the last week. So glad to meet you. Come on in. You'll have to wait a minute." Judy pointed to the dance floor.

"Ms Ginny?" Rachelle asked, smiling.

"The one and only." She smiled back.

"How sweet," Rachelle said as the two of them sat down to listen to the music and watch Ginny and the gentleman finish dancing. When the song ended, and they separated, the man held her hand up and gently kissed the back of it.

"Are they together? Married?" Rachelle asked.

"Oh, no. Just best friends. They met here about three years ago when he moved here. He had lost his wife the year before. Ginny was the first to introduce herself to him. She's been there for him ever since."

Rachelle listened to the story. She wondered if they loved each other. She made a mental note to ask Ginny on the way home.

Ginny spotted Rachelle and walked to the back of the room to meet her. Rachelle stood up and walked to meet her. She held out her hand to shake it. Ginny took her hand in hers. "Rachelle?"

"Yes, Ma'am."

As soon as Ginny was sure it was Rachelle, she pulled her into a hug.

"None of this hand-shaking stuff. You are family."

Rachelle accepted the embrace and didn't try to deny being family. It could have been her cover story to get away from the Assisted Living home for a few days.

"I'm so glad you are here. I've told everyone that you were coming. I told everyone that you were my granddaughter. I hope you don't mind." She whispered.

Rachelle had thought correctly about the hug.

"What all did you tell them?"

"Just that you had been away for several years and just reunited with my daughter. They don't know much about my daughter." She added. "It is my son that is the one who has me here and comes to see me. So don't worry about questions."

"Okay, if you say so."

"We'll talk in a few. Let me tell Judy we're going to my apartment."

A few minutes later, they were in Ginny's small apartment. It was an oversized bedroom divided into a bedroom, bathroom, living room, and a small kitchenette.

"This is so cute," Rachelle said as Ginny gave the brief tour.

"Thank you. I did the best I could with the space I had. I had to sell most of my stuff. Some of the treasures are at my son's in storage."

270

Rachelle listened as Ginny told her a little bit about living here.

A knock at the door interrupted them

Ginny opened the door to Judy standing in the hall.

"Are you ready to see where you'll be staying tonight?" Judy asked Rachelle.

"Sure."

"I'll take you there, and then we can meet everyone in the dining room."

"Perfect. Grandma, are you coming along?" Rachelle looked at Ginny. Her eyes were pleading with her to join them. She didn't want to say the wrong thing and ruin Ginny's cover story.

"Of course." Ginny grabbed her sweater and joined them as she closed and locked her door. She walked with them to the end of that hall to guest housing, where Judy showed her where she would be spending the night. It was more than a room. It was a full-size apartment.

Rachelle easily found her way around the little apartment after Judy's short tour. They all walked around the corner to the dining room. Rachelle kept an eye out for the man Ginny had been dancing with earlier. She then noticed a man give a small wave and a smile in their direction. She turned just in time to see Ginny wave back with a big smile.

"We can join him if you want." Rachelle offered.

"Are you sure?" Ginny asked, hanging her head like a small, shy child in disbelief she was getting to go somewhere.

"Of course. I want to meet him; he makes you smile."

Ginny smiled up at Rachelle. There was a gleam in her eye. "That he does."

They walked over to join him. As they approached the man that made Ginny smile, he stood to greet them.

"Hello, Grant." Ginny held out her hand to him. He raised it to his lips and kissed it while reaching for Rachelle's hand.

"Grant, I'd like you to meet Rachelle. Rachelle, this is my good friend Grant."

"Good to finally meet you, Rachelle. I have heard so much about you."

"Good to meet you as well, Grant. I saw you dancing earlier; you're pretty good."

"Thank you. But I'm afraid I've slowed down a lot over the years. I still like to move with the music, and Ginny makes it easy for me." He had let go of Rachelle's hand but was still holding Ginny's in his.

Rachelle smiled. She could see the silent connection between the two people. Yes, she thought. I will have to ask Ginny for more details about their friendship.

Chapter Thirty-One

The road was calling their names. Rachelle and Ginny ate breakfast, put their suitcases in the back of the SUV, and were on the road early the next morning. It would be a long trip, and Rachelle would take full advantage of it to get to know Ginny and tell her all about Bella Rose Manor and the family she was about to meet.

Grant had joined them for breakfast and bid them farewell, telling Ginny to make sure she came back. They hugged goodbye, which was so sweet it made Rachelle feel guilty for separating them. She almost wanted to invite him along. Almost.

For the first several miles, Ginny talked about the area, pointing out different buildings and some other special places not on the roads they were driving along. Rachelle was so impressed she hated to get on the interstate. Once they were, Ginny began asking questions about Bella Rose.

They talked some about Bella Rose and Ginny's life at the Assisted Living Home on the phone, but there was so much more to both sides of the story. It was a wonderful time to chat, with many hours ahead of them, stuck in a vehicle with few interruptions.

All it took was one question from Ginny, and Rachelle began telling all about it. She began by telling her the complicated story of how she got there. Ginny had stayed there when Robert and Rose owned it; before Susan was born, she did not know any of the stories of Susan and Glen. It took several questions from Ginny before she finally figured out the love story of Susan and Glen.

Ginny listened as Rachelle explained how Susan and Glen were married, had two children, divorced, and remarried. She explained how Glen had married her mother, Hazel, while Susan and Glen were divorced. Then about how Glen and Hazel had a little girl, but Hazel and the little girl were killed in a car accident a few years later. Then she went on to explain how she went to live with her uncle. She omitted the part of how horrible her childhood had been living with him.

Ginny was taking it all in. With only a few questions along the way to clarify things. It was rather confusing when she thought about it.

"So, you are not a blood relative to the Rose and Robert's family?"

'No, not blood. And no relation at all. I was Glen's stepchild. When my mother passed away, it wasn't up to him to take me in, so he let me live with my aunt and uncle. He thought it best that I stay with my biological family."

"That was nice of him, I guess." Rachelle didn't correct her and tell her it was the worst thing he could have done. She just let it pass.

"So, how did you get to Bella Rose?" Ginny asked, now more curious than before about this wonderful lady taking her back to her own childhood.

"Well, a few years ago, I got a call from this attorney named Randall. He said that he had found information about me through his searching the history of Glen. And that Glen's family was searching for information about what he was doing while he and Susan were divorced. When it led him to me, he asked to bring Sara to meet and talk with me. I told them to come down; I'd love to talk. I was running an assisted living facility in Florida at the time—one left to me by my aunt. When they arrived, we talked, I told them my story, and they invited me to visit them sometime. The three of us had an instant bond. I saw the love they had for each other and listened to how that love seemed to be all around this Bella Rose place, and I wanted to be part of that."

"You didn't have love where you were?"

"No, I hadn't had love in a very long time." She was doing her best to keep the complete truth from her.

"That's a shame. A family always needs to show and share their love." Ginny said as she placed her hand on Rachelle's arm. "I hope you found the love you needed."

"Oh, I certainly did. The family is wonderful. The funny thing is, I saw that true love shining between Randall and Sara when they first came to see me only to find out later that they were just friends at that time." Rachelle laughed. "I could tell they were in love with each other, and they didn't even know it."

"Observant of you. They are married now, right?"

"Oh, yes. And just adopted a little girl." Rachelle was getting ahead of herself.

"They adopted a baby?"

"No, actually, they adopted an eleven-year-old girl."

"Nice. I look forward to meeting her. Was she in trouble like the other girls that came to the manor when I was there?" Ginny made quotation marks in the air as she asked.

"No, just a little girl who had lost her parents a few years earlier. She is a sweetheart. You'll like her. Her name is Gayle."

"You told me about Glen when he was divorced. What about Susan? Did she marry anyone?"

"No, she didn't marry anyone, but she did have a child. She spent a lot of time in Pennsylvania when Glen left her. Robert had friends up there, and they sent her there to just get away for a while. The divorce hit her so hard she was miserable. While she was there, she met a young man, and they got close. Too close, you might say. Susan returned to Tennessee and had the baby. Larry, the father of the child, never asked her to marry him. The little boy, Andy, didn't find out about Larry until, oh, five or six years ago."

Ginny was sitting there listening and just shook her head. "What a messed up world in which we live. Always have, so it seems."

Rachelle went on to fill Ginny in on the details of finding Larry and Grace. Some of the back story of Andy and how he and Glen were never close. About Andy running away for all those years.

"So how did everyone get together to run Bella Rose? If Andy was gone, the girls had moved away. What happened? You talked on the phone as if they all love each other, and it is a happily ever after family now. Is it?"

Rachelle then explained how Susan's will was written. And then about how they had to wait to get into the attic, and when they finally did, it led them to the secret room, where all the history was discovered.

Ginny laughed through some of the stories and cried during other parts. Rachelle was doing her best to fill in all the gaps as she went along and didn't realize how some of it may affect Ginny. She knew the memories of the secret room would touch a heart cord.

"I didn't mean to make you cry," Rachelle said at one point when she noticed Ginny wiping a tear.

"Oh, at my age, sometimes it doesn't take much for a tear or two to escape. Don't worry about me. It's just the memories of that secret room. It's like it was yesterday sometimes when I think back to those days. I know it was a lifetime ago. I've done well for myself after I left there. I can honestly say it was the love and caring of Rose and Robert that changed my life."

"Tell me more about you, Ms Ginny. I've been talking for miles. Shall we stop for a bite to eat and to stretch our legs? I think my car is ready for a refill as well."

"I could use a bit of a walk. And something to eat sounds good too."

Rachelle pulled off onto the next exit. It had all they needed—a gas station, restaurant, and a small park-like perfect for a short walk.

When they were back on the road, Ginny took over the conversation and revealed her life story.

When I was way too young, I did something stupid and thought I was in love. I told a boy yes when I should have said no. We were too young to know any better, and I soon found out I was pregnant. When he found out, he dumped me. When I finally told my parents, they were embarrassed and did not want me to ruin their family reputation. Mom somehow heard about what Rose and Robert were doing to help young girls in my situation, and Mom took me there. She told me it was for my own good. Mom also insisted that I give the baby up for adoption. If I didn't give the child up, she told me that my father would never let me back inside the house. I loved my father and hated to disappoint him. So soon after I gave the baby up for adoption, I contacted my Mom, who came to pick me up. We never talked about the baby or of me being anywhere except away at school. That was the story they made up to save face—their face.

"How horrible."

"Yes, I saw that years later. After I found my true love, I got married and had two kids. When my daughter was my age, it brought back the childhood memories that I had suppressed. I'm not sure how my family dealt with me through that year. I guess because they let me talk about my past and loved me through it."

"Did you ever want to find your firstborn?"

"Yes. After I told my family about having that first baby and giving it up for adoption, we tried to find him, but it was hard to trace adoptions back then. So we just gave up. I kept praying that he was being raised well and was successful with a family of his own to love."

"You are a remarkable woman, Ms. Ginny." Rachelle was truly impressed with her.

"Besides getting married and having a family, what did you do? Tell me more."

"Well, for a while, I was what is now called a stay-at-home Mom. Back then, it was just what most women did. They stayed home, took care of the children and their husbands. I had a garden and raised my vegetables, canned most of them. I had a good life. After the kids were grown and moved away, it was just my husband and me. I started to volunteer at the local shelter for women and children." She stopped talking for several moments. Rachelle stayed quiet. She knew Ginny was thinking back.

Ginny gathered her thoughts and continued. "After my husband died, I lived alone for many years. My kids came to visit now and then, but we were not close." Ginny was quiet for a few minutes, spending the time watching the scenery as Rachelle drove in silence.

Ginny spoke again when the view had changed. "My daughter went to college for business and now is a CEO of some big company in New York City. I don't even remember which one. She is single and has no kids. When we did speak, I accused her of being married to her job. I guess she didn't like my opinion. I miss our relationship and pray she comes around eventually. I hate to see what she will go through if she doesn't come around before I die. Of course, maybe she won't care."

She continued, not waiting or expecting Rachelle to comment. "My son, on the other hand, lives closer. He is a pediatrician. He and his wife have two kids, a boy and a girl. They all come to visit me from time to time. They are busy, which I understand. And it's not like they live around the corner. It's about an hour away."

"I'm so sorry you are not in touch with your daughter."

"It's okay. I'm used to it by now. I've not heard from her in about three years now. My son is in touch with her, so I know how she is doing. I still send her cards and little gifts from time to time. Just to let her know I love her no matter what. I am her mother, and that love never ends."

"You are amazing. Can I adopt you?"

Ginny laughed. "Of course you can." She placed her hand on her arm. "You are amazing as well. I think the whole family that surrounds Bella Rose is amazing."

"You know I'm not a blood relative to them."

"I know, but it doesn't matter. You are there now, and from what you told me, the family has taken you in as if you were one of them."

"I guess you are right. It feels like home and like family."

"And that is what matters."

They made another stop before they started the last stretch to Bella Rose. Once back in the car, they were both quiet for a while. Not that there was nothing else to talk about. It was that they were both getting tired and still had several miles to go. Rachelle looked over at Ginny after several miles along their final stretch had gone by in silence. Ginny had fallen asleep. She looked so happy even while she slept. Rachelle hated to wake her when they approached the land of Bella Rose. She gently called her name, and Ginny easily woke up. "I wasn't sleeping." She lied. "I was just checking my eyelids for holes. The good news is, there were none." Ginny laughed. "Where are we?"

"We are about to turn onto Rose Lane."

"Rose Lane? Named after Rose, as in Rose and Robert?"

"That's the one. When Robert changed the land and planted the rose bushes, he made a sign naming the driveway Rose Lane. Over the years, they widened and paved the driveway."

Rachelle made the left turn onto Rose Lane, driving slow so Ginny could experience the beauty, even in late fall.

Ginny was speechless at first, just taking in the beauty.

"This is beautiful. Who planted all the rose bushes? And the landscaping is amazing."

"Robert started it back in the day. Currently, it is Ben who is taking care of it. Ben is in charge of all the landscaping, maintenance, and remodeling here at Bella Rose. He used to have his own company but sold that when he and Heather moved back to help run the place after Susan died."

"Ben is Rose and Robert's grandson-in-law. Did I get that right?"

"Yes, you did. You were following along when I did my best to keep the family straight."

"Not easy at my age. I try."

Rachelle made the last corner to face the Manor. "Remember, I have not told anyone who I was bringing home. All they know is I'm bringing home an old friend."

"So they don't know you literally meant 'old'?" They both laughed.

"No. But that's not the point. The family doesn't know your relationship with Bella Rose either. I'm going to try to sneak us in directly to my apartment. There we can rest up a bit before dinner." She glanced at the clock in her car. They had an hour to hide.

Ginny didn't say anything. "Are you okay?" Rachelle asked.

"Oh yes. I'm fine. I'm just amazed at all of this. It is beautiful. So different from what I remember. Nicer. Much nicer."

"Wait until you see the inside and the newest additions."

"There's more?"

"Yes. Sara, Heather, and Andy added a chapel and a fellowship, slash, reception hall. There is even a hiking trail just off Rose Lane. Not a very long one, but a nice one."

"They have church services here?"

"No. Heather uses it for special events—weddings mostly. Sara and Randall got married there."

Ginny just shook her head. So much to take in.

Rachelle drove her car around the back to her apartment, so hopefully, they would go undetected until dinner time. As she opened her door to get out, she looked around. No one was around. They were safe. Now to hide for an hour.

Chapter Thirty-Two

The family was gathered in the kitchen and dining room. Everyone was helping set the table and get ready for dinner. They knew Rachelle was bringing a guest staying for a few days, so they set an extra place at the table.

"Do you know who she is bringing?" Heather asked Sara.

"No clue. She told me on the phone yesterday that the friend she went to see wanted to come here for a few days and see where Rachelle lived. I'm assuming it's an old friend from college. Maybe it is someone from where she used to work. I didn't even ask if it was a male friend or a female friend. I must be slipping in my investigative work."

"You certainly are." A voice from the side door called out. Rachelle was standing in the doorway. She had only heard the last part of the conversation and was amused. Her mind thought, 'wait until they find out who it is.'

Everyone turned toward her as they looked beyond her to the older woman just a step behind.

"Everyone, meet Ginny." Ginny stepped into the kitchen with Rachelle. "Ginny, meet everyone." She motioned around the room at everyone. "Including the little kids over there playing." She pointed into the living room play area.

"Hello, Ms Ginny. Glad to meet you." Sara said as she reached to shake her hand.

"Hello, everyone. It is so good to put faces to all of you finally. Rachelle has told me so much about each of you."

"Uh oh. We're in trouble now." Andy said as he wiped his hands on a hand towel and then shook her hand. "I hope she only told you the good stuff."

"It was all good." Ginny shook his hand and smiled. "You must be Andy."

"That's me." He then proceeded to introduce everyone else as they each shook Ginny's hand and welcomed her.

"So, how do you know Rachelle?" Sara asked as they all went into the dining room. Andy and Karen carried in the serving dishes of food and set them on the table.

"I will explain all of that after we sit and have grace. I'll tell you the whole story as we eat." Rachelle answered for her.

Ginny leaned into Rachelle as they sat next to each other. "Do you think we have enough time to tell them the whole story?" She smiled.

"They don't need to know 'everything.' Rachelle teased.

Once everyone had their plates full and started to eat, the room grew silent as they waited for details.

"I'm not sure where to begin to tell you about Ginny. She lives across the state in an assisted living facility. Much like the one I ran in Florida. That, though, is not how I know her. I just met her yesterday."

Everyone stopped eating for a moment and looked at her. She continued.

"I will tell you this. Ginny is living history, and she has a story to tell."

"Don't we all?" Ben asked.

"Yes, you are right. We all have our stories. Ginny's, however, affects us all."

Everyone looked at Rachelle. How could this woman, who was a stranger until yesterday, affect them all?

Rachelle saw their curiosity. "I was working on the Bella Rose history book and came across her name. I decided to try to contact her. Are you ready for this? Ginny is one of the girls that stayed here under the care of Robert and Rose." She put her hand on Ginny's shoulder and let her statement linger in the air.

"You're one of the girls who," Heather caught herself and redirected her words. "stayed here back in the day?"

Ginny smiled. "Yes, Heather, I am one of *those* girls." She used quotation marks in the air to emphasize the meaning without saying the words.

"Wow. Now we've met two of the girls. This is wonderful." Sara said.

"After we finish dinner, maybe you can tell us your story," Karen commented. She didn't want Ginny to feel pressured to tell her life story at the dinner table.

"I'd be more than happy to tell my story. It may wait for full details until tomorrow. I'm quite tired from the long trip."

"Understandable. We can wait. If we must." Andy said.

"I will say that I am impressed with what you have done with Bella Rose. I've not seen a lot yet, but Ben, the landscaping I have seen is beautiful. And to keep you all from guessing my story, I will tell you that, yes, I was one of the girls who stayed here for a while when I was a wayward young girl. This place, Robert and Rose, changed my life. For the better. Long story short, I've had a great life."

"I am so glad Rachelle found you and brought you here. I look forward to hearing your story when you are ready to tell it. How long are you able to stay?"

"Only a few days. Through Thanksgiving. That is if you will have me."

"Of course, we will have you. You are welcome to stay as long as you like."

"Well, the home does expect me back at some point. They think I'm spending time with my granddaughter." She winked at Rachelle.

"Granddaughter?" Heather asked.

"It was the only way they'd let me leave for longer than overnight. They are a bit restrictive. I do see their point, though. You never know when strangers may want to kidnap an old person." She laughed.

They all laughed.

After dinner, they gathered in the living room, where the kids went back to playing. The twins were starting to craw all over the place, so everyone was looking out for them.

"That dinner was delicious, Andy. If I still cooked, I'd ask for the recipe."

"Funny you should say that, Ginny," Karen said. "His cookbook is at the publisher as we speak. Last I knew, it had gone to the printer."

"I'm just waiting to hear that the books are ready to pick up," Andy added.

"That's great. A published author." Ginny said.

"It's just a cookbook," Andy replied.

"That's what you may think, but it is still quite an accomplishment. I used to wish I had written a book."

"What would you write about?"

"My life. It has been a great ride."

"Rachelle is writing one about the history of Bella Rose. I have a feeling you may be in it."

Ginny looked at Rachelle. Her eyes asked if she was in it.

"I've changed most of the names, but yes, you are part of the book."

"I'd like to read it."

"Well, it is just in a three-ring binder. Not a book ready for major publication at this point. I hadn't even written it for that. Just for the family."

"You should publish it. I'm sure others would like to read it."

"I'm not so sure about that. I don't think even a lot of the local people know what went on up here years ago."

"Really? It was that secret?"

"We are finding a lot of secrets about this family."

"Rachelle told me a few of them. You have quite a family."

They all laughed. It all had been hard to accept in the beginning, but they were at a place now that they could laugh about it. Some of it was still painful, but they could now laugh at the fact that it was kept secret for so long. Their family was amazing—at keeping secrets.

As they sat in the living room enjoying cups of coffee, Sara asked Ginny if she was up to telling them some about her life. Ginny took a sip of her coffee and said she would tell a little, but most of what she had to share would have to wait.

I know you all want to know my story as I do all of yours. Rachelle and I had a long time to talk on the way here, so I do know a lot about each of you."

"Sorry, everyone, but she asked." Rachelle defended herself.

"Be glad she did. Otherwise, I'd have a lot of questions. Instead, you get to hear my story."

"Which I've already heard too," Rachelle interjected. "Hey, what? It was a long trip." She added when Sara gave her a suspicious look.

Ginny began to tell her story as she had already told Rachelle. After she had talked about her current life and her children, she stopped.

"The rest I'll share tomorrow or over the next few days. I am tired and think it's time I call it a night."

Everyone said goodnight to each other and went their separate ways. Ginny followed Rachelle to her apartment. It didn't take either of them very long to fall asleep once they laid down.

Andy was in the kitchen early to make breakfast for the family. All their guests had left a few days earlier to head home for Thanksgiving. The family was alone for this Thanksgiving. Ginny being with them was a bonus. She was also a great reason to make a family breakfast. He didn't do that very often anymore since everyone had kids, and getting everyone together was difficult.

Rachelle and Ginny were the first to arrive.

"Something smells good. What are you making?" Ginny asked.

Rachelle raised her head, putting her nose up in the air, allowing her to take in the aroma. She took a deep breath. "Gingerbread Pancakes! To be served with Ginger Molasses Maple Syrup."

"Good nose, Rach!" Andy said, calling her by a nickname he had never used for her before.

"Rach?" Rachelle asked.

"Sorry, Rachelle. It just slipped. I didn't mean anything by it."

"No, it's fine. Don't worry about it. It's just that I've never had a nickname before. I kind of like it."

Andy smiled. "Okay, 'Rach' it is. Yes?"

"Sure."

"Now, back to the pancakes, Ginny. Andy only makes them at this time of year. They are a favorite around here."

"If they taste as good as they smell, I know why they are your favorite. Is that one of the recipes in your cookbook?"

"Yes, ma'am."

"Please call me Ginny."

"Yes, Ms Ginny," Andy replied with a grin.

"Good enough," Ginny smiled.

The door opened, and Sara, Randall, and Gayle walked in, followed a few minutes later by Ben, Heather, Marc, and Maddex. As they all helped set the table, Karen came in, pushing the twins in their stroller.

Ginny looked around at the beautiful family that had gathered. A tear slid down her face. She did her best to wipe it away, but Rachelle noticed. She went to Ginny and put her arm around her shoulder. "You okay?"

"Yes, Dear. I just wish my family was like yours."

Rachelle hugged her a little tighter. "You can borrow ours if you like."

Ginny smiled. "Thank you," she whispered as she leaned her head on Rachelle's shoulder.

Andy served the pancakes, fresh-squeezed orange juice, and fresh fruit. A simple but delicious breakfast. One that was easy to make but made a lasting impression.

Following breakfast, the older kids went to the living room to play. Karen put the twins in the play pen so they could play, and she wouldn't have to worry about them crawling away. Gayle had become a built-in babysitter when she was around them. She loved to hold them, play with them, and just watch them. Sara watched her as she played with the little ones. She had come a long way in the last six months. She was very proud of her daughter.

While the adults were cleaning the kitchen and dining room, Sara asked Ginny what she would like to do that day.

"I think I would like to tour the Manor and the grounds."

"We can do that. Are you ready to visit the upper room and the secret room?"

"I have been thinking about that since I first spoke to Rachelle on the phone. I had spent my life wanting to come back here, and I'm not sure why." She stared off into the space of the room. "When Rachelle called me, it made me start thinking and remembering back when I was here and what I gave up. I was saddened by those memories and wasn't sure I wanted to come here. But, Rachelle convinced me that what I did was because of love. After seeing your family here last night and this morning, I am reminded of Rose and Robert's love for all of us girls that just showed up here. And it is that love that has been passed on to all of you. That love helped me get through the roughest time of my life and learn and grow from it. I say all of that to say, yes, yes I am ready to visit the places of my childhood, though briefly here, it was the place that changed my life."

Sara could feel the love as Ginny spoke. She understood a bit more of how her grandparents not only helped the girls with their babies and found them good homes, but they did change the lives of those girls. Her heart was full as she walked with Ginny into the part of the Bella Rose where it all began.

Chapter Thirty-Three

Sara led the way to the third floor. She had already given Ginny the tour of the guest rooms and the main living area. Now it was time for Ginny to find closure with her past.

They stopped on the second floor to look at more of the guest rooms. Ginny loved that each room was named after a quilt pattern and that each room had that quilt on the bed. A touch of home, a touch of memories passed for all the guests. Ginny knew that if people didn't know someone who currently quilted, they most likely had a grandmother or great grandmother who did. It was that personal touch that helped make Bella Rose what it was. A home away from home for travelers from all over the world.

At the base of the steps to the third floor, Ginny hesitated. This was the point of no return. This was the place that saved her life. Up those stairs were the memories. Many memories that she remembered, and some she knew may come back to her once she climbed those stairs and opened that door one more time. She told Sara that she wanted to be the one to open the door.

Sara didn't ask why; there was no need to know. She did know that Ginny would share if she felt she could. And that she might not say a word to any of them about her thoughts or memories from that time in her life. She was okay with that. Sara knew all too well the pain a negative past could bring. Her abuse during her first marriage had left those scars. That was in her past, yet she still felt the pain from time to time. Some called it PTSD. She didn't like being included in that classification. To her, that was for the soldiers who fought the wars. Sara had learned over the years, and through a few sessions with Joe McBride, that what she went through certainly left scars, and yes, it was PTSD. She looked at Ginny and wondered about her painful memories. Were they mostly good memories? Or did she, too, suffer, even after all these years. She would not pry. It was not for her to ask. She would listen if Ginny wanted to share. She would comfort, if and when she could.

Ginny took one step up. Then another. She held tight to the railing, the railing that had not been there when she was a little girl. The room had been added just before she found herself dumped there. Having something new along the way helped.

Ginny took the final step. Standing up as tall and straight as she could, as if preparing herself to stand tall in battle, she reached for the doorknob. This was going to be the beginning or her ending. She prayed a silent prayer. Her mind took her back. She struggled to turn the knob. Sara waited, reaching behind Ginny without touching her. Unsure what her reaction would be. This room was the upper room. What would Ginny do when she then got to the door to the secret room?

Ginny closed her eyes, took a deep breath. Then she opened her eyes, turned the doorknob, and pushed the door forward. It opened easily, revealing what the threshold of her safety was. Now it was a beautiful room set for a country queen. Ginny smiled and turned to Sara.

"Thank you."

"For?"

"For making the changes you did. This is beautiful. The sun filtering through the window cast a beautiful streak of bright light across the queen-sized bed. Covering the bed was a quilt like the quilts in all the other guest rooms. This one was an antique quilt. Ginny could tell by the fabrics and the stitching. She glanced briefly around the rest of the room. Her eyes landed on the other door. She knew it led to the secret room. She was surprised, for some reason, that they had made the door opening full size. She remembered it being so small when she was a child that she had to almost crawl through the opening. Weren't things supposed to seem smaller when you got older? She smiled to herself. Another great change, she thought.

Ginny inhaled. She reached for that doorknob, and without any hesitation, opened the door. And stopped. Her eyes were closed as she looked back through the years to the last time she had walked into that room. She was so scared. She had been crying. She had been holding her baby still growing inside her. She had never felt such deep fear. Now she shuddered. She was afraid to open her eyes. She had seen the changes to the upper room. Did she want to see the changes to this room, or did she want to see it just the way it was? She closed the door and took a step back. Her eyes were still closed.

"Ginny?" Sara whispered and touched her elbow to steady her. "Are you alright?"

"Can I have a chair?"

"Yes, of course." Sara brought over the desk chair to her and helped her sit down. She reached for Ginny's hand to hold it, but Ginny pulled away from her.

"I need to remember. I need to feel it again." She whispered to Sara. Her eyes were still closed. Sara patted her hand gently and then stepped back. She walked quietly to the bed and sat down on its edge, giving this beautiful lady the space and time she needed. She understood.

They sat in the quiet stillness. No words. No music. No noise. Just sitting. While Ginny remembered, Sara waited. No pressure.

"It was a stormy day. Complete with thunder and lightning. The dark clouds had rolled in about noon that day after a morning of bright sunshine. It wasn't supposed to rain that day, but it did. Boy, did it. We heard a loud knock at the front door. At first, even Robert thought it was the wind. Then we all heard it again. It was an angry knock. Robert and Rose were both with all of us in the living room. The knock sounded again, only this time it came with a loud voice. A man's voice, yelling for Susan. Us girls were quiet. I could see fear in our eyes, as I'm sure mine showed the same. Robert pointed to Rose and then to the stairs. She got up and motioned for all of us to get up the stairs quickly but quietly. We tip-toed as we ran. We hunched down so we could not be seen through the window." Ginny was whispering her story.

She took a brief moment before continuing. "Rose led us to the secret room. She shooed us inside. It was pitch black inside. She whispered for us to be silent and not move until she or Robert came for us. Then she closed the door. I heard something scrape across the floor outside the door and then gently tap the door or wall. I knew she had barricaded us inside. There were three of us girls here at that time, and we huddled together. We were all shaking."

Ginny lowered her head that she had raised while taking in all the visions, the sounds, and the feelings of that one moment in time. She kept her eyes closed. She said nothing for several minutes.

"We could hear muffled voices. Yelling. We heard a scuffle. Sounds of furniture being tossed," Ginny jumped suddenly. "No. Not gunfire. Could there have been? Is that why we were so scared?"

Sara was by her side in an instant. She didn't touch her as she didn't want to pull her out of her trance, but she was there if she was needed.

"Again, the gun fired. The door slammed shut. I heard footsteps. We all waited. We didn't know who was coming for us. The blockage was removed from our door. I heard the latch turning. And we heard her voice. Rose had come to get us out. We asked where Robert was. She told us he was fine. The three of us nearly knocked her down in one mass hug. We were all crying."

Sara wiped a tear from her face. She was glad Ginny still had her eyes closed.

Ginny shook her head. "I'm ready now." She opened her eyes, stood, and walked to the door. She opened the door and peeked inside. She smiled.

"Again, thank you." She reached for Sara, who returned her hug as they both stood and cried.

Back downstairs, Ginny and Sara sat in the main kitchen. No one else was around. Sara looked at the clock above the sink and realized they had been upstairs for nearly two hours. It had been an amazing two hours. She hoped that Ginny saw it that way as well.

"Are you okay, Ms Ginny?"

"Yes, dear. I am fine. I didn't imagine what I would feel going up there, but it was so worth it. To see the changes you and your family have made to those two rooms." She took a sip of the coffee that Sara had just set in front of her. "I was not quite ready to see the remodeled secret room. After seeing the changes to the upper room, as we all called it, I knew you must have changed the secret room as well. I had to go back in my mind to the original and chase the demons away first. I think they are gone now. At least for a while." She took another sip.

"It's none of my business, and you don't have to tell me or anyone, but do you ever wonder?"

"About what happened to my son?" Ginny finished the sentence for her. "Yes, I do. For a while, I tried to locate him, but back then, it was impossible. And now, I don't know. What would be the point? He is grown. I hope he is doing well with a loving family of his own. He may even have grandchildren by now. Would he even want to know about me? Did he ever know he was even adopted? So many things to consider. I like to think that whoever he is, wherever he is, that life has been good to him, and he was loved."

Sara sat and thought about that for a moment. "I guess you're right. Did Rachelle tell you about Ben's history?"

"Just that he takes care of the grounds and is married to Heather, father of two boys. Adorable boys at that."

"Ben was adopted by one of the sons of one of the girls who were here. His adoptive grandmother was Rhea. After leaving here, she went on to get married and have two children. Her son, from that marriage, adopted Ben."

"Oh my goodness! How did you find that out?"

"Rachelle was researching for the Bella Rose History book and did some tracing, and well, the rest is history."

"Small world."

"Yes, it is. Rhea was here earlier this year. She and Ben got to know each other. They stay in touch. She lives out West and doesn't travel much."

"So she found her true love and got married and had more children as I did."

"Yes, she did. It was because of her granddaughter that we found the connection. Her granddaughter stayed here and told us that her grandmother told her if she ever had the chance to come to visit Bella Rose. She never told Laura, that's her granddaughter, why she was here, but we figured it all out. So Ben and Laura are cousins!"

"Small small world," Ginny said again as she shook her head. Her mind drifted back again.

"What are you thinking, Ms Ginny? I can see those gears turning."

"Oh, nothing."

"Ginny?"

"You are a stubborn one, aren't you?"

"I've been called worse."

"I was just thinking, 'what if.' And I know those thoughts are usually useless."

"Usually, yes. Impossible, maybe. Worth the time and research? Could be."

"No." Ginny shook her head. "I'd rather keep my thoughts as positive and not risk finding out he had a rough life or that he's already dead. I don't think I could handle that."

"That is up to you. However, I do know this great detective. She may not have her license, but she has shown some good results." Sara winked at Ginny and grabbed the coffee carafe. "Refill?"

"Please. Thank you. You all have been so kind."

"Thank you for being here. It has meant a lot."

The door opened and closed with a bang, and in walked Marc with Maddex in tow. Heather followed right behind.

"Sorry, ladies. The boys found out about hidden cookies here somewhere, and I could not catch them in time. I hope we are not interrupting anything."

"No. We are done. Coffee? To go with the cookies the boys have found?" She added when she saw Marc lifting the cookie jar off the counter and placing it on the island.

Heather scolded him for lifting it while she laughed inwardly. He was such a handful but so smart. And he was getting so big. All too fast.

"He is quite a little man," Ginny said as she helped herself to a cookie when Marc carefully lifted the lid off and tilted it toward her first.

Heather just shook her head as she took a drink of her coffee. 'Ahh, that hits the spot." She held onto her mug while she sat down. "These two are wearing me out."

Ginny smiled a big smile. "Little ones have a way of doing that. I remember my two. I had a boy and a girl, but they still wore me out when they were young. Can I share something I learned?"

"Sure, please do. What's the secret?"

"Oh, Heather, there is no secret. The truth is all mothers go through the struggles of the energy of the little ones. No, the thing that mothers learn way too late is to enjoy all the moments. Pick your battles. Don't fight or argue over the little things. And lastly, all too soon, they are grown up and gone, and you will wish for the little ones to come back."

"And here I thought you had a secret to help me get through this stage." Heather slumped forward.

"No, there is no secret. Just love them."

"Thanks, Ms Ginny. I know they will be grown before I know it. I'm already stunned that Marc is in first grade." Heather took another sip of coffee as she watched Marc offer Maddex a cookie. Yes, she loved her boys, and they really were good kids.

The ladies finished their coffee. Marc put the lid back on the cookie jar and put it back on the kitchen counter without even being asked. Heather smiled and shook her head. Ginny reached over and patted her arm. "See, they are good boys."

"I know. I just have to remember to pick my battles."

As they were about to get up, Rachelle walked in. "Hi, ladies and boys. Did I miss a coffee and cookie meeting?" She looked at Marc and winked. Marc looked at his mother and asked if he could get the cookie jar down again for Aunt Rachelle. Heather was so impressed she told him, "Of course, you may." He reached the cookie jar and handed it to Rachelle.

"Thank you, Mr. Marc. I appreciate that,"

Marc smiled. "You're welcome. Mama, can we go play?" he asked Heather.

"Of course. Play nice."

The three ladies watched in silence as the two little boys played together. They were laughing as they shared toys and chased each other around the room playing tag. After about fifteen minutes, they heard the door open, and Andy walked in.

"Hey, ladies! Just who I wanted to see."

"Why?" Heather asked suspiciously.

"Can't it be 'just because?'"

"Not with you," Sara added.

"Funny. Okay. Truth be told, I need your help. With Thanksgiving dinner."

"What do you need?" They all turned toward him.

"I've got most of it covered, but I could use some extra hands to get it all made."

"Isn't the saying that too many cooks ruin the broth? Or something like that?" Sara asked.

"True, but I think it will be fun. We've all worked together in here before."

"I think it is a great idea. I'm in." Ginny volunteered.

"You are more than welcome to help. You may know some secret ingredients we don't know. Thank you."

Chapter Thirty-Four

All too soon, Thanksgiving was over, and Rachelle was loading Ginny's luggage into the SUV for her return trip home. It was a sad time for the family. They had instantly bonded, and taking her home felt like a part of the family was leaving. Even Ginny was having a hard time saying 'goodbye.' She told them she would stay in touch as much as she could and hoped to be able to return sometime. She thanked them for all they did for her, especially all the love they shared. With tearful hugs, she climbed into the passenger seat of Rachelle's SUV and closed the door.

The trip back home for Ginny held mixed emotions. She enjoyed where she lived, but her family was not close to each other nor her. In less than a week, she had found true family love. She talked to Rachelle about her feelings as they traveled.

"I know exactly how you feel. Remember, I'm not a blood relative to any of them either."

"That's right. I keep forgetting that. To the world, you are one big happy family. Never lose that."

"I don't think we could if we tried, Ms Ginny. And please know that you are now a part of our family."

"Thank you. That means the world to me."

They spent the rest of the trip talking about kids, more about Ginny's life, and plans for another visit. When they reached Ginny's home, the man she had been dancing with when Rachelle first saw her met them. She looked over at Ginny and smiled when she saw the smile on her face. Rachelle knew Ginny would be okay.

Her trip home seemed like such a long trip the next day. She had stayed in a hotel instead of at the assisted living home to get an earlier start. Plus, she didn't think she could go through another goodbye with Ginny. She was going to miss her so much. They had learned a lot from her. Mainly about the love Robert and Rose had for the girls they took in. They also learned that Ginny had never found her son. Rachelle was going to do her best to follow any lead she could find on him. Maybe she could bring the two together after all these years. Maybe not, but she was going to try.

Andy sat at home playing with the twins, who were standing and walking while hanging on to furnishings when his phone rang. It was his publisher. His cookbook was ready to pick up. He called out to Karen and told her he had to go pick up the book. Karen offered to pack up the kids and come with him. He hesitated a moment before telling her to grab her coat and the kids. He had learned one thing from Ginny. Family time was important.

Sara watched as Andy and his family left. She sat at the window in the living room at the manor. It was so nice to see them all together. She smiled and waved, even though she knew no one was looking in her direction.

She turned and looked around the room. It was time to decorate for Christmas. She picked up her phone and called Heather. An hour later, they were in the craft supply room, pulling out all the Christmas decorations. Heather had called Ben and talked to him about going for a tree for the Manor. They agreed to meet the next day after Rachelle returned home and go to the local tree farm to find a tree together. It would be fun. Heather and Sara set about cleaning and taking down all the other decorations and knick-knacks until then. The decorations for the manor took over the place. Even the guest rooms if they had guests. And this year, they had a few staying for at least part of the season.

Andy and his family pulled into the parking lot of his publisher. He turned the car off and just sat there.

"Are you okay?" his wife asked.

"No, I'm nervous."

"Why?"

"I am about to pick up copies of the book I wrote."

"The cookbook you put together."

"Okay, reality check downer."

"I know it's a cookbook, but there are personal stories attached to some of those recipes. So in reality, okay, I wrote some of it."

"I know. I am proud of you. You know that, right?"

"I know. You have been my best supporter and encourager. Without you, I never would have finished it."

"Oh, yes, you would have. I wasn't the only one pushing, I mean nagging, I mean encouraging you to continue making it."

"I'm so glad you did whatever you want to call it. It worked. Now I just hope people buy it."

"Why would they not buy it? Our guests are always asking for it. When we get home, or over the next few days, you need to put it on the website so people can know where to buy it."

"I will."

Andy drove them to the local dairy bar to celebrate with ice cream. "Let's celebrate the final step."

The next day, Rachelle arrived earlier than they expected, and although she was tired from her trip, she agreed to help pick out the Bella Rose Christmas tree. It was a special family event, and this year Marc and Maddex were old enough to appreciate helping. It was always fun to watch small children during the holidays. Their sweet innocent faces, their eyes lighting up with the glow of the lights, the seemingly magic of Santa Claus and the reindeer. The music and the snow. The snow didn't always show up in Tennessee for the holidays, but the thought of it helped. And where it was necessary, fake snow was used to cover the decorated landscapes in store windows and homes alike. Bella Rose was no different. Fake snow would have to do again this year.

Andy had not told anyone that he had picked up his books just yet. He was waiting for the reveal but didn't know when to present them, maybe after they got the tree up. Maybe once they were done with all the decorations and were seated enjoying a cup of cider or hot chocolate, he knew it had to be soon.

As they walked around the tree lot, the kids were oohing and aahing at the trees, the Snowmen, Reindeer, and other decorations. The magic of Christmas was in their eyes. Even Gayle was enjoying the spirit of the season. Sara had found out that she had not had a real Christmas since her parents had died a few years earlier. This year Sara hoped to change that. She wanted to make this Christmas the best for her daughter. One she would remember for the rest of her life.

Ten days before Christmas, Sara had a last-minute errand to run. Gayle was in school, and everyone else was busy. It was her opportunity to take care of something. She would be home in plenty of time to turn around and go pick Gayle up from school. She drove to town to pick up her final gifts for Randall and Gayle. She had ordered them a week before, and they were ready. Sara had been concerned when she had not heard anything about the Father/Daughter ornaments and was so relieved when she finally got the call.

On her way home, she pulled onto Rose Lane and looked up. The lights from the manor glowed through the dusk that was coming far too early now that winter had set in and the time had changed six weeks earlier. As she turned that last curve and caught sight of Bella Rose Manor in its glory, she stopped her car and put it into Park. She knew no one would be coming up the lane, and no one would notice her just parked there with her car off and her lights off. She just sat in awe.

What a year. What a life. The last several years had been life-changing for all of them. Had someone told her five years earlier that she would be married, have a child, be a co-owner with her siblings of Bella Rose, she would have told them they were crazy. She was happy with her life the way it was. Had they told her that there were papers telling the truth of how her grandparents had risked their lives to save little girls and babies, she would have called them liars. She would have told them to read some other fantasy book. And yet, that is what happened. She was married, she had a precious child. She had her siblings around her. There were secrets about the family.

The family she thought was so simple and perfect were anything but either of those adjectives. Her family was, what could she call them? What could she call her grandparents? Brave. Courageous. Risk takers. Life savers. Heroes. Wonderful. Full of love. Caring. And her parents? Ha, they were something else. Hard workers. Loving—sort of. Caring—maybe. Secretive—definitely. They had somehow made it work. They had been very successful despite all they had done. Her father's investments had allowed the family to live a good life while operating the manor. He had made sure his daughters were taken care of.

Sara shook her head. She wasn't sure what to think of her parents. And yet, if either of them had done anything differently, the life they all had now would have been totally different.

Then she thought about their lives since they had been in charge. They had all decided and agreed not to keep secrets from each other. They had seen what secrets did to a family and knew it would be better not to keep any of them.

In the past five years, there had been a lot of changes. They had found their long-lost brother; put additions on to Bella Rose Estate; found people who had been at the manor generations earlier; found Rachelle living in Florida, and taken her in to be a part of their family. She had fallen in love with her childhood friend and married him. They had found and fallen in love with Gayle.

Sara's dreams had all come true. Even those she had not known she had dreamed. God had blessed them all. She whispered a prayer thanking God for all He had done for her family and asked Him to watch over them over this holiday season and for years to come.

As she said amen, she noticed car lights behind her. She started her car and drove the rest of the way to her house. She would get Gayle in a few minutes. Gayle was staying with a friend after school, where they were practicing for a Christmas program set for that weekend.

The car that had followed her home was Rachelle. She had also been out shopping or rather picking up secret gifts for everyone.

That night everyone was eating in their own homes. The last of the guests had left that afternoon. Christmas, like Thanksgiving this year, was just going to be family. Having Ginny there for Thanksgiving didn't count as a guest. Ginny was family. Christmas was going to be a special one with the three new family members, River, Ryan, and Gayle. It required lots of kid toys and more gifts from Santa Clause. They were all ready for it. The kids were excited. The kids had already visited Santa. The ones who were old enough had written him letters.

Gayle, who had not celebrated Christmas in the few years since her parents had died, had mixed emotions. Sara had noticed her mood changes and went to talk to her one night after she had changed for bed. It was a routine of theirs since Gayle joined the family. Sara would sit with her and either read to her or just talk for a few minutes before her lights went out and she drifted into dreamland. A few days after Thanksgiving, Gayle's usual smile had diminished.

"Gayle," Sara said quietly as she sat on the edge of her bed like every other night. "What's wrong? Why are you sad?" She had an idea what was on her mind, but she didn't want to voice her opinion in the case that was not it.

"I miss my Mom and Dad," Gayle said quietly. She wasn't sure how her new Mom would take it.

She looked up at Sara with such a sad face. Sara moved closer to her and wrapped her arms around her, pulling her close. "Gayle, it is okay for you to miss them. After all, they were your parents. I would hope that you do miss them. It shows me that you loved them. I know this year will be hard for you. You have memories of the Christmases you had with them when you were younger. Cherish those memories. Keep them a part of you. Never forget those." Then Sara had an idea. Why she had not thought about it before, she didn't know. "What are some of the memories? Maybe we can do them here? With you?"

Gayle looked at her new Mom. "You would do that for me?"

"Of course. Why not? It will help you keep those memories alive and cherished. So, what would you like us to do? Or what would you like to do that we can make happen? I do not promise anything. Not yet. I need to know what they are and see if we can do them first."

Gayle looked down. She thought for several minutes. She lifted her head when she had made up her mind about what she wanted to do. "Can we buy gifts for a little kid who needs something? A kid who doesn't have parents to buy things for her, or him?"

Sara was speechless. Of all the things she had running through her head that Gayle may have wanted, this was not one of them.

"You don't want anything else for yourself? You don't want to do anything? Not a special ornament or a tradition? You want to buy a gift for someone else?"

"Yes, Ma'am." Gayle lowered her head as she spoke quietly. Maybe that was a bad idea, she thought. Maybe she should have just asked for something else. She waited for Sara's reaction and answer.

Sara held her daughter even closer to her. Showing her how much she loved her and hiding the tear that was falling down her cheek.

"Of course, we can buy something for a child in need. Do you know someone specifically?" She loosened her grip, wiped her single tear from her face, and hoped she had hidden it well.

"No, no one specifically. Maybe someone who lives at the home where you found me? The group home place?" She asked as she shrugged her shoulders. "I know it was a rough time for me when I was there. Being an orphan and all."

Sara let go of Gayle and stood up. She reached for Gayle's shoulders and held them. "That's it! That's perfect!

Gayle just leaned back and looked at her. She thought Sara had just lost her mind. Who was this woman?

"That's it? What's it?"

"What a great idea!"

"It was? It's just that every year Mom and I would buy something for a kid on the Angel trees at the mall near our house. I thought we could do the same. Nothing drastic."

"No! Don't you see? We can, oh yes, this is perfect!" Sara let go of this little girl genius that she was so proud to call her daughter. Especially at this moment.

"How about we invite all of the kids from that home here for Christmas?"

"All of them? Here?"

"Yes! We can have our own Christmas at the manor with just family. But maybe the day before or even later that day, we can have a Christmas party for them in the fellowship hall. Complete with Santa!"

"Santa too?" Gayle winked at her Mom. She did realize she didn't believe in Santa anymore, didn't she?

"Of course. Santa will have already delivered all the presents around the world; then he can make it here." Sara laughed. She knew Gayle was too old to believe, but suddenly even she believed in Santa. All Sara had to do was find one, find him. She noticed the time on the clock.

"Oh, dear. Look what time it is. You need to get some sleep. So do I. We have a busy day tomorrow. She motioned for Gayle to lay back down. "Do you think you can get some sleep?"

"I will try," Gayle said as she thought about a big Christmas party. "Do you think you can pull it off?"

"Pull what off? A Christmas party for all the kids? Not on my own, but look at the family we have! Of course, we can pull it off!" Sara pulled the covers up for Gayle. She was so excited she could not wait to tell the others. "Now, you get some sleep. You do have school tomorrow."

"I love you, Mom. Thank you." Gayle said as she snuggled under the covers. "Good night."

"Good night, sweet child. Sweet dreams. I love you." She bent down and kissed her on the forehead. "See you in the morning." She stood up, turned her light off, and left her room, gently closing her door.

When she reached the living room, Randall was busy reading a book. He looked up and saw the biggest smile on his wife he had ever seen. "That must have been a great bedtime story!"

"What?" Sara asked.

"Your smile. Why so big?"

"You will not believe the conversation I just had with our amazing daughter."

"Tell me about it." He motioned for her to sit next to him, then he set his book aside on the end table.

Sara proceeded to tell him about the entire conversation, hardly taking a breath between sentences. Randall could see how excited she was about the idea. He also thought about the time they had to plan it all. It was a lot to get done in a short amount of time. Then he smiled.

"You think we can do it?" Sara asked after she finally took a breath. "You are smiling; that's a good sign."

"Well," Randall said as he sat front. "While you were rattling away, at first, I thought it would be impossible to do it this year. The smile came when I realized the family I was dealing with. So far, nothing has been impossible for you. Or your family for the last few generations. Let's do it!"

"I have to make some phone calls." Sara stood up.

"Sara, my love," Randall said calmly.

"Yes?" Sara asked as she took a step toward her phone.

"You need some sleep first. It is late, and everyone else is in bed."

Sara looked at the clock. He was right. Gone were the nights her siblings stayed up late. Once they had kids and those kids finally slept through the night, so did the grown-ups. It was a new way of life, for everyone, even for her. She needed some rest. She didn't think she would sleep much, but she would try. "Okay, dear husband of mine. Let's get some sleep, and I can start making phone calls in the morning.

Chapter Thirty-Five

It took some planning, but the day had arrived. The children's party was going to be on Christmas eve day. They could not get it planned for Christmas Day, but the day before worked perfectly. It would mean the kids at the group home would still be at the group home for Christmas, but they would have their new toys and gifts to enjoy.

Heather had been thrilled to be able to plan the event in the fellowship hall. Andy was making the food and treats. Ben was making some of the decorations, so it looked like a Christmas toy land. Randall and Rachelle were helping anywhere needed. Randall had contacted the home and taken care of any legal papers, insurance, and such that needed to be in place. Rachelle put herself in charge of contacting people to play elves and finding the perfect person to play Santa. The first person she thought of was someone she had not thought of since Sara and Randall's wedding. Bob. He was perfect. Size, laugh, fun. Yep, She had called Bob, who was more than happy to help out. It turned out that Bob played Santa at one of the stores in town, so he already had the suit, beard, and all.

The day of the party arrived. Everyone was excited. Especially all the children. All fifteen of them. Ten of them were from the group home.

It had not been easy to plan in such a short time, but Heather was good at her job. And when all the family chipped in to help such a good cause, it all fell into place.

Bob arrived just in time dressed as Santa. Rachelle was playing Mrs. Clause and having a great time. The children gathered around Santa as he and Mrs. Clause handed out gifts to each child. The joy and laughter continued as the gifts were opened and games and toys spilled out. Sara and Heather helped clear up the gift wrapping and bows so the gifts would not get mixed up with the papers and thrown away. Then they sat back and watched as the children played. So much laughter and smiles from them all that it made them smile as well.

"This was a good idea, Sara," Heather said.

"It wasn't all my idea. It was Gayle that wanted to buy gifts for a needy child. I just decided to take it a step further."

"A step? You took it a lot further."

"And I think it was a good step."

"Yes, it was. We should do it every year. You know it is a continuation of what our grandparents used to do. Helping out the girls. We just are helping the girls and the boys."

Andy and Karen had been busy making the last special treats for the kids and came in with a large tray of cookies, brownies, and little pies. Afterward, the children were served lunch, complete with ham, mashed potatoes, macaroni and cheese, green beans, and fresh bread. There were enough leftovers to send back to the children's home for them the next day.

The children gathered around once again when the sweets were served.

While they continued to play, Sara watched as Gayle spent time with them all. She may have adopted Gayle out of her situation, but she could tell that a part of her felt for those still living at the group home with no family to call their own. She wondered what Gayle would choose as her future career and thought it might have something to do with helping kids who had been through what she had been. She knew she might be way off her mark in thinking that way, but she would try to remember it when the time came later in life.

All too soon, it was time for the kids to return to the group home. The Director had them help with the clean-up, thank everyone for the party, and bid everyone a Merry Christmas.

It was the best Christmas some of them had had in a long time.

Back inside the manor's living room, the family had gathered for their traditional reading of the Night Before Christmas.

After the story, the children were sent to bed. They were half asleep before the story had ended. The party earlier had worn them out. They were ready for sleep and dreaming of sugar plum fairies and Santa coming by reindeer to leave their presents.

When morning dawned, Sara looked out her living room window across the mountain and saw light snow falling. A very rare occurrence on Christmas day for Tennessee. It would not last long, but watching as the large flakes floated down to the earth was beautiful. It was time to wake the rest of the family and gather for breakfast and the children to see what Santa had left each of them. She woke Randall and Gayle, and soon the three walked hand in hand through the fallen snow to the manor to be with the rest of the family.

The kitchen already smelled wonderful as Andy had breakfast cooking and coffee brewing. Karen and the twins were sitting in the living room admiring the tree with all the gifts piled high. Heather and her family came in a few minutes later, and the boys rushed to the tree. Ben hollered to them not to touch any of the gifts until it was time. Marc picked up the empty plate where he and Maddex had set out cookies and milk for Santa. He carried the plate to show everyone that Santa had eaten all the cookies.

Rachelle had been sitting in the living room the whole time just watching. Her family. She loved being a part of them. She loved belonging to them these past couple of years. She had a smile on her face, but inside she was beaming ear to ear and then some. It had been a good year for all of them.

"Breakfast is served," Andy called from the dining room. "Let's eat and then see what Santa brought." He said as he filled the glasses with milk for the little ones and orange juice for the adults and Gayle. When all were seated, Ben asked if he could say the prayer.

"Dear Heavenly Father, we come to you this morning with such joy in our hearts. We want to thank you for the blessings you have given us all this year. Thank you for our family, our health, our lives. Thank you for this food. Bless it, Lord. Bless each of us. Take care of our children. Let them know that Christmas isn't all about the gifts under that tree but about you and your love for us. Be with us throughout this day. Amen."

"Let's eat," Maddex said as he took a drink of milk.

"Yes, young man, let's eat. Andy placed a helping of his special one-dish casserole onto his plate. Then he filled the other plates and passed them around. Everyone helped themselves to the Danish and the fresh fruit salad that Karen had helped make. In a few minutes, there was quiet, except for the sounds of everyone eating. Anyone looking in on them would have seen the love.

"Can we go open presents yet?" Marc asked as soon as he finished eating.

"No, you must wait for the rest of us," Heather told her son.

"Hurry up, everyone," Maddex added as he also finished eating. It was obvious they could not wait for the chaos of opening gifts.

"Okay. Let's go!" Andy said when he saw all the empty plates. "We can clean up this mess later. Time for the gifts."

"Now, boys, you know the rules."

"Yes, Mama," Marc said. "One at a time. Can I play Santa this year?"

"Of course you may." She saw the disappointment in Maddex's face. "You and Maddex can work together this year. How about that?"

315

"Okay." They both rushed to the tree and started pulling gifts. Marc would pick them up, read who they were for, and Maddex would take them to the right person. A great plan that usually worked and was working well this year too.

When most of the gifts had been handed out and opened, Andy stood and said he had one more gift for the adults. He reached behind the sofa and pulled out a cardboard box. He reached inside and handed Sara, Heather, and Rachelle a wrapped gift. They instantly knew what it was. It was Andy's cookbook! A published cookbook! Inside each one, he had autographed it with a personal note to each.

"This is so sweet! Thank you Andy! In all the fuss since Thanksgiving, I had forgotten about your cookbook." Sara said as she thumbed through hers.

"Does this mean I have to do my own cooking?" Heather asked.

"No. But if you want to, you may. All the favorites that we like and our guests have asked for are in there. Along with the back story, if there was one."

"This is amazing, Andy. Thank you so much." Rachelle said. She set hers aside and stood up. "Now I have something special for each of you as well. As you know, I have been doing a lot of research. I've been reading the letters and journals that you all have also read. I've researched online, researched in town, and looked at old documents at the courthouse. I have been busy. I wasn't planning to make a big deal out of it, but as time went on, I found it to have such a special meaning to the family that I contacted the man who published Andy's cookbook and found a publisher who would publish mine as well."

All eyes were on her in amazement. They had put the cookbooks down and listened. Even the kids were quiet.

"Now, no, I don't have it published into a 'real' book. At least not yet. I have a copy of my work for each of you in binders. I wanted you all to see it, read it and give your opinion." She began passing around the binders to everyone, including Gayle. "I want you to read through them. See if what I have included is correct, and let me know if you approve of having it published. The publisher I am in touch with has read it and wants to make it a book for print that can sell. He says the story of Bella Rose is an amazing one. One that the world should read about."

Sara looked at her siblings. She was excited about the book, but she was concerned. Did they want the public to know the secrets of Bella Rose? She could tell by their looks that they had the same thoughts.

"Rachelle, this work looks well put together. Our history is unique. Personal. I love the idea of having it in a book, but I'm not sure it is for the public. What do the rest of you think?" Sara voiced her initial thoughts.

"At first, I thought the same thing," Andy said. "But, when she and I spoke more about it, I can see where a book about the history here, the love of our family, the stories from the girls could appeal to others. It is heartwarming."

"About those letters from the girls. Don't you need permission from them to write their stories?"

Rachelle nodded her head. "Yes, and surprisingly I either have their permission or the permission of a family member. There are still more letters that I have not included or stories I have not told because I have not found the person who wrote them. That is another reason I have held off on making it an official book. I think it needs to have more. I promise not to take it any further until you all agree it is ready for that final step."

"Rachelle, you have done a great job with this," Sara said after looking briefly at most of the pages. "I do agree you need to see if you can find more of the girls or the families and," she hesitated. "And I think it will deserve to be published."

"You do?"

"Yes, I do," Sara said as she then looked at her siblings. "Don't you agree?"

"I don't know Sis. Do you know what that could do?"

"To what?"

"To Bella Rose and all of us?"

"Make us more popular? Bring us more business?"

"Yes. Or it could work against us."

"How could it work against us? It's not like the place is haunted."

"Are you sure?"

"Yes, I'm sure. I think if it were haunted, we would have figured it out by now. No, Bella Rose has a great history. It is filled with love—from its beginnings. Granddaddy and Grandmama started with just about nothing and risked everything they had. Because of their love and their willingness to help others, well, it brought us to where we are now." Sara responded in defense.

"Very true," Andy said.

Heather looked at them both. "IF the book gets published, it may bring in more business to the events here as well. Life as we know it could change for the better. Sure we have guests, most of the time. We are not at 100% all the time. Between this book on the history," she held up the binder, "and Andy's cookbook," She picked up the new cookbook, "We could become THE place to stay in our area." She hesitated. "Are we ready for that?"

"Well, we can only fit so many people in our guest rooms. I can only do a certain number of events in the chapel and fellowship hall."

"And I can only make so many cakes," Karen added as she realized how it could affect her as well.

"One thing we do need to keep in mind is our families. We still need to put our families first. The kids come first. Always."

"I agree. We have to keep the kids our number one. If it means we hire more help to run this place, then that is what we will do. I didn't adopt this beautiful little girl to get so busy with work and running this place that I ignored her. She needs me, us." Sara said as she looked at her daughter and her husband.

Rachelle had been sitting back, taking in the whole conversation. This little task of hers had just become something major. At least it had the possibility of something major. She was glad she had contacted a publisher already who wanted to publish her book if she wanted it. The way things were going, she was almost certain that was going to happen.

Sara looked through the binder pages once again. It was a great little book. With some additions, a few more stories, and especially if they could find more of the former guests to include their stories, this could change Bella Rose as they knew it.

"I say we all read through this. Make notes of what might not need to be included, and we, mainly Rachelle, hunt down more of the former guests. Whether they be more of the young girls from when our Grandparents started it or when our parents had it. Then we see where it is and make the decision then."

"Sounds like a plan."

"I agree. There is no rush."

"Alright," Rachelle said. "I will wait to hear from each of you. Then I'll take it from there. In the meantime, I will contact the publisher and let him know it is a possibility."

All were quiet for a few moments as they were all leafing through the binder and the stories.

The phone ringing broke the quiet. Sara went to answer it. It was several minutes before she returned.

"Who was on the phone?" Heather asked.

"That was Laura wishing us all a Merry Christmas. She said that Rhea sent her good wishes as well."

"That was sweet," Rachelle said.

"She also said that in the new year, Rhea was going to be moving east to live with her."

"That is wonderful. It will be good for Rhea and Laura to be together." Heather smiled. "It's always good to have family close."

"I agree," Andy said. He set the binder down that he had been reading. "I hate that it took me so long to realize the true meaning of family." He turned to Karen. "I know that if I had stayed here my entire life, I probably would not have met you, and yet somehow I would have. There is no stopping finding your soulmate. But, " he turned to the rest of his family. " I wish I had not missed so much of the life we all could have had."

"I know what you mean. I also know that our lives would not be as they are even if one thing had been changed. You all know that. A minute later and we may not have met that one person that changed our life. God has a plan for us from day one. It is up to us to make the most of it and to follow Him through everything." Heather said.

"You have a special way of viewing this, Sis. I admire you for your faith. It is your faith that helps get us all through the tough times. How do you do it?" Ben commented to his wife.

"For me, it just comes naturally. I guess I just know God is there with me. He saw me through a near tragedy when I first remember praying a lot and hearing others pray for me. As I healed and we worked through our struggles, I knew it was God in control."

"You are amazing, Heather," Karen said.

"No, not really."

"If you say so. Whatever you are, I admire you."

"Thanks."

A few minutes later, after such a calm Christmas day, the two boys were fighting, the twins were crying, and Gayle was asleep.

"It may be time to take the boys home for a nap," Heather said as she tried to get Marc and Maddex away from each other. The boys were best friends but mostly brothers, and brothers fought occasionally.

"I think I'll take the twins home for a nap as well," Karen said as she picked up River.

"Make sure everyone comes back later for dinner," Andy said.

"Oh, we will be back. We can't miss eating dinner."

"We'll stay and help get it ready. Gayle can sleep where she is. When she wakes up, she can help us too." Sara said as she reached for Randall's hand."

"I'm here to help too," Rachelle said. "You all take the kids for naps." She got up to help Karen with the twins. "They are getting so big. It won't be long before they are walking."

"They are trying. It won't be that much longer." Andy said as he put Ryan into his side of the stroller. Rachelle put River on her side while Karen gathered their favorite blankets to cover them between the manor and their house.

Andy walked into the kitchen after Karen and his kids had left. He checked the ham in the oven and started preparing the potatoes as he looked out to see more snow falling. It was already the perfect Christmas.

Chapter Thirty-Six

There was a sense of peace surrounding Bella Rose. A gentle snow was again falling from the sky. The family, gathered in the living room, sipped the last of the eggnog and apple cider. The children all had fallen asleep underneath their new quilts, resting their heads on the matching pillows. Christmas day had come and gone; the year was coming to an end.

What began as a year of hopes and dreams and complete unknowns was now a year closing with dreams come true that had not been dreamt. It had been a year of secrets revealed and truths told. A year of stories, lots of love, joy, and even sadness—a life experienced by a growing family.

Three siblings, their spouses, a stranger who became counted as a sister, and five beautiful children filled the walls of Bella Rose. No more secrets, no more hidden truths. There was peace on top of the hillside. A peace that had never before been a part of that land. Land that overlooked such beauty that people came from miles and miles around just to stay and experience the sights, the love, the family known as Bella Rose. She finally was that Beautiful Rose that Robert saw two generations before when he stopped to visit a friend on leave from his Army duties. Little did he know the life that would come from that sparkle he saw in her eyes.

New Year's Eve at Bella Rose was a time for celebration. The family had opened the fellowship hall to the public for a New Year's party. The guest rooms were booked. Andy had prepared special snack food to serve. And for the first time since they had taken ownership, Champagne was being served. Andy had told his family he was fine with that as they also were serving sparkling soda for those who were not drinking the alcohol. He had done so well for the last several years.

Guests started arriving early in the morning. They wanted to have time to settle in, tour downtown, enjoy the views, even take a short hike through the woods even with the snow that had stayed since Christmas. It wasn't much snow, but it had stayed in the wooded area making for a perfect holiday touch. The roads had all been plowed and salted, and traveling was easy for everyone.

Heather had talked her family into helping her decorate the fellowship hall. Included in the decorations was a small table set up with Andy's cookbooks for sale. They had left the Christmas tree and other decorations up but added gold and white streamers, white paper bells. Another table held the party hats and noisemakers. Ben had set up a large flat-screen TV so they all could watch the ball drop in New York City's Times Square. The TV would be staying so Heather could play videos and streaming photos at her special events.

They had even set up a corner with toys for all the kids. Most of the guests were adults, but they made the event very family-friendly and inviting since they all had kids.

The party began at 9 PM with food, games, and music. Guests were having a great time. Dancing, talking, eating, getting to know each other. The kids were all playing nicely. Gayle had put herself in charge of the smaller kids, as she was one of the oldest ones there. Sara was so proud of her. The year had been a good one to her and all of them.

Games for the kids and the adults were being played. Bag toss competitions were started between families. A few kids were playing twister.

At eleven-thirty, Heather replaced the music with the TV show so they could all watch the ball drop. It had been a family tradition for as long as Sara and Heather could remember. They remembered the thrill it was to be able to stay up so late with their Mama and Daddy to watch the ball drop and cheer in the new year. Sara remembered the kiss between her parents and the warmth she felt. She always thought her parents had the perfect marriage. All Sara had thought about them had changed over the recent years. That perfect image had become tainted and what she had viewed as perfect turned out to be either a facade or just in her vision. She had talked with Heather about it and found that she felt the same way. When they were growing up, their life had been great. Perfect even. They thought it was normal to spend the summers with grandparents. Normal to start working at a young age. Normal for parents to spend time away once in a while. Little did they know the hidden secrets. Little did they know what was going on. And now, as parents themselves, they were determined to have the life they 'thought' they had had, but better. They would be honest with their children. They did not want their children to look back with great memories only to find out that their parents had kept secrets.

Andy was looking around at everyone who was there to celebrate with him and his family. What a difference this year was from just a year earlier and the last several years. His family was truly blessed. He looked at Karen sitting near his twins. He never knew life could be any better than when he and Karen had married until they had the twins. What a love that was. He looked around again and back to Karen, who was looking at him and smiling. His smile was full of love for her.

Rachelle was busy picking up a few things to get a head start on the cleaning. When the music ended, she looked up and saw the TV show had started. She took a deep breath and smiled to herself. Or she thought it was to herself. She didn't realize that Bob had come over to her side. He put his arm around her shoulders. She looked at him and smiled a bit bigger. The year was coming to a good ending.

Randall had taken it upon himself to pour everyone a glass of champagne. It was the first time that alcohol had been available on the grounds of Bella Rose. The 'dry' rule had been in place in respect of Andy. He had come such a long way since returning home. He had been sober for five years now. He had gone to the meetings when he needed to but had not been in the last two years. The desire to drink had disappeared the busier he got and especially after the twins were born. He did not want to ruin the life he had. So he was the one who suggested offering to bring alcohol back for this occasion. People were lining up to get their glasses. As they picked up their glass, they saw the Bella Rose Manor etched on each glass, complete with a rose. The glasses were beautiful.

A few minutes before midnight and the door opened. A gust of cold wind blew in, making everyone standing close to the door look, including Andy. His first thought was that the wind had blown the door open. Then he saw Larry and Grace walking in. His Dad and step Mom had made the trip from Pennsylvania to spend the new year with him and his family. He looked over at Karen, who had a sneaky smile as she walked with the twins to meet them all.

"You knew about this?" He asked.

"Maybe," She said as they all gathered in a group hug.

"Larry, Grace! What a surprise! I'm so glad you are here!" Andy said as he broke loose from their embrace.

"So are we. We were supposed to be here sooner, but the traffic and weather held us up on the way."

"I can't believe she was able to keep a secret that you were coming !" Andy looked at Karen again.

"It was not easy," Karen said. "Did you not wonder why there was one guest room at the manor left vacant?"

"No, not really. I just figured someone had not shown up." He laughed, realizing that is what happened.

The rest of the family had come over to join in greeting Larry and Grace. Andy watched them all and realized that he was the only one kept in the dark. "Wow, I can't believe you all were so good at keeping this secret! What happened to this family not keeping secrets?"

"There are exceptions to that rule, little brother," Sara answered. "If the secret is revealed within a month, we can keep it." She shrugged her shoulders. "Sound fair?"

"Sure. But."

"No buts. Besides, this was a 'good' secret."

"Yes, it was."

As they were still gathered around in their small family group, someone yelled out that the countdown was starting. Randall had sneaked away and brought back two glasses of champagne for Larry and Grace. They took their glasses and clinked them together. Then they quickly joined everyone else standing and watching the countdown show on TV. Together, with the announcer, they counted down the ending of another year—a wonderful year at Bella Rose Manor.

Five, four, three, two, one. Happy New Year!

Noisemakers, whistles, cheers, kids jumping, adults kissing. The perfect way to begin a new year. A year with just a few expectations but mostly a year everyone was just hoping would be a normal, quiet, family year.

The party quickly wound down after midnight. Guests who were staying at the Manor started to help with the clean-up. Those who had just driven in left to go home. The kids even pitched in and helped clean up. Karen excused herself to take Ryan and River home to bed. Grace offered to join her and help, which she appreciated. Andy told them he would be home shortly. With everyone helping out, it did not take long to pick up most of the mess. They would return later in the day to finish cleaning. Heather didn't have another event for a few weeks, so there was no hurry.

Rachelle was surprised when Bob offered to stay and help. The two of them had started to learn more about each other over the last year but had not become what would be considered an item. When she watched how he just pitched right in with the family and how he was always willing to be there to help out, such as being Santa for them, she started to think that, maybe. She quickly turned her head when she realized he was looking in her direction and walking toward her.

"I guess I'm going to call it a night, or day, as the case may be," Bob said to her. "Can I call you later?"

"Of course." She said, then added, "Anytime."

He reached over and kissed her cheek. "Thank you for a lovely night. Happy New Year, Rachelle."

"Happy New Year to you too," was all she could get out. She felt something she had not felt before. As he walked away, she watched his every step until the door closed behind him.

"That's enough for clean-up, everyone. Time to go get some rest." Heather announced. "Thank you all for helping."

"Don't forget brunch will be served at 10 AM in the Manor dining room," Andy added.

One by one, all the guests that had stayed to help clean up left to head to their rooms or home. Heather, Sara, and Andy were the last to leave.

"Happy New Year, y'all," Sara said. "I love you both."

"Love you too Sis. It's been quite a year. Let's hope for a better new one."

"I think it will be"

"Me too. As long as all the kids stay healthy, we'll be fine." Andy said.

"Brother, we will be fine, no matter what happens." Heather reached out to put her arm around him. Sara joined her, hugging Andy. This family was going to stick together no matter what they faced.

"Let's go home and get some rest. I'll see you all at brunch." Sara said.

"Good night, Sara," her siblings said in unison.

"Good night Heather. Good night Andy."

The three siblings walked out the door and headed to their homes. Sara closed and locked the door as she was the very last to leave.

Sara walked to the Manor before turning toward her home. When she got close enough to see it, she stopped and gazed at the scene. The moon shone bright and cast a beautiful light with amazing shadows from the trees over the front. She smiled. This place was home sweet home. This year she finally felt her family was complete. This year all the secrets had been revealed. The heartache and pain from losing their parents were still there but becoming more bearable. The joy her growing family brought her erased any sadness and loneliness she had left over the last several years. God has truly blessed them all. And He had blessed Bella Rose.

"Good night Bella Rose," Sara quietly said as she walked to her home to join her little family.

Epilogue

Bella Rose had been in the family for four generations. The youngest generation that would inherit the property was still too young to understand that it was not just a fun place to live and play. They didn't know any other way of life than having family all live close to each other.

The future of Bella Rose looked bright. Everyone was ready to settle down to a normal life—one of raising their children, entertaining more guests, and holding more events.

Each family member went to bed on that first day of the new year with gratitude for everything of the past year. They also hoped the dream of their life of secrets, sudden changes, and the mystery was over.

Ben was thrilled to have made a connection to his past, but something about his meeting with Rhea and his adoptive dad, David, not being willing to meet his mother after all the years apart, had him curious. Was something missing? Was there something David was not telling him? Did Rhea know and understand what it was?

Larry and Grace loved being there for New Year and spending time with their grandchildren. Larry loved being there, although he never told anyone the real reason. Larry felt close to Susan when he was there. A lifetime ago, he could have made a different decision and life as they all knew it; well, it didn't matter anymore because he did what he did, and there was no changing it. He was happy to have his son know him and to be able to get to know his grandchildren that Andy and Karen had blessed them with.

Rachelle had become so much a part of the family everyone forgot that she was not a blood relative. They had stopped trying to explain the truth, and that was the only secret the family continued to keep. She was looking forward to whatever the future held for her, as long as she could stay at Bella Rose.

Randall watched Sara sleep. He sensed that as the past lives of the family he loved so much had changed over the year, they were not done discovering more about Bella Rose. He couldn't say for sure. Nor could he tell what he knew. He hoped the hunch he was investigating was true.

While everyone slept, Bella Rose seemed to settle a fraction. The foundation clung tighter to the earth. No one felt the movement, but she felt restless.

Tomorrow was a new day—a new beginning. So much had happened at Bella Rose and with the family over the generations. The truth had prevailed at Bella Rose.

As each family member closed their eyes with smiles and anticipation of dreamland, none of them realized that there was much more to come.

Coming Next:
Standing Alone
The Mysteries of Bella Rose Estate
Book #4

Acknowledgment

Thank you to all who continue to read the story Bella Rose Estate and get caught up in their lives, full of twists and turns. And to all my readers who contacted me, wanting the next book. The Hidden Truth came to life with even more surprises, thanks to you.

A special thank you to Ellen Peck and Cynthia Risk, who helped me with small portions along the way with their input.

I appreciate all of you who go out of your way to let me know how much they enjoy my creations.

It is thanks to you that what began as a trilogy will now continue to become a series.

Yes, there is more to the mysteries involving Bella Rose Estate and the family.

About the Author

Phyllis Dewey has a passion for writing that began when she was just eleven years old when she wrote her first poem. Three of her poems were published in different Anthology Books. She stopped writing for several years while in school and then with her growing family and working.

In 2019 she returned to her love of writing with a simple story idea that became the series: The Mysteries of Bella Rose Estate.

She has a college degree in social work/mental health. She draws on her experiences in that field, her life adventures, and her imagination in her writings.

Her passion for writing continues as she continues writing this series. Her first non-fiction book, *Her Turn* is published. and she is writing more fiction.

Ms Phyllis lives in East Tennessee, enjoying time with her family and friends. She also enjoys her gardens and photography hobbies, the view of the mountains from her home, and traveling.

www.ingramcontent.com/pod-product-compliance
Lightning Source LLC
Chambersburg PA
CBHW030414180626
46812CB00005B/1997